W9-BOO-810

One Man's War

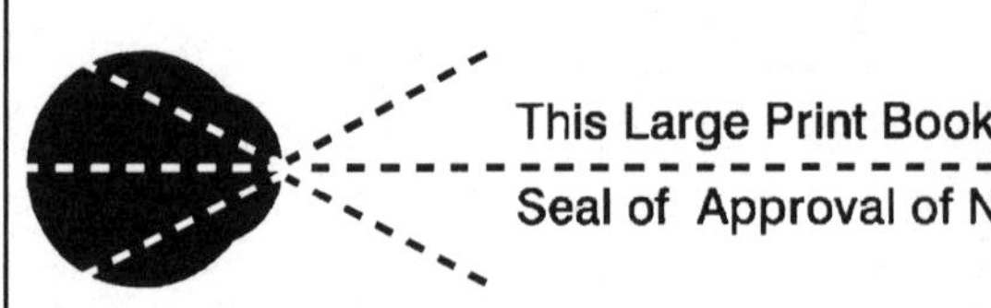
This Large Print Book carries the
Seal of Approval of N.A.V.H.

One Man's War

Annabel Johnson

THORNDIKE PRESS
A part of Gale, Cengage Learning

Detroit • New York • San Francisco • New Haven, Conn • Waterville, Maine • London

Thorndike Press, a part of Gale, Cengage Learning.

Thorndike Press® Large Print Clean Reads.
The text of this Large Print edition is unabridged.
Other aspects of the book may vary from the original edition.
Set in 16 pt. Plantin.
Printed on permanent paper.

LIBRARY OF CONGRESS CATALOGING-IN-PUBLICATION DATA

Johnson, Annabel, 1921–
One man's war / by Annabel Johnson.
p. cm. — (Thorndike Press large print clean reads)
ISBN-13: 978-1-4104-1102-0 (hardcover : alk. paper)
ISBN-10: 1-4104-1102-8 (hardcover : alk. paper)
1. World War, 1914–1918—Veterans—Kansas—Fiction. 2. World War, 1914–1918—France—Fiction. 3. World War, 1914–1918—Psychological aspects—Fiction. 4. Psychological fiction. 5. Large type books. I. Title.
PS3560.O37134O64 2008
813'.54—dc22 2008036539

Published in 2008 by arrangement with Annabel Johnson.

Printed in the United States of America
1 2 3 4 5 6 7 12 11 10 09 08

This book is dedicated to my father.

His memoirs provided the
detailed background on which I relied.

One

Early in the year 1918 thousands of us shipped out for Europe to try to end a filthy war that had shattered a whole generation of French and British soldiers. They called us "doughboys," for some reason, maybe because we were half-baked. It's true we jaunted off like kids on a camping trip. But we soon found ourselves mired in the stinking mud of the trenches with mortar rounds falling on all sides and the smell of death in the air. Some were killed, many were ruined by gas or shell shock. Those of us who survived that last awful battle called The Argonne were left stunned and uncertain of who we were or who we had been. Some asked for God's help; many just wrote it all off as the Devil's doing. I'd agree — at least I knew that I had walked through Hell and lived. But the truth was, I didn't believe in the Devil. I didn't believe in anything.

It was in that state of confusion, with the

guns gone silent and little to do but the sorry job of packing up to go home, that I bought a notebook and began to write. Just making a few sketches, jotting down notes, it brought a return of some sort of order to my mind. I finished this record after I got home, a personal catharsis which was never meant to be shared. Mainly I was trying to understand the progression that brings a kid to manhood, and why that doesn't necessarily make him a hero.

Hero was a word that loomed large over Ookey, my lifelong buddy and fellow warrior. He saw himself, I think, as some sort of mixture of Captain Kidd and Teddy Roosevelt and Jim Jeffries combined. When I thought back to him I sketched a cartoon — of a wild-haired idiot in a pilot's jacket with scarf, gun in one hand and a cigarette in the other. The caption is: *One man's war is another man's piece of pie.* His grin is full of the joy of the kill. Is that what creates a hero?

When I try to remember my own early struggles with that word I return to a day in the summer of my thirteenth year, the moment when I first realized I probably was a coward.

The moment of the shotgun. There was

something about the weapon that made me shudder — with excitement, a mixture of delight and fear. A birthday present to Ookey from his uncle, it was dreadfully beautiful.

"Come on, you can touch it." But he held his hand cupped over the trigger mechanism as if I might fumble around and do something stupid. The stock was polished wood with a graceful grain; it felt warm to my fingers, but the steel barrels were cold as death. I drew back and caught a flash of contempt in his eyes. Dark eyes, almost pure black, when Ookey got excited they snapped like flags in the wind.

How he got the nickname was supposed to be a mystery. The gang would speculate that once he stepped in a pile of horse manure and said, "That's ookey." Another story was that his mother spoke the word when she first saw her new-born babe, which was just kidding I think. I never met his mother. She was dead long before I met him, but he said she was nice. The real truth he confided to me: when he was two years old he couldn't pronounce "Luke" so he called himself "Ook." He swore he'd kill me if I ever told.

In fact he was more secret than anyone I ever knew. Older than the rest of us who were about to enter the eighth grade, he'd been kept out of school for a year with the smallpox. It had left him with a scar on his cheek, looked like a seven. He called it his lucky mark and would touch it when facing a tough shot at marbles. He never beat me playing marbles, but he could mop up at mumblety-peg. Threw that knife down with a wicked skill that seemed born in him. When I would have to pull the peg out of the dirt with my teeth he would grin like a fiend.

His own teeth were brilliantly white, due to the fact that he drank a lot of milk. None of the rest of us did, it cost too much. But living on a truck farm, he had ticket to a cow. His dad made a little money on crops, a few chickens and pigs. His granddad had homesteaded the land back in the days when Kansas City was still just a frontier town on the edge of Indian country. It was one of those rambling frame houses that had grown ungracefully to suit each generation's needs. Ookey had a great room upstairs above the back porch, all windows.

It was flooded with light that day of early summer, sun glinting off the twin barrels of the shotgun. "Ain't she a beaut'?" He shucked the thing in his hands, sighting down it at his bed, which was a flop of sheets. When there are no women around to keep washing and scrubbing everything a room takes on character. The place smelled like socks and stale soda pop and gun oil.

"Pa wasn't too happy that Uncle Pete gave it to me, but Pete said every boy ought to have a scattergun when he turns fifteen. He said it's full-bore. I wonder what sort of pattern she'll spread." Putting the gun to his shoulder he blew a hole in the ceiling.

You could see clear into the attic. As I stared up at the ragged dark gap with stippling all around it I said, "Mmm, yep, pretty good spread." Odd feeling right below my ribs, kind of like little mouse-feet hopping around. "What'll your dad think of that?"

"He's gone to Springfield, big poker game over there." Mr. Marlowe was a professional gambler. "By the time he gets back I'll have some butcher's wrap over the hole. He'll never notice it. He don't come up here much any more, this is my place. Anyway I'm near as big as he is. Last time he got likkered up and came after me with his belt, I told him to cut it out, and he did."

I had to admit I wouldn't want to get into any arguments with Ookey while he was cradling that gun. He looked pretty primitive. His black hair was shaggier than usual now that school was out. He usually cut it himself, sneaking the teacher's scissors out of her desk. She caught him at it once and took him down to the shower room in the basement, gave him a proper haircut using a bowl to get it straight all around, and for a while he looked almost normal. But by now the elf locks were long, he was being Deerslayer.

"Wonder what kind of range this thing's got." He took the shotgun over to the row of casement windows, standing open as if they were pleading for a breath of wind. Dead quiet lay over the Missouri hills, the leaves hung motionless on the sycamore trees. Beyond the farm acres of purple thistles stood stiffly, covered with summer dust. Below us the barnyard was a barren pitch where half a dozen leghorns scratched in the dirt, hens mostly, a few young cocks. And one old red rooster limping about, pecking at the dried manure.

"Want some chicken for supper?" Ookey sighted down the gun.

"Uh — no thanks," I said. "We don't eat a lot of chicken, and Grossmutter is making a mutton stew tonight and . . ."

The shotgun went off in a blast and the rooster was headless, floundering around in the dirt, a thing of antic feathers.

". . . and that reminds me, I'd better be

getting home. I promised her I'd pick some apples for pie."

Ookey gave me an amused glance. "Apples are still green."

"That makes the best pie," I said harshly. "Don't tell Grossmutter how to cook."

"You look a little green yourself," he went on carelessly. "I bet you never shot a bird. It's high time you became a hunter, kiddo. I've got a great idea. I have to stick around here and feed the stock until Pa gets home next Friday, but Saturday we could go out, take the streetcar to Waldo and walk across to that place where we used to raid nests. There's whole coveys of quail out there. Even a few grouse. What do you say?" The gleam in his eyes taunted me: *Are you a yellow-belly?*

All I could think was, I wished I could give somebody a look like that. Ookey was a walking dare. "Sure," I said. "Sounds good."

"Maybe a couple of squirrels." He knew I like squirrels. Right where they're supposed to be, up in the trees. "You ever eat squirrel? They're a little gamy, but they're different."

"Or rabbits," I shrugged. I think I shrugged.

"Now you're talking." He followed me on out the back door onto the porch. A few feet away the rooster lay still now, like a worn-out feather duster.

"Aw, don't worry about that, he was getting old. I think he had the pip."

"Who's worried?" That time I know I shrugged. You had to shrug a lot around Ookey.

And we eat chicken every Sunday for dinner, so why did I feel queasy as I hoofed it back down the long dirt track to the county road? It's just that one minute the rooster was alive, kind of dignified in its old age, and the next it was flopping all over the place. It was comical, and dying shouldn't be funny. I tried to tell myself, *Oh, grow up!* But it didn't work. Come Saturday I was going to have to do it myself, shoot the gun with the nice spread that was so wide you could hardly miss anything you aimed at. I had to kill some happy dumb squirrel . . .

From behind me I heard the clop of horse's hooves, the rattle of a buggy. A glance back and I recognized Doc Hainey's rig coming along. On an impulse I stuck out my thumb. Who else might be able to discuss sudden death? He slowed the bay mare to a walk — an old animal, gray whiskers on her chin and she was blind in one eye. But old is okay. Old is Grossmutter. You don't just do away with old things.

"Hop aboard, son. You're a long way from home."

Three miles or more it was, to my house in the new part of the city, an area they were starting to call the Country Club, though there wasn't anything ritzy about our neighborhood. It was made up of solid folk like my father, who was manager of the Iola Feed and Grain Company. I wondered if I should ask him about my feelings, about the gun and all. But Dad liked to hunt himself. He went down to the Ozarks every year and brought us back twenty pounds of venison steaks. I didn't mind eating them, not a bit. I like mutton too, but that doesn't mean I want to go out and shoot a sheep. I kept picturing myself looking down the barrel of that shotgun at a rabbit, minding its own business, thinking, "What a great day." And then I shoot it and it's just a piece of raw meat. It made me feel downright sick, which meant I really was a yellow-belly at heart.

Doc kept glancing over at me. Tough little man, he'd been a medic in the Mexican War, so he must be pretty old now. Hidden behind a bushy beard, his face was mostly unreadable, but the blue eyes were wise, alert. "Well, m'boy, you wreck any bicycles lately?"

"No, sir." When I was eight I had borrowed my sister's bike and run it into our apple tree, thereby breaking my arm and incidentally falling on my head, which caused me momentary unconsciousness. I wakened to see Dolly jumping up and down — she'd have been about eleven — her long braids rising and falling as she screamed with horrified delight.

"He's dead, he's dead, he's dead."

Since the Doc lived right across the street from us, he'd got over there fast and told her I'd just had the wind knocked out of me. I didn't even know I was in pain until he began fiddling with my arm. Then I knew all there was to know. But it didn't take long, in no time he had splinted it with some slats off an orange crate. Those stubby fingers knew exactly what to do. When he finished the beard split open and I saw his gold tooth, I guess he was smiling. "You'll live." I didn't like to remember that day. I had cried. Pure weakness.

What the Sam Hill am I going to do Saturday? I said to Doc, "Don't you sometimes get bothered by all that blood and stuff you see?"

"Blood is a normal bodily fluid. Ever cut your finger? But that's not the point, is it? You and all the other young cubs — what you really wonder is, what's it like to see a man die."

I wished he wouldn't invent things for me to wonder about.

"Dying is a natural event. Sometimes it hurts, sometimes not." He shot me a beady look from under bushy eyebrows. "But you've still got a way to go. You aren't worrying about dying yourself?"

"No sir. I feel fine." Well, of course, once in a while you think about it. You can't help that.

"Good. Go to church?"

"Yes sir."

"Glad to hear it. That's where you'll find all the answers."

I doubted that. The last time I asked God for anything He hadn't come through. I asked Him to make me six feet tall and here I was, stuck at five-ten-and-a-half.

"Or maybe you're thinking about taking up the medical profession?"

"No sir," I told him emphatically.

"Just as well. I don't think your pap would approve."

My father had gone off like a skyrocket when Doc sent him a bill for five dollars for my arm. Dad claimed he could have done the job for nothing. We had a Complete Encyclopedia of Human Diseases and Their

Cures. You could find every ailment in there from catarrh to lockjaw (which it says you can't fix). The book had even brought Dolly through diphtheria. I wondered if it told how to treat plain old cowardice.

I blurted it out before I thought. "Don't you ever get scared? Like when you're called out on a job and something you do might make a person die?"

"All you can do is try," he said bleakly. "As for 'scared' — without fear there's no courage."

Maybe he was the wrong person to ask, or I didn't really have the right question. "I'll just get out here," I said. It was our corner.

Doc laughed at that. "I bet you don't want to be seen in my company. Your pap's still sore at me over that bill I sent him? Wouldn't want you accepting favors from the old doc." He pulled the mare to a complete stop and dug down in his pocket, got out a fiver and handed it over to me. "Give this to your old man and tell him he was absolutely right. I should have got his permission that time before I did any doctoring on you. I should have let you suffer for five or six hours until he got home from work. Of course, by then maybe a bone is sticking through the skin, dirt get in there, infection, so forth. Never mind. Now we're all square.

I don't want any hard feelings from my neighbors."

That word "suffer" twisted my brain some more. Does your body suffer even after your head has been blown off? The rooster had flopped around as if it were in terrible pain. Confused, I stuck the fin in my pocket and jumped down from the buggy. "Thanks for the ride."

"Glad to help out. Next time maybe you'll tell me what's really on your mind." He clucked at the mare and she moved on.

Two

I can still recall the way that fiver felt in my hand, like a key to my whole destiny, that night as I sat in the treehouse, waiting for the rest of the gang. Shoes dangling forty feet above the traffic below, I was literally on top of the world. Take a wrong step and you're down there under the wheels of the buggies. I knew people who had lived crippled all their lives, like Zoobird's dad, who had worked in the coal mines down in Joplin until he got the black lung. You couldn't imagine him looking anywhere above his belt line, much less at a great punching sunset.

We had built high and secret, slinging the lumber across from the heights of a hillside right behind the big walnut tree using a winch that Ookey had acquired from a construction site a couple of blocks over. We had borrowed some boards and two-by-fours, too. As he said, they certainly didn't need all those nails just to put up a streetcar barn. The furniture we had gathered cautiously from around the neighborhood, a mattress we had rescued from somebody's trash and an assortment of chairs, a spittoon for decoration. But the main luxury of the clubhouse was its privacy. No telltale steps nailed to the tree, we reached it by the sling, fitted now with a seat and a piece of clothesline to pull it back and forth between the tree and the hill. Those poor fools down there in their surreys had no idea I was perched way above their heads, watching their lives unfold.

It was still early evening. I sat there alone with a lot of thoughts that grew bigger by the minute as the golden leaves hung motionless around me and the sounds of the town were far away. It was a moment in time that came back to me on the eve of battle, the way your life plays out on the moving-picture screen in your head. It was at that moment I'd had my idea — the inspiration came over me like a load of coal down the chute, rough and crude, but fuel for thought. A simple enough plan, it would keep me from facing the prospect of the hunting trip on Saturday. Only it became much more than that as I considered it.

On one level it was a chance to lead an

adventure. On another it was a step into the mysterious adult world where men made decisions and had to struggle to survive. In my pocket I had a talisman, a medal that my uncle had won in a fierce war where he had charged up a hill beside Teddy Roosevelt and got himself killed. It was always with me, and when I touched it I was filled with sadness and the magnificence of one man's bravery. Now, in my solitary spot above Gillham Road, I kept a tight grip on it as I saw the chance to do something important. Next fall we would be entering Central High, a melting pot of neighborhoods. Kids from all over the west end of town were sent there. Our gang might get swallowed in the crush, lose track of each other, the old ties broken. This, my plan, would weld us together once and for all.

I wished the gang would hurry up and come, all except Ookey. He was usually late because he had to hike all the way in from the farm. I hoped tonight he'd take his time so I could get my piece said before he arrived and turned the project into a safari to go kill something. I even resorted to an unusual expedient. I said, inwardly, *Lord, I don't ask you for very much, but tonight would you please find a way to slow Ookey down?*

At least one thing was going right. I saw

Zoobird up on top the hill, pulling up the sling by its rope to come down and join me. When I had passed his house awhile ago I'd given a whistle, but got no response. He was probably still out delivering his mother's work. Mrs. Fleischman was seamstress to the whole neighborhood. Everybody knew she had to support the family. His old man could hardly get out of his chair, breath coming so short it was painful to watch.

The Bird came down the cable in a rush, landing lightly on the tree branch. A big gawky body, it was easy to see how he got his nickname. Long bony legs, elbows sticking out like flustered wings, and his straw-colored hair rising in a giant cowlick like a crest. But it was the nose that clinched the title, beaky and red, thrusting out to a point from which the rest of his face receded. His chin faded into his collar and his forehead went up into that shock of hay, ears a prominent adornment. He knew he looked comical and sometimes acted like a clown to divert people from pitying him in his homeliness. But under the horseplay he was smart. I happened to know that he could do math faster than the rest of us put together.

As he joined me I said, "Zoo, you know all about sums. How many potatoes does it take to feed six, seven people for a week?"

"Depends how hungry they are." He had a funny little hooting laugh that made his shoulders shake. "Whatcha cooking up, Bernie?"

As I laid out my plan for him the birdy face took on a gloss as if it had been polished. He always was the cleanest guy I ever knew. His Dad was a kind of gray color that wouldn't wash off, which is why Zoo scrubbed down so hard.

"Except how are we gonna buy the potatoes?"

I showed him the fiver. "Doc Hainey," I said and told him the story of my ride that afternoon and the broken-arm thing. "When I tried to give it to Dad he wouldn't take it." My father's Welsh, not very tall, but he can get square and hard as a sack of tight-packed winter wheat.

He said, "I was sore that day, but I wasn't home and Doc was and he fixed you up pretty well, so he had a right to send me the bill. No, I don't want it." Turning away, he left me standing there with the five-spot in my hand.

"I knew Doc Hainey wouldn't take it back," I explained to Zoobird. "And you can't just leave money lying around. So I figured, it was my arm, my suffering, maybe I should just call it all even. Anyway, it will buy us some provisions. Maybe the others can chip in —"

Shades of poverty dimmed his look.

I hurried on. "So we buy some food, but what we really need is somebody to cook it." I knew that would make him happy. Zoobird made all the meals at home, while his mother was at her sewing machine. He was a terrific cook.

"Takes a lot of money to buy meat."

"Well, that's the good part. This place I had in mind, there's a stream running through. Can you make stew out of fish?"

"Oh, sure. Put in some onions and potatoes and . . ."

With a thump we were joined in our roost by another member of the gang. Deke — his real name was Daoud, he was Jewish, but we called him the Deacon because he was an expert on sin. He actually read the Bible. That night the setting sun made a little halo around his curly black mop of hair. He usually hung out with Dollars.

"They're up there fighting." He jerked a thumb toward the hilltop. It was the only rule we had, no slugging or wrestling here in the tree, lest we go through the skimpy railings and plunge into the street below. That would draw attention to our hideaway, which nobody wanted. Might incidentally break your neck, too.

"What's it about this time?"

"Dollars called Pug a 'harp'. Why is that so obnoxious to Irishmen?"

"You got me." They usually got over their tempers fast. We heard the sling being drawn across to the hill, and in a minute Pug came down first, so he must have won the fight. He usually did, a big husky kid with hair the color of a sweet potato.

"Hi, guys," he said, as casually as if he didn't have blood running down from his nose. Deke handed him a handkerchief.

By then Dollars had joined us, a wiry type who was all mouth and grass stains. Got his monicker by his favorite expression: "Dollars-to-doughnuts you're wrong about that." His father was a lawyer, which explained a lot.

"Where's Fats?" somebody asked.

"He's coming along, bringing some stuff from the store. They're taking inventory over there." Fats Mayhew was son of the owner of the grocery at the end of our block. We all lived on Magee Street, had grown up together, fought our way through the lower grades, and forged a kind of bond that went beyond a few games of Sow-in-the-Hole. We were old enough by then to mean it when we used the word "friend."

But how long would that last when we were surrounded by a crowd of new faces over at Central next fall?

"Listen, everybody," I began. "I got this idea . . ."

When Fats hit the tree limb the whole platform shuddered. He wasn't really fat, but he was stocky and solid. I bet he weighed twice what I did. Good-natured as a pony, and just about as dumb, for a minute he was the center of attention. He was carrying a bag that turned out to be full of fractured cookies, bruised fruit and a piece of moldy cheese, which Zoobird skillfully scraped clean with his pocket knife.

"Nothing wrong with a little mold." He cut it in chunks and handed them around.

"So, as I was saying —" The itch of leadership was growing stronger. "I had this idea, something we could do to have a little fun and make our parents realize that we are too old for these darned knickers." That was last-minute inspiration — we all hated our knee pants, symbol of childhood. It got their attention.

I was about to go into my pitch, when somebody said, "Hey, wait a minute. Here comes Ookey."

So much for asking favors of the Lord.

Down at the foot of Gillham Road, he

came loping along, then stopped short and seemed to be jawing at somebody. Out of the shadows into the street came the lamp lighter. His job took a special skill, the way he'd run the long stick with the match on it up the post, turning on the gas just at the right minute for it to catch fire. Those lamps were his pride and joy, and Ookey was an expert at breaking the glass globes. The two of them were old enemies. Now, the old man was making threatening gestures — not a good idea. Ookey bent down, scooped up a stone and shied it at the nearest lamp. He was a dead shot, of course. The rickety old timer went for him waving that stick and Ookey ran — the other way. He'd never lead anybody near our hideout.

"Look at the old geezer rattle his shanks," Dollars marveled.

"I hope he doesn't pass out," Zoobird said soberly. "Old people have bad lungs sometimes."

"If he died, would that make Ookey a murderer?" Pug wondered.

"No," Deke said flatly. "He didn't force the guy to chase him. But he'd be a sinner, for sure. It's wrong to tease a person into a rage. He could go to Hell for all eternity."

Pug snickered. "Not in my church. He'd just go and confess his sins and say a few

Hail Marys, he'd be forgiven."

Deke gave him a scathing look. Being Jewish he didn't Hail Mary. "Sin is something you should take seriously."

Which is exactly why I have a problem with church, if Doc Hainey should want to know. It never had the answers to any of my questions, it just made me feel guilty. About everything on earth, going back to the Garden of Eden. I said, "Would you guys shut up and listen? We've just got until Saturday to plan our camping trip. All by ourselves, for a week, out in the country. I know a place with a fishing stream, spot to pitch a tent, a whole field of corn just coming ripe."

They grew rapidly interested.

"Who's going to get our parents to agree?"

"You can tell them my father okayed it." Needless to say I would never have gone forward with this if I hadn't got Dad's permission. I'd followed him out to the back yard after supper where he always smoked a pipe. When I put it to him he frowned and puffed. Not a big man, but square and solid as a sack of oats. Tufty eyebrows drew into a knot, and then his blue eyes lightened as he began to nod. "He even said we could use our big tent."

"Where'd you learn about this place?"

"How do we get there, walk?"

"That's the first thing we have to figure out," I told them. "We're going to need a horse and wagon."

Pug spit some chewing gum juice at our spittoon. "I can get that. A fellow over in Westport owes me a favor. I helped him muck out his stable."

Dollars began to get into the spirit. "Ma just put up some crabapple jelly. She'd let us have a couple of jars."

"We can catch fish in the stream. Maybe borrow a little of the farmer's corn if it's ripe enough. I'll buy coffee and sugar. Fats, will you or your dad sell us some canned goods at half price?" I waved my fiver and they began to grin: this could work.

Zoobird put a cap on it. "I say it's a great idea. I nominate Bernie to lead the expedition."

At that point we heard the sling being drawn up and in a few seconds we were joined by Ookey himself. "Hoo boy," he breathed. "That old codger chased me four blocks."

"I hope he didn't drop over dead," Deke remarked darkly.

"Naaah. Old people know when to quit. That's how they get to be old. What's up?" He looked around at us, sensing that he had walked in on a serious discussion.

In a spate of talk the others told him, while I stood off to the side and waited for my moment to collapse. Ookey eyed me and put on his best swagger. "Well, hey, don't worry about food. I'll just bring my shotgun along. Plenty of birds out on those prairies."

Zoobird glanced over at me, a look of total comprehension. He said carelessly, "No guns. This farmer wouldn't appreciate us shooting up his corn fields. Guy with a family, he's looking to bag those birds himself. Stream's a different matter, fish come and go. He'll never miss them." His voice was suddenly so authoritative I was amazed.

Ookey, too. "Who made you top dog here?"

"I did." I said it flatly, borrowing my tone from Zoobird. "He's my trail boss. This is my expedition."

The others stood silent, looking at Ookey to see how he'd take it. I had fought him a few times. He always won, he was ten pounds heavier, but it didn't keep me from wading in. Now he stood fingering his scar. Then, slowly, he took off his ragged old baseball cap and swept the floor with it in a great bow.

"Lead on, O Leader. I am at your service." But his grin was crooked and his eyes gleamed with some private emotion. He hadn't conceded a thing.

Three

There was a horse, in a place called Grange-le-Compt. But that's another story which I will have to tell eventually. My first equine experience was with a hip-shot, bald-faced roan mare by the name of Sweet Adeline. Pug was inclined to baby her, but I could see that was wasted on the old girl. She had a rolling eye.

As we gathered around the wagon parked in front of our house, we were joined by half the neighborhood. The long block of homes was a congenial place of front porches and pitched roofs, swinging hammocks and lemonade pitchers in the afternoon. At seven on a Saturday morning people were inclined to congregate if given a reason and our expedition was a thing of speculation and some wagering.

"Bet they don't last three days."

"I got a dollar says they'll be home by tomorrow."

"Five p.m. tonight, you watch, they'll come dragging in."

The Lord had come through and granted me my chance at leadership, only now I was beginning to understand that old phrase: be careful what you wish for. I had a feeling He was having Himself a laugh.

Then Dad crawled out from under the wagon where he had just affixed the tent pole and stood up. His Welsh rose and he said, "I'll cover all bets." I could have licked his boots.

The wagon was piled high with bedrolls and bags of personal belongings. Deke was wearing his skull cap from synagogue, and Dollars had the paperweight he'd got at the St. Louis World's Fair. Pug had brought along a stereoptican viewer and some slides. I was going to sneak in my entire marble collection, but it weighed a ton and I got a vision of Sweet Adeline lying down quietly in the traces and refusing to haul the ever-increasing load. So I settled for my uncle's medal. Zoo, I knew, had brought his own, the medal he'd won in the high jump in seventh grade. He carried it everywhere — nobody knew that but me.

"What you need," Dad says, "is a bucket of ice. I'll give you some from our box. I can go over and get more at the ice house later. You'll need to keep your eggs and bacon cool on the way over."

Eggs? *Bacon?* There hadn't been enough money for that. I was lucky Mr. Mayhew had donated a bunch of groceries, some broccoli that had aphids on it which he couldn't sell, a box of peaches that had arrived green, but would ripen in the heat by the end of the week. Dollars' folks had staked us to three cases of soda pop, strawberry, cream soda and sarsaparilla. At the last minute Zoobird brought a proud sack of coffee. I just hoped the fishing would be good . . .

"Who-all's the Booshway here?" The cracked old voice cut through the chatter. It was Grizzard, the most ancient man any of us had ever known, said to be a hundred hard years and he looked it. All wrinkles and liver spots, muscles in his arms that stood out like ropes, he peered around with faded eyes as he plunked himself down on our front steps.

"What's a Booshway?" somebody asked in hushed tones.

"You darned fools, you ain't got the sense to blow smoke. Ever' outfit needs a booshway to run the show."

"That's me," I came to stand before him. I always respected the old man. I wished I knew half the stuff that he did. He could talk sign with real Indians, and they say he had trotted across hundreds of miles on foot to escape some Pawnees that stole his pack mules. "You got any advice for us, sir?"

"You ain't gonna live long enough to hear all the advice I got in me. But I can tell you one thing, you better make your camp-kickers walk. That old hayburner ain't got many miles left in her. She won't never get you to Rendezvous."

"We aren't going very far . . ."

"A thousand miles," he said dreamily. "That's how fur it is to the Siskadee, and don't let me hear you callin' it the Green River."

They said old Grizzard was actually at the Grand Rendezvous of 1833. Just the thought stiffened my spine on the spot.

I called over to Deke. "Don't bury that soda pop too deep. We're all going to need some on the road."

About then Sweet Adeline deposited a steaming heap in the street in front of our steps. From the porch came a small strangled noise from my mother, who stood with Dolly, both of them frowning at the mob in our yard trampling the petunias.

Mother looked her usual imposing self. She never left her bedroom without being stiffly buttoned up to her second double-chin, leg-o-mutton sleeves perfectly puckered, curls piled high. Her hair was brown, but sometimes it took on odd tinges of red. I never knew why until Dolly tried it, spilled the stuff and came forth looking as if she had run foul of a bottle of catsup. After that she proclaimed that she would be a blond and bought some peroxide, but that didn't work either. She stood there now, hair brown and stringy, a tall girl in a long straight dress of dowdy blue material that hung crookedly around her shins. She had to take sewing in high school, it was required of the girls, and her attempts were laughable. Except that you didn't laugh at Dolly unless you wanted to get pummeled about the ears.

I had recently drawn a cartoon of her — it has always been one of my pastimes, to sketch. It used to drive my teachers crazy when I drew little pictures on the margins of a book. This time I had taken a pad of writing paper and doodled a small cat with a mean face chasing a large dog that looked something like me with its heels up around its ears. She happened to see it — what she gets for trespassing in my room — and since then we hadn't been speaking.

Grossmutter was nowhere in sight, to my

disappointment. I had been at her to let us have her favorite frying pan. I mean, you can't fry eggs on the end of a stick. But she had sent me scooting with a whole barrage of German. That kitchen was the bridge of her ship from which she ran our household, and the big black iron stove her helm. Then at the last minute here she came, bearing the beloved skillet, thrusting it at me. Gnarled knot of an old woman, she exploded into German: *Here, you little bean-face. Get on with you! Go with God.*

I yelled after her retreating figure. *"Danke."* Now, if we actually had a few eggs and some bacon. I guess I said it aloud, because Zoo-bird looked shocked.

"You mean you didn't get bacon? What am I going to cook things in if I don't have bacon grease?"

Good question. Answered, of course, by Ookey the Great. He came peddling into our yard on his bicycle, saddlebags of food hanging on either side — a crate of eggs, slab of bacon, a small ham, which I doubt his father knew he had contributed. He was juggling a pail of butter. "Where's your ice bucket?"

Dad came forth lugging a small wash-tub with several large chunks in it. "You better put some heavy cover over it, or that ice will melt before you get to Allen's Hill."

The only hill between us and the hundreds of miles of flatness that was Kansas, it almost proved fatal. Pug was driving the wagon, his voice the only one that Sweet Adeline recognized. But even he couldn't persuade her to tackle that long slope.

Ookey jumped down off the wagon. "I'll find a stick."

Pug said curtly, "Nobody better hit Sweet Adeline. She will lie down right here in the road, believe me."

Zoobird sidled up to me. "Maybe she's thirsty. Did we bring any water?"

Oh Lord, did you know I wasn't up to this? Water for the horse never entered my head. There would be plenty where we were going. I said to Pug, "Do you think she'd like a little soda pop?"

"Beer," he said. "She's crazy about beer."

I reached under the tarp and found a bottle — it turned out to be sarsaparilla, which was probably more like beer than grape soda. "Pug, you want to give it to her?"

He shook his head. "I'll encourage her from up here. You're the Booshway. See if you can get her to drink some."

Responsibilities weigh heavy. I approached the old mare cautiously, those yellow teeth were big as dominos. Dribbling some pop on the whiskery lips, I was ready to retreat in haste if she didn't like it. Her huge tongue licked thoughtfully. Then she reached out, took the bottle by the neck and tipped her head back, glugging it straight down in a matter of seconds.

The guys fell all over the ground laughing.

Getting a little bit impatient I went and got another bottle, prepared to make her sip it while I tempted her up the hill. To the rest of my crew I said sternly, "Okay, men, let's each get on a wheel and push." Pug got into the spirit and slapped her briskly with the reins and we began to move slowly a step at a time. It took a third bottle, but we finally topped the brow of the rise and let out a cheer.

"Well, done, guys," I told them in my best Booshway tone. And we rolled out onto the prairies of Kansas singing.

"Oh, me name is Sam'l Hall, Sam'l Hall.
Oh, me name is Sam'l Hall and I hates
you one and all, Damn your eyes!"

Ookey offered a new sea chantey called "Fifteen Men on a Dead Man's Chest." Drink and the Devil had done for the rest.

It got us started on a discussion of Satan, does he really exist? Ookey said it was like fairy tales of ogres and trolls, a total fraud.

"Well, you can't deny that there's evil in the world," Deke protested.

The discussion took us all the way to Pinkerton's Farm, a spot I had noticed the year before when our church rallied a harvesting crew to help the owner, who had a broken leg. As we left I'd seen the spot by the creek, with an abandoned fire place, looked as though fishermen had come and gone there. It was perfect, with a spreading tree above us and the stream not a hundred feet away. All the sign said was, "Please keep the gate closed." The minute we unhitched Sweet Adeline she headed into the water, drinking and peeing simultaneously.

"Well," said Zoobird, "I guess we won't be making coffee from the creek." He was inclined to be finicky about such things.

"There are springs all over the place," I told them. "In fact they said the best ones are up on the high ground." A grove of trees stood on the crest of a rise about a hundred yards away. I headed up there and found a lovely cold clean bubbler where we immediately cached our butter and pop and the ham. Zoobird was already building a fire, while Ookey was lunging through the brush, yelling, "Snake, snake! Can't pitch a tent until we clear this area of snakes."

In a half an hour a total of fifteen dead rattlers hung on the fence gate as a terrible object lesson to all other intruders. Ookey chased the last one across the stream, splashing in its wake like a fiend, snatching it by the tail and swinging it around his head before he cracked it, like a whip, against a rock.

"Oh, man," he called back to us, "that water is perfect for swimming."

I was choosing the site for the tent. "As soon as we get camped, we'll join you," I said, trying not to sound sarcastic.

The others didn't even hear me. They were already tearing their clothes off.

Well, I couldn't put the tent up by myself. I ran for the river and was naked before I got halfway there.

Scenes from that week will never be erased by time or cynicism. You only have a certain amount of storage space in your brain; I am glad that the early days drown out the images that gave me battlefield nightmares. I'd much rather remember the picture of Zoobird coming back from a foraging expedition, pants tucked into his boot tops and bulging with dozens of small ears of corn, such a load he could barely walk. Or the vision of Deke, his turn on the revolving clean-up brigade, scrubbing the huge frying pan and stepping backward into a hole in the creek bottom. Came up, trying to swim with ten pounds of iron in his hand. Or the night the rain came and the tent collapsed. We had put it up after dark that first evening and it never was well balanced or taut. We spent a wet night and did the thing right the next morning. On the whole I was satisfied with our experiment as we ambled down our home street that following Saturday, seven days and five hours on the prairie, and never mind that we had to subsist on crawdads and peanut butter the last day.

It was a triumphant parade, with the neighborhood turning out to greet us and settle bets. I was on the driver's seat, Pug having gone back to take a nap. Beside me was Ookey. He could afford to let me drive. He had saved my life.

At least that's what he claimed. It had happened on the last day of our stay, my turn to get water from the spring. We shared the pasture with a couple of mules, but they had left us alone until then. I had hardly filled my milk can when I looked up into a pair of mean black eyes. A huge brown beast with black shadings, he had decided to contest my right to share his watering hole.

My "Shoo!" sounded weak, even to me.

Another monster was ambling over to join him, even more surly of look, huge hairy ears laid back on his neck. Their feet were shod and were the size of dinner plates. I backed off with what dignity I could. They followed, I broke into a trot, they picked up speed. The gang was yelling encouragement — I don't know why I didn't put the water down, it seemed like a point of honor. Abruptly Sweet Adeline let out a long feminine whinny, which seemed to rouse a fury in the mules. They broke into a gallop. Zoobird was yelling something about tent ropes — I hit them full speed and spun in an arc, water flying everywhere. Landed on my back.

The next thing I knew I couldn't breathe. I was lying face-down and there was a terrible weight on top of me. Hands pushed the air out of my lungs faster than I could draw it in. Distantly I heard Zoo yelling, "Ookey, let up! His eyes are open. Give him some air."

"Shut up! I know what I'm doing."

"I tell you, you're suffocating him." All at once the weight was gone. They told me later, Zoobird attacked Ookey bodily and hurled him off of me.

I managed a thin trickle of air. "I'm . . . okay."

I tried to muster a proper gratititude. But my days of leadership were over. On the way home Ookey outlined a plan of his own, for a baseball team. Which, of course, was just what we needed.

In the days that followed he assigned us all positions, said he would hustle us some games from the ads in the papers. He even managed to talk a local business into buying us uniforms. We were called the Ogallala Warriors, (and please buy Ogallala plumbing fixtures). By late summer we had formed into a tough unit, taking on such formidable opponents as the Westport Wild Cats. Westport was the meanest neighborhood in our vicinity. It was a memorable game in which the Wild Cats threw bean balls at us, enfuriating Zoobird, our hurler, who threw strikes that nobody could even see going past, ending in a free-for-all where the field was covered with bare-knuckle contests that left us covered in blood and joy. Nothing ever welded a group together the way that did.

We took the valediction of that summer clear on through high school and into a war, where friendship took on new dimensions and the action wasn't kid-stuff.

Four

Once you have lived in an Army uniform for eleven days straight without taking it off, the stink of desperate sweat and mud and other men's blood lingers strong in memory. It's hard to conjure up the juvenile elation of your first long pants. It was a sack suit of brown wool, woven with small checks of black in it, the legs tapering down to the tops of my shoes. Dad had bought it from the family of one of his customers, Mr. Dillon, who had hardly used it before he passed on. It had been too big for me, but Mrs. Fleischman had altered it to a perfect fit. She'd even given it a bit of swagger. Or maybe that was me. After a couple of years of high school I was beginning to strut a little.

Grossmutter grinned wickedly as I strolled into the kitchen, one fateful day. In a firecracker burst of German she said, *"The girls will lust after you."* Actually it isn't a good translation. I can speak the language like a native, but I couldn't write a line if my life depended on it, and a lot of it doesn't translate well into English. But I appreciated the sentiment. I had never had a date with a woman at that time. Girls were a kind of mystery. I couldn't see why they giggled so much as if I'd said something funny, when all I was asking for was tomorrow's history assignment. The truth is they scared me to death and those dire words would sometimes haunt me: *yellow belly.* There must be some way to approach them . . . ?

The thought made me shiver. Not just to approach, but to — well, what I wanted was considered very sinful by our church. And yet there was something in the Bible about being fruitful and multiplying. You don't get there without some physical contact. You don't have children unless you . . . I heard my mother's footsteps in the hall and shuddered. My father must have courted her, he must have — I couldn't imagine it.

She sailed into the kitchen like a great ship, her collar a bow wave of white lace and below it streamed a gown of blue silk, the bodice glittering with rhinestones, narrowing to a flow of dark blue taffeta that even made a tidal sound as she walked. It was hard to believe that she was Grossmutter's kin. The old lady was tough as a burl of walnut, she was little and sneaky. Mom was lofty and somehow noble. Her lifelong ambition was to be mentioned on the society pages of the Kansas City Star. She, and the rest of her friends in the Delphian Club, aspired to be part of the city's elite, and today they were taking a run at it.

Looking me over, she said, "Straighten your tie, young man, and you watch your manners when we get there. This is a very posh affair, organized by Mrs. Dwayne Forrest herself. She's the wife of a judge, a member of the D.A.R., the W.C.T.U. and the Colonial Dames of Virginia. Be careful of those cakes."

It was a high-class cake sale that was being held at a downtown hotel for the benefit of the starving Chinese orphans. I had asked why the Chinese, when there were plenty of local orphans? That got me nowhere, of course.

"We'll need help to carry the cakes," I said. Mother had volunteered to donate three, which Grossmutter had baked, grumbling all the way.

"And you keep off the fingers from the icing," she snarled as I hovered over one, a gorgeous chocolate creation with white

swirls all over it. She really loved making cakes.

"I'll get Zoobird," I offered.

"That poor boy? His clothes look like discards," Mother said, not unkindly. "He can't walk into a grand place like the Coates House."

"He's got a good suit." His mother had made it for our graduation from the eighth grade, two years ago. Zoo had bought the cloth with money he earned on Sundays at the Grover's Bank. They paid him fifty cents to mop the marble floors and polish the brass fixtures. They even let him keep any small change he found that had rolled into the corners. I wanted to get a job like that myself, but my father wouldn't hear of it. Sunday, he said, was for going to church. When I mentioned it to Zoobird he said he got plenty of religion at home. His mom read the Bible every night, and he really needed the money.

That day when he got dressed up (the prospect of riding in Mrs. Petty's Daimler was irresistible) he was so neat even my mother was impressed. "Calvin, you look — very nice." She eyed his yellow polka-dot tie, but it was as straight as geometry could make it. "You boys be careful of those cakes." Taking one, she led the way forth down the front walk to a car of breathless beauty. Mr. Petty was in railroads.

"You kids, don't get icing on the upholstery," he warned. It was handsome cream-colored leather that matched the automobile's exterior. A town car, it had golden-plated door handles inside and a great horn that blasted lesser vehicles out of the way with its AA-OO-GAH.

At the hotel there was a traffic jam of buggies and surries and horses kicking at the traces, shying away from the snorting of the Daimler's exhaust. Mr. Petty steered clear of the mess and found a place to park well over on the far side of the street.

Zoobird marched through the grandeur of the Coates House lobby, carrying his cake with nonchalance as if he did this every day, while I tried to keep from ogling the elegant chandeliers dripping with cut-glass prisms, and the potted palms, the huge Persian carpet. When we had got our cakes settled in the ballroom, Mother took a deep breath.

"Well, that's that. You boys can go home now." The streetcar ran not two blocks away, so it was no problem. But Zoobird had veered off in another direction, toward a smaller salon off to one side where an orchestra was playing. I made my way over there, too, sidling between the rich people.

Those men in tall hats, with their gold watch chains strung across big bellies, looked like they could have run the city with a cigar in one hand and a glass of brandy in the other. Women sprouted egret feathers from their sweeping bonnets, long white gloves up to their elbows. I thought, Mom will be needing some of those.

I never understood why she wanted to be one of the upper crust, but now I believe it was partly because she never went past third grade in school. She had worked to learn everything she could from books, magazines, she cut pictures out of Harpers and Leslies and made scrapbooks. She read the classics, which is how I came to be christened George Bernard Jones, after some author. My father put his foot down on calling me George, said he had a boss once named George who was a complete idiot. So I was stuck with Bernard, and sometimes I wondered why she couldn't have got impressed by Jack London instead.

As I strolled through that crowd I got a sudden shiver of maturity. It had been slow coming. High school had been a disappointment. They keep you in an eighth-grade frame of mind for the first two years, with sentences to be parsed and elements to be memorized. Now in my junior year I had begun to find trigonometry a challenge, and the Civil War was actually interesting. Also Zoobird had insisted that I go out for basketball. It was a brand new sport, and when I pointed out that it was obviously for tall people, he corrected me. As the center, he said he needed a smaller, faster person to take the pass and dribble the ball rapidly down the floor to the basket. I found I wasn't bad at free throws either; in fact by the end of the year I had worked up a certain amount of self-confidence.

But socially I still felt backward. Maybe because our gang members had all blossomed into young men with clever advances toward the girls in spite of all that giggling. Even Zoobird, who never had time for dating, was speculatively eyeing the crowd in the salon who moved to the tune of the orchestra. Now there, I thought, are women.

"Ballroom dancing" had become a craze, ever since Irene and Vernon Castle had come through town with their exhibition. Everybody had to learn the fox-trot. Dolly had collared me, under pain of dire retribution, to learn to dance with her. She thought she might get asked to in college — she was now up at Missouri U. I put up a fuss, but I really didn't mind. I might want to go on a date myself one of these days, and it turned out to be fun. The people out on the floor were laughing, swirling and dipping, full of gaiety.

Zoobird was transfixed. The band was playing the Missouri Waltz now and the skirts flared, showing a few ankles, pretty golden slippers on the girls' feet. "Bernie," he breathed, "I got to learn that. I want to do that."

"Get Dolly to teach you. She'll be home from college soon, and she's always looking for a partner to try new steps out."

"Your sister despises me."

"Yeah, she hates me too. What you do is make her a deal: tell her you'll help her with calculus. She's no good at math."

"Okay, I can do that." He still stared hypnotized at the dance floor. I was thrilled too at the sight of those moving bodies, the gowns clinging to them. I thought, *some of those girls aren't wearing corsets.*

"Aren't they beautiful?" A small voice rose beside me. "I'm going to have some golden slippers myself some day." She was a very neat child, dressed in a Navy-blue middy blouse and pleated skirt which came just below her knees. Long brown stockings, her own shoes were black patent leather with a strap. A plain face with a snub nose and long braids the color of red squirrel's fur, with eyes to match, she watched the dancers wistfully.

As an act of charity I asked her, "Would you like to dance?"

She glanced up gravely. "Thank you, I wish I could, but my mother hasn't sent me to dancing school yet, she says I'm too young. I just came along to carry the cake while she drove the electric."

"Me, too," I told her. "My name's Bernie Jones."

"How do you do?" The sudden smile brightened her eyes. "I'm Belinda Forrest."

Of course she was. A little princess from the royalty of Kansas City, Missouri, but it was doubtful that she would ever grow a glorious bosom to match those women on the floor who were bourgeoning out of their low-cut bodices. I went back to trying to figure how to get one to lust after me.

They seemed very human, gliding so easily in their partners' arms.

After a while I became aware that an older lady had come to stand with an arm around Belinda. "Someday soon, dear, you'll be out there," she said kindly. "Right now, I want you to come and recite for the ladies." A pale handsome woman in a simple yellow silk gown that fell in a shining column around her, she was topped by a small velvet hat with but a single rose on it. Almost seemed puny, so why did it make her look extra rich?

"Oh, let me introduce you, Mother. This is Bernie Jones."

"How do you do, young man." Mrs. Forrest shook my hand firmly. "Are you an usher?"

"No, ma'am. I came to help my mother — she donated three cakes," I said, hoping it might make an impression. Anything to help Mom get ahead. "She's with the Delphians."

"How lovely. It's nice to meet you." She said it very sincerely, and if my mother should want to know, *that's* elite. "Sorry to interrupt your fun, but I need Belinda now." And she led the little girl away, but not before the kid gave me a small wave *goodby.*

Zoobird had gravitated over to get closer to the band, so I left him and followed into the ballroom, just curious to see what kind of recitation rich people listen to. On a stage at one end, Belinda stood so straight I thought she was going to recite the pledge of allegiance. Bowing to the audience, she took a deep breath and began, in a slightly artificial tone:

"This is a poem by Mr. William Wordsworth, titled *The Daffodils.*

'I wandered lonely as a cloud
That floats on high o'er dales and hills,
When all at once I saw a crowd,
A host of golden daffodils . . .' "

It was nothing. Just the kind of thing you have to memorize in high school, so I don't know why I hung around. The crowd liked it, though, they clapped prodigiously afterward. I finally slipped out and went in search of the Zoo. I thought, some day for a laugh, I would say to Mom offhand, "Oh yes, I've met Mrs. Forrest." My mother would go into a swoon.

Zoobird was out on the veranda by then, frowning and shuffling his shabby old shoes — he had never saved enough to buy good ones. With the big feet he looked like a duck trying to do the quick-step.

"I'm going home," I announced, and he followed. We didn't bother with the streetcar, it was only ten blocks. Silently we walked, somehow overwhelmed by our thoughts. The afternoon seemed to have taken on an importance, but we'd have laughed if anyone told us it would change both our lives.

Five

By the time I reached my senior year of high school I was having weird dreams about women, usually prompted by some lurid tale of Ookey's. He had hinted that he "knew" quite a few of them and had nothing but contempt for the lot. But a man's got needs, he always said. I more or less understood what he meant. The sight of their bodies undulating under thin materials that clung and flowed, suggesting warm, soft flesh that smelled of lavender, aroused in me a positive thirst to embrace them. I thirsted for lips, not the real red ones, but the pink kind without a lot of paint on them . . . Not a suitable fantasy for a quiet Sunday afternoon.

Quiet no more. I was startled out of my day dream by an inhuman racket that seemed to be approaching, sounded like the banging of hammers on all the barrels in the world. I rushed outside and gave a whoop. You might know Ookey would be the first of us to acquire a car. The Shoemaker, a sorry green roadster, let out a tremendous indigestive backfire and grunted to a stop at our front walk. Nifty in a green-and-white checkered touring cap, Ook climbed over the door, which was held closed by baling wire, and jumped down proudly.

By then my father had joined us and the neighbors were gathering. "Hello, Ookey, where'd you get the tin lizzy?" Dad shook one of the fenders cautiously.

"Uh — over in Kansas, sir." Ookey gave me a look. He was hedging, of course. "Thought Bernie might like to come along for her maiden voyage."

"If that's a maiden, she's a little long in the gears," Dad kidded. You could see he was dying to delve into the engine. The other neighborhood men stood around kicking the tires, stooping to peer underneath at whatever was grinding around down there.

I was already up into the passenger seat, feeling ten feet high above the crowd. *Tomorrow I am going to find somebody to teach me to drive one of these. Anybody but Ookey.*

He was back on board now. Shoving in the gear with a terrible screeching noise he let out the clutch and we lurched down the street, rattling and clacking, back-firing every hundred yards or so.

"So how did you come by this monster?" I shouted.

"Won her in a game of call-shot last night. Some hustlers came over from Topeka, thought they'd take us rubes for a ride. I covered their bets and ran the table. Good thing I won, I couldn't have paid off." He chortled with sheer delight. We were approaching the hill that had almost done in Sweet Adeline. "Okay, Bunk," he yelled, "get ready to jump out. When I tell you, get a rock and shove it behind the rear wheel. The brakes on this thing aren't too good." He took a run at it as fast as he could force the old bucket of bolts to go, but it still only got us halfway up. As the engine neared its final gasp, he hollered, "Now!"

I leaped from the seat and found a great round stone to brace the wheel. He had managed not to kill the engine, but it was taking both hands to change to some extra low gear. Slowly the car began to crawl forward while I pushed from behind. At the top we paused and I got back on board. *If the brakes are that bad, what'll happen when we hit the crossroads down at the bottom?*

Too late to speculate. The Shoemaker felt the downgrade and took the bit in her teeth.

Ookey began dragging on the brake stick with both hands. "Steer!" he yelled at me.

I leaned across and tried frantically to keep us from veering into the ditch. As we approached the intersection I fleetingly saw a couple of cars stop in sheer terror, while we blazed on through. Finally the roadster began to slow to a limp.

"Flat tire," Ookey laughed like a little kid. "Good thing. Man, I never traveled that fast in my life."

"What do we do now?"

"Change the thing. Don't worry, I brought along a couple of spares."

He knew what he was doing, stripped the shredded rubber off the rim, pried some of the dents out of it and got a new tire on. And it only took him about a half an hour. I pumped it up and he pulled the jack out from under, then strolled over to sit down under a big sycamore tree, rolling himself a cigarette. Offered me one.

"Nope," I said carelessly, "Championship playoffs are coming up. I'm in training. Coach says smoking shortens your wind."

"Which is why I wouldn't come out for basketball," he commented. "Always somebody telling you what to do. Baseball's my game. Lots of chance for initiative. Need that in the Navy." He threw the remark away so carelessly I paid attention.

"You going to go be a sailor?"

"I'm heading for Annapolis," he said. "Been studying my head off. You have to pass some stiff exams to get in there."

"Crying-out-loud!" I mean, he couldn't have mentioned it to me before this? "Why the Navy?"

"Get a free education. See the world, like they say in the ads. And it'll keep me out of the mud when we go to war over in Europe. I'll be sailing the high seas."

"Who says — ? Listen, President Wilson promised us he wouldn't let us get into all that." The pictures in the rotogravure section showed ruined villages in Belgium, refugees crowded on boats and men slogging along the trenches in France.

"Don't be stupid, Bunk. We'll have to get in. They're running out of foot soldiers over there, getting killed off by the thousands, and it's still a stalemate. Who else is going to put an end to the thing?"

I never much liked the nickname "Bunk." I said, "Well, if you go off on a ship you could end up like the Lusitania."

That had been the headline in all the papers recently. The huge ocean liner, carrying ammunition and passengers, had been sunk by a German submarine. It went down so fast, they lost hundreds of people. Made everybody so mad at the "krauts" that I was just glad my last name happened to be Jones. I even tried to get Grossmutter to learn English so nobody would know I was part-German.

"Na-a-ah," Ookey said. "That's what we'll be putting an end to — the Navy, I mean. We'll be out there chasing those U-boats with depth charges. I bet I'll get my own destroyer."

I wasn't all that convinced. "My dad says the Germans and French have been fighting wars off and on for a century. It's in their nature. Nothing to do with us."

"Go ahead, think like that," he said smugly. "I'll talk to you in a couple of years, if you don't get sunk in all that mud. I met a fellow other day, he'd been over there, a place called Passchendaele on the border between France and Belgium. They'd been shelling it for months, churned up the earth twenty-feet down. And it's still raining, the ground is like quicksand. It swallows up whole caissons, mules, driver and all. Imagine drowning in muck? I'll take the good clean ocean any time."

"Not me," I said with a shudder. That much water, there was no bottom to it.

"Sure, you'll do the easy thing. Go to

M.U. like a good little boy and turn out to be a sales clerk at the haberdashery with a wife and two kids and a dog."

"Nothing wrong with getting married." My voice came out thick and unnatural.

Ookey gave me a shrewd look. "You picked her out yet? The little woman?"

I had to laugh. "I think I will have one of those cigarettes."

Once before I had started to take up smoking. I'd swiped one of Dad's stogies, took it out to the barn to give it a try, but I couldn't get it lit. Until Grossmutter showed up, muttered some German profanity, took it from me, bit off the end and spat it out. Then sheltering the match in her bony hand she got the thing going. *"Here, that's how it's done."* Ten minutes later I had given up smoking forever. Now, I managed not to choke, though the taste was raw.

"Actually," I said, "I might go to college." It was taken for granted that Dad had only enough money to send one kid to M.U. and Dolly was not only the oldest but the smartest. "If we win the playoffs the first team will probably get scholarship offers."

"Great, you can take advanced backslapping and graduate in ass-kissing and become a politician, or be a barber or start a little ice cream shop. Bunk, we don't have money, we don't have power, we don't even have talent. The only thing we got is time, so think before you waste it. Or you will lie on your death bed and never have tasted a moment of glory. Your life will flash before your eyes and it will only take about ten seconds, because it's never been all that exciting." He squared around and looked at me, those dark eyes judicious. "Trouble with you, you need a woman."

It came out of the blue, but instantly I knew he was right. I had sulked around the edges of the dance floor instead of getting out there and hoofing it. Even Zoobird knew how to grab a girl and swing her. Dolly had taught him to dance, though after a few lessons he was teaching her some new frills he made up. But I hadn't been in tune with the music, including the background score of my entire life. The piano player was ripping off ragtime and I was still waltzing around and around, in circles.

"I don't seem to make much hay with the girls at school," I admitted, in a tough voice. "Oh, I went to a few hops, but they seem pretty juvenile."

Bernie, you bad boy, you're holding me too tight.

But Bessie — or Junie or Katie — that's what clutch dancing is all about. You're sup-

pose to touch chests.

Not my chest, you don't.

Ookey snorted. "Sweet little innocents, you don't want to fool around with that kind or they'll have you at the altar. If you need sex, go down to Twelfth Street. Or if you want to just fool around I can take you to a place where the good times roll."

Fiercely I envied him that off-hand confidence, to come out with a remark like that. *Go down on Twelfth Street.* As if I had ever been near the red light district. But fooling around I probably could handle. I said, "Sounds good. Let's go."

Six

It was coming on dark as we parked in front of the roadhouse. Ookey said, "This is a great place to pick up a girl, learn some lady-killer technique. Just don't get cold feet on me, Bunk."

My feet turned instantly cold. It was a low-life place on a side road over near Olathe. Cars lurked crookedly in the shadows behind the building and the out-house over to one side. As we walked into the half-light of the bar I saw a group of guys who looked familiar. They were from Westport, some of them on the basketball team. I recognized one I'd had a few brushes with. He had given me an elbow in the ribs last time we met, for which I had accidentally stepped all over his shin. Name was Nuck.

When he saw me his seamed face took on a look of evil recognition. His pals stood up, too, and Ookey fingered the lucky scar on his cheek. "You take the one on the left.

I'll handle the other two." He was tense as a dog ready to attack.

The toughs strolled toward us and Nuck bantered, "Well, well, if it ain't the Central High hot-shot." To his pals he added, "That little squirt runs around the boards like a jack-rabbit. Name's Bernie Jones, ain't that right?"

"Yep," I said, "and in a few weeks we're gonna lick you like a kid licks a candy cane."

"Lick my boots," he snorted. But he was hanging easy now. "I'll say this, you guys got spunk. And you got one good tall old skinnymarink for a center. Come on, I'll buy you a drink."

I could feel Ookey eyeing me as if I'd just popped out of a box of Crackerjack. He said, "Thanks, guys, but we're joining some friends over there at the table." And led me toward the back of the saloon, where a couple of guys and several women sat. All of them older than me, they looked fairly spiffy in their tailored suits and polished shoes. It was a fad, those days, for rich people to go "slumming," which I bet was the case.

They greeted Ookey with the condescension of the wealthy. "Here's the chap who relieved me of my cash in that poker game last week."

I was being introduced all around, looked at up and down, especially by one small pert girl. No floozy, her black hair was held up by a handsome enamel comb and a spill of enamel beads hung across the front of her dress, which was emerald green sateen. She pointed at me and said, very distinctly, "I want that one."

"He's all yours, Darlene." Ookey shoved me down into a seat beside her and took one himself on the opposite side of the table. "Beer for everybody. I'm buying."

"On my money," added the languid fellow who had spoken to him first.

When the bartender came over, I stopped him briefly. "Make mine a sarsaparilla," I said in a low tone, which managed to fall into a gap in the conversation. Everybody heard it and hooted.

"Hey, don't sell Bunk short," Ookey warned. "He's the star player on our basketball team, going to take us to the championship. He's in training, no booze, no cigarettes. Next month they're gonna play those bozos over at the bar, bare-knuckles and down and dirty."

"Ooooh, that sounds exciting." The girl hitched her chair up tight to mine, leaning close so I could smell her perfume. Somehow the green dress had inched up to her knee, showing a thin white silk stocking. Down there in the dark under the table her foot nudged mine. My belly did a flip. "I love sportsmen," she went on in a coquettish tone, but her green eyes were sharp and hungry. "What else do you do for fun?"

"I do push-ups," I kidded.

"Then you must be strong." She delicately reached out and squeezed my arm. "You're cute. Why don't you and I get out of here? My car's right outside. Let's speed off into the night and break some rules."

I must have looked dumbfounded, because Ookey was laughing as she tucked her arm in mine and guided me out the door.

Back in the days of the tree house we had held many discussions on the subject of good and evil. Pug claimed we were all sinners, implying it was Eve's fault that we weren't still living in the Garden of Eden. Deke protested that it was Adam too who sinned by letting her talk him into disobeying the Lord. I kept my mouth shut because I always secretly figured it was pretty sneaky of God to put a beautiful apple tree into His garden and then tell them not to eat the fruit. Deke said it was our fate, to be tested. I never took that personally until I met Darlene Puckett. I mean you've got to feel sorry for Adam.

She overthrew all the conventions I had been taught, to treat a woman with respect, escort her to your auto, make her comfortable before you take the wheel and so forth. Not a chance, not with that girl. She sashayed her little backside across the yard and got in the driver's side of one great automobile — a Jackson touring car with spare tire mounted on the side door. I had to climb past it when I got in, and sit down fast as she ripped on out of there.

"There's a new moving picture downtown," she was saying. "It's called 'A Fool There Was.' " She invested the words with extra meaning.

After years of Our Gang comedies and Chaplin, I wasn't really ready for Theda Bara. In the darkness of the movie house I could feel myself blushing as she flared her nostrils, giving sultry looks at the poor besotted man. Her makeup was painfully seductive, and when she sank into his arms I felt odd sensations in my gut. It didn't help that Darlene's hot little fingers were interlocked with mine in a grip that was both sensuous and demanding. Only I didn't know what she was demanding. I just knew that when the piano player would twist the melody a certain way she'd wriggle and sigh. By the time I got out of there I felt like ten pounds of hot coals in a five-pound hopper.

All the way home she kept glancing over at me — I wished she would keep her eyes on the road. I felt embarrassingly edible. When we parked in front of my house, I saw a light on back in the kitchen, which meant Dad hadn't gone to bed yet. He sometimes smoked a final cigar on the front porch. Might be there in the dark right now watching.

I struggled to get out. "Uh — thanks for a nice evening."

But she had leaned across and blocked me bodily. "Wasn't it a great movie? Didn't you love that line: 'Kiss me, you fool!' " And with that she planted her mouth on mine, her lips moving, searching. I felt the fire flare under those embers of mine and reached blindly for the door handle.

With an odd laugh, she drew back then. "You are a real challenge, my boy. Don't worry, there's plenty of time. This basketball practice of yours, when does it let out?"

"Around five in the afternoon."

"I'll pick you up at the school gym, five-oh-one. And be sure and get me a ticket to that big game."

As I said, poor Adam.

Hard as I tried, I couldn't put Darlene in

a category. She wasn't a chippy, but she certainly wasn't one of those china figurines you picture standing with you at the altar. Not a stupid bar-room wench, Darlene was about as dumb as a team of engineers. In fact, she had a kind of classy air about her, but what class I wasn't sure until one day she took me home with her. Drove right on in the driveway of one of the new hotels that had gone up on Linwood Boulevard.

"My folks are out," she was saying as she let herself into the apartment. A whole suite of rooms, rented by the year, she explained; they did that because her father traveled a lot, he was in oil. He had residences in Tulsa, California, and Mexico City. There were curious gew-gaws, tin candle holders, little clay idols with big bellies, and heavy throws that looked like saddle blankets, she called them serapes. But all of it looked like money.

Especially the grand piano in the corner over which was flung a red silk scarf with fringe dangling. Darlene plunked her rear end on the bench and carelessly began to rip off a tune with a hard beat and a sad sound. "Oh, I hate to see that evening sun go down." She sang it in a hoarse throaty voice, but mainly she played the paint off that piano. Better than the guy in the movie house.

When she paused to light a cigarette I said, "Where on earth did you learn to play like that?"

"My mother. Mom was a cabaret performer, you should hear her! Songs that would knock your pants off." She said it proudly, as she sank down beside me, her hand on my knee, progressing upward until she was fiddling with some very personal buttons. I wanted to bat her away, but it would be rude. Wouldn't it?

Thank goodness at that moment her folks came home. They didn't seem at all scandalized to find me there. In fact her father shook my hand enthusiastically. A sturdy man with muscular grip, he could have done a patch in the oil fields himself, I thought. Her mother was so heavily rouged it was hard to tell what kind of face she had. I was pretty sure she was wearing a wig. And yet I liked them. I liked the way Mr. Puckett was proud of his company.

"Oil is going to make this world run, you'll see. Coal will peter out and wood's a thing of the past. Yes, sir, in fifty years oil will fuel every house and every business, not to mention our automobiles. There'll be thousands of cars some day, all running on gasoline."

I didn't even know that gas came from oil. I asked him questions and we talked for maybe an hour as the evening wore on. Mrs. Puckett went off to bed. Darlene kept pacing the room, giving me grim looks. I wasn't paying enough attention to her, I know. Finally she made her exit.

"It's been a real great evening, Bernie. Call me up some time." Her voice was hard as a grinding stone.

Mr. Puckett didn't seem to notice. He was saying that once I was out of high school I should consider going into the oil business. Always a place in his company for up-and-coming young men.

Later when I told Dad about it he seemed troubled. "You never brought this young lady home with you. Why don't you ask her for dinner?"

The thought of Darlene in our humble house with its painted wooden floors and antimacassars on the furniture, Grossmutter grumbling in German and my mother putting on airs, as if she were a Colonial Dame or something, it made me shudder. "The Pucketts are kind of over my head," I said. "Shoot, I don't even have a car. I have to let her drive me everywhere."

It was only a day or so later that my father stunned us. He drove into the yard in an

Abbott-Detroit, a black sedan with wooden spoke wheels and only one dent in the rear fender where a horse had kicked it. He got the thing cheap because the flame squealed unmercifully on the chassis.

"It just needs a little work," he told us cheerfully. And the next weekend he invited a couple of friends over and we lifted the body off the undercarriage, put in leather padding all around. By the time we got through the car moved like a whisper.

It was one of the high points of my life to drive that auto into the barnyard where Ookey was bending over the engine of the Shoemaker, greasy and angry and baffled. When he saw the Abbott-Detroit, me behind the wheel, his whole face went crooked with jealousy. Which was what I wanted, but I didn't want to lose him permanently as a buddy.

Very quickly I spoke up. "So, whatcha think? This is my old man's car. He decided we need one."

Putting it that way allowed Ookey to be generous. "Very nice for an older person. Very respectable." Which meant he wouldn't ride in it if he only had one leg.

"Also, I think he figured I shouldn't be dependent on Darlene to chauffeur me around."

"You shouldn't be dependent on Darlene for the time of day." He turned away sourly and began to fiddle with his engine again. "You're spoiling that little floozy to death. Treating her like gold, when she's actually just yard trash. If I'd known you were so dumb I wouldn't have ever introduced you. I mean, why don't you grow up?"

I began to burn. Because he was right, I did feel stupid around the girl. She was full of strange moods. Sometimes her hands were all over me and when I wouldn't get fresh back it made her mad. "Good God! Didn't you ever learn to neck?"

Taking the Lord's name in vain worried me. I had a hunch He didn't look kindly on people who did that, and I still needed Him occasionally for advice and assistance. Like the big game coming up, I kept hinting to Him that I'd really appreciate His help.

I didn't argue the matter with Ookey, he was obviously in a grim place that day. "So," I said, "any word yet from the Navy?" I knew he took their examination.

He scuffed his knuckles on the engine block and cursed, with all the ugliness of a bull-driver. After a minute he asked, "What about you? All set for M.U., rah-rah-rah?"

"Dolly goes there," I reminded him. "I'm not even thinking Mizzou. In fact what I thought was I'd probably take a job for the summer. Dad thinks he can get me a place on the loading dock over at Kansas City Bag Company. He knows the boss."

"That'll be a great and noble career, pushing a broom for a buck a day."

"Seventy-five cents," I said. "It would only be temporary. Give me time to figure out what I want to do. I'm not like you, I don't have any great goal."

"Are you making fun of me?" he snarled, turning around in a black fury.

"Naaah," I said, "no more than you were trying to make me feel like a worm for wanting to earn a living." My own insides were bracing up now. "I ought to bust your jaw."

"Try it, you little Missouri puke!"

I threw my best punch into his gut as hard as I could. It was always important to land the first blow with Ookey. You needed all the edge you could get. He staggered, but came back fast. I ducked his roundhouse, came in under it right into his jab, which was short and powerful. For a minute I was seeing double. But I had learned to take a pretty good hit. All that training I did for basketball kicked in and for a few minutes I even matched him. Then he tripped me and followed me down onto the dirt where his weight was an advantage. Even so, I almost pinned him once, but he slid aside and was on my back, got me in a neck hold. For a minute everything stuck. I could see the pigs over in their wallow, watching us like spectators. Then my eyes started to get spots in front of them. I wasn't going to holler "uncle," not if he killed me.

Then abruptly it was over. He rolled off me onto his back. We lay there panting while out across the fields a crow called. With the world silently spinning, I fought to get my breath back. Somewhere in the distance Ookey spoke.

"I got turned down by the Navy."

SEVEN

I've seen New York City spread out across the night sky, an amusement park for the Wall Street gods. I've seen London like a huge grimy magnificent etching out of a Dickens novel. I've seen Paris. We covered a lot of ground on our way to the killing fields, us doughboys.

And yet, the building that jolted my heart the most was in Kansas City the day the Muehlebach Hotel opened. Right there in our own front yard, a ten story palace. The lobby was massively elegant, the dining room a dazzling sight of white napery and electric chandeliers. We'd had lights in our house for some time now, but nothing like this. The ballroom had a hardwood floor as shining and as broad as our basketball court. A small string orchestra was playing garden music the day we took the tour, Darlene and I.

"Well, we've got to come here," she informed me. "Make a reservation right now. Dinner and dancing."

"Listen, I'd like to, but I can't afford —"

"Oh, can it, Bernie. My father's already got an account here. I'll just sign the tab." Her scorn was coming through oftener these days.

"All right," I sighed. "I'll pick you up Saturday night around six."

"I'll pick *you* up," she snapped. "That dowdy thing you drive, it's an old-man's car."

So I guess I knew our days were numbered. I was even ready for it. When she arrived that night I didn't even get in beside her. She was wearing a get-up that would have embarrassed me if we'd been going to a bawdy house. The thin yellow chiffon dress was coming apart in rifts around her shoulders, trailing little ruffles, and open down the front as far as I could see, held together with a couple of flogs of gold braid. The skirt was so flimsy it revealed every inch of the legs beneath it, clear on up to forbidden territory. On her black hair a gold tiara was overbearing, and her black-shadowed eyes and rouged cheeks were in the style that was Theda Bara's trademark. I wouldn't have been seen with her at a dog fight.

"Well, get in," she demanded irritably.

"Uh-uh. If you want to go to the Muehlebach dressed like a vamp you'll have to find another escort."

As easy as that. She drove off in a flush of gravel and was gone. I felt a little sad. It was like losing a front tooth that's killing you. The pain is over, but you doubt if you'll ever smile again.

I glanced up at Zoobird's window next door. It was dark. Saturday night he usually went down to the dance hall he had found off Twelfth Street, spending all his small change on partners that cost but ten cents a dance. There was a certain wisdom in that, I reflected.

What I needed to concentrate on was the championship game which was coming up next week. That and my future were pretty much linked. I hadn't decided yet which school I'd like to be invited to, if any. If the summer job turned into something more serious next fall, I'd be on my way to a bank account. Money appealed to me right then. It was the only thing you could count on, not school, not friends, certainly not women.

I decided maybe it was time I went to church. Lately I'd been ducking out on that, using homework as an alibi, the only one

Dad really accepted. But the minister didn't exactly help me that next morning, he was all about Samson and Delilah. So at least I'd had the sense not to snuggle up to Darlene. I still had my hair, I sort of kidded myself sadly as we filed out of service. Doggone, religion was a constant reminder of all that could go wrong in life, I thought. It's depressing, church is. I should have stayed home and studied for my final exams.

I didn't really need to. What I needed was to practice my moves with Zoobird over at the gym. We spent most of our spare time that week gearing up for the game. The team was tight as a laced shoe that night. Coach called us to order and handed out chocolate bars as we stood there in our new uniforms, orange shirts and green padded pants to the knee above orange socks. We looked good. I began to feel good, keyed up to the right pitch the way you should be before a great game.

The roar that went up as we took the floor sent my blood surging. This was my world, the push and shove and skill of a long shot, the slap of tennis shoes on the hardwood floor, the scream of the referee's whistle. This was the stuff of manhood.

Westport was menacing in blue and silver. The band was playing the Star Spangled

Banner, but I was too moved by it all to join in. I scanned the crowd for my parents — they were out there somewhere. As my look careened along the rows it snagged on a bright scarlet dress just below the basket at one end of the court. I had forgotten that I'd given Darlene the best ticket in the house. It astounded me that she had come. We hadn't spoken since the night our date blew up..

Well, let her watch, I thought. She will see me in action for once. I took a deep breath and squared my shoulders. Zoobird gave me the sign: *Get ready for our move.* We had a sequence that we only used in the most important games. On the tipoff he would knock the ball backward into the adept hands of Deke, who would sling it to me with one long under-hand throw. I'd be halfway down the floor by then — one bounce and I'd lay it into the basket before the other side caught on. We'd be two points up. It demoralized our opponents. Sometimes they were too flustered to take the rebound and Zoobird would steal it from them, get in another basket while they were floundering.

That night it worked smooth as grease. Deke put his throw right into my numbers, I took my dribble. Easy shot.

I missed.

A dead hush fell over the crowd. And in that silence Darlene's voice rang out like a gong. "Next time get a step ladder."

After we lost the game to Westport our lives all went into limbo. We didn't even meet at the treehouse any more, kid stuff. We had given it to a young cousin of Pug's who needed a hideaway. Fats was working full time in his dad's grocery, and Deke was attending synagogue every day, thought he might just be a rabbi. Zoobird got a couple of scholarship offers, M.U. and Kansas State, but he turned them down.

"I can't leave Mom." His father had died the week after graduation. Instead of being relieved to be free of her burden, his mother had gone to pieces, weeping her heart out. "I got a good job offer from the bank," he told me. "Bookkeeper. Pays fifty dollars a month. We can live off that and she won't have to take in sewing."

Dollars got a job down at the stockyards. They were right across the street from Drover's Bank. Since Pug was in the same neighborhood, I went on down one morning and hired on at the Kansas City Bag Company, which was around the corner on one of the railroad sidings. The gang was still more or less together, but hardly glorious. Ookey was nowhere to be found.

I kept remembering his careless remark, that if I needed a woman I should go on down to Twelfth Street, so one Saturday afternoon I did just that. We got off at three o'clock, and instead of heading for the street car I strolled in the direction of loud music and damnation.

I had been listening to the guys on the loading dock, their exploits made me feel like a mere child or a monk or an idiot. I didn't even know their vocabulary of sin. What they said they did with women made me sick, with a horrid sort of curiosity, almost like the queasiness that still came over me at thought of using a gun on some animal. The dock workers were all great hunters. They had tattoos and they chewed tobacco which they spit expertly right where I was sweeping. Their laughter had a nasty ring. It was time to start taking steps to grow a shell of maturity, even if I was secretly still soft inside. I was reconciled to the fact that I probably was a yellow-belly and would be forever. But I needed to start putting on a tougher face.

Along Twelfth Street you could hear some of the best jazz in the country, so they said. The open doors of the saloons let it pour forth, the honkytonk piano, the booming doghouse, the wailing bone and the fiery horn, all played by the top musicians in the business. As I walked down the street I vibrated to those drums, midnight music played at four in the afternoon.

The best house of prostitution west of the Mississippi was said to be our own pride and joy, Anne's Chambers. It was a surprisingly modest hotel with no gaudiness about it, just a row of windows that looked out on the Street. The women who lounged there were lovely, modestly folded into kimonos and with well-groomed hair, nice jewelry on their hands that sparkled when they waved to me. My heart was pitching like a rowboat in a storm as I walked in. To be met immediately by a handsome woman, her robe an expensive unrevealing gown of soft rose-colored velvet.

"Hello, sweetie," she said to me gently, turning me around and escorting me back to the door. "You come and see us in about five years."

It rattled me. I must have some sort of baby face that made her think I couldn't handle the job. But that was Anne's reputation — she was very careful about the men she let in. I didn't have the look, and I'd better find some way to acquire it.

Wandering aimlessly along the Street I stopped in front of a vaudeville house and stood gawking. The signs depicted voluptuous women in scanty scarves and veils and not much else, seductive faces with secret eyes and flaming hair. Their bodies — I never realized the human female body could look so decorative. But there it was again, a big sign on the ticket booth: NO MINORS. I didn't know I was one still, I had turned seventeen.

Down the alley I saw a side door ajar to let some air into the old theater. The manager, who usually stood there, had taken a few steps away to talk to one of the show girls. In the flick of an eye I slipped into the dark hot shadows within while he was telling her off.

"Now you listen to me good, Millie. You are out on that stage to entertain the customers. You flash them bazooms."

Lurking behind a rack of costumes I could see the stage. The foot-lights shone blindingly bright up into the faces of the women, who flounced and wriggled to the tinny piano music, opening their costumes to reveal their bodies to the audience of men, who hooted and whistled. As they came trooping off they didn't bother to cover up. I could see their fat flesh sweating, sagging, patches of glitter stuck on crucial parts of their anatomy. But what shocked me most was their faces. Under the grease paint they were old, as old as my mother! To think they were so needy that they had to take a wretched job like this — it made me sick to my stomach. I stumbled out into the street. Even the jazz had gone sour.

Riding the streetcar home I stared blindly at the city as if I had never seen it before. Not until I turned in at my own house did I begin to feel a sense of recognition. I headed for the kitchen where Grossmutter was making crabapple jelly. *"Gut!"* she said. *"You can help cut the worms out of the fruit."*

I wished I could cut some worms out of my inner mind. As I dug the white little slugs out with a knife I ruined quite a few crabapples, which doesn't matter when you're making jelly. I slashed at them pretty wickedly, until the old woman peered at me.

"What's the matter with you!"

"Nothing," I snapped back at her. *"And you? How makes the new stove."* I knew she hated it. A gas stove had supplanted the old wood one, burners that turned on at the strike of a match. But it was too hot sometimes, others not hot enough, and there was no reservoir of warm water. The German language gives itself to *sturm und drang.*

Listening to a long spiel of it made me feel better.

"I have to new recipes make up, nothing tastes right," she growled.

"I know how you feel." I flipped a worm clear across the counter and onto the floor.

"Take that job out onto the back porch," she ordered, and went off to the front of the house.

As I sat on our rear stoop I gave our whistle, just in case Zoobird was home. But he often worked late on Saturdays, catching up with last-minute bank business. He liked his job — I envied him that. And I wished I could lose myself on a dance floor with some faceless partner who only wanted a dime. By now he had found a permanent girl, her name was Nadine. He said they were the perfect fit. She was tall, too, and danced well, and didn't want to do anything else. *Watch out, old buddy, you'd better look way beyond her foxtrot.*

I said something of the sort to Dad, who had wandered out to join me on the steps. "I'm really worried about Zoobird. I mean he's so darned innocent. This girl has got him dancing around like a puppet. I'm afraid she'll get her hooks in him."

Picking up a short stub of dowel he began whittling on it with his pocket knife. "Yep, that's the way it goes sometimes. Young fellows have to learn to deal with the opposite sex, and it's not easy."

"You said it. I mean, I almost got serious with Darlene. Man, would that have been a mess."

"Was she the one in the red dress at the basketball game?" When I nodded, he went on, "You're right, that's the kind who can wreck your whole life. Any woman who would put a man down in public isn't worth a bucket of spit."

The good manly words braced me up a little. "Of course, in private she could be very lovey-dovey. Too much. She seemed to expect me to —" I couldn't say it, not with the memory of her fumbling at my buttons and so forth. "Listen," I blurted, "do women ever actually want to be disrespected? Why would they want you to take advantage of them?"

"Well, I guess they enjoy a little flirting."

"I'm talking way beyond flirting." A vision arose in front of me, of her in that feathery costume. "I'm talking about a girl from a nice family with respectable parents, and all at once she's getting fresh. She's making moves that I can't — I don't think I should — I mean, I didn't want to — I'm not even sure I could if I tried." There it was. The thing that had been gnawing at me like a crabapple worm. Angrily, I dug deep and nicked my finger.

"Ought to sharpen that knife," Dad said. "It's the dull ones that slip and cut you." He had turned the stub of wood into a clothespin. "I can see your problem: you've been brought up to be decent, you go to church, you know what sin is. Doing the wrong thing doesn't come easy to you, thank the Lord. If some woman tries to get you to go beyond your best instincts, then she's in league with Old Bug and all you can do is pity her and head for the door."

Actually I had figured that part out. Darlene had called me a couple of times since that night, and I had shut her down fast. The last time she had said, "Bernie, I'm very disappointed in you." I think she was crying.

Dad stood up and put the clothespin on the line. "Don't worry, you'll have better times than that. Women can be fun."

"I don't know. Dad, what do they really want?" *And how can I learn to give it to them, what's the secret?*

His face flushed slightly. "You have to do a lot of guessing. But I can tell you this: when a certain one comes along, you'll hear a kind of jig in your head and you will suddenly know the right steps. Count on it."

After he'd gone in I sat there, still confused. Did he hear some sort of music when he met my mother? It seemed unbelievable. Besides, I already knew how to dance, that wasn't my problem. I decided he had no idea what I was really asking, and it made me feel very deserted.

Now, of course, I understand it all. A war is a shattering way to learn, but it's effective at demolishing your immaturities.

Eight

With summer drawing to an end I had to face a decision — whether to go on with my schooling or not. I had been offered a sports scholarship by a small college in Arkansas, tuition, but no room and board. By then I had saved up a few dollars — over at the Bank my salary was deposited by Zoobird with ceremony each payday. He was now a Receiving Teller and making sixty bucks a month. He said he liked the job just fine. I didn't know whether he meant it. His fingers got pretty inky in the course of a day and that bothered him, I think.

For me, the prospect of more books and tests was not appealing. But then nothing was at that moment. I had been about to quit my job on the loading dock when the Bag Company offered me a position in the bookkeeping office with a desk and a calendar and a nice raise. For lack of anything better I stayed on, much to Ookey's disgust.

"Go on, scribble up your ledgers, that'll make you feel like a hero."

He himself was a walking case of frustration. He had taken a job in the train yards as a switchman, shunting cars around the sidings. It was hard, brainless work, and when his shift was over he would disappear into the dusk of evening to find a poker game or shoot some pool. Then he disappeared, left the railroad and nobody saw him for a month. I figured he had done it, gone off and joined the Foreign Legion. I almost wished I had gone with him.

There was no drive in my life, no great game to train for, nothing to look forward to. So I was ripe for action that afternoon in April when he suddenly showed up on my doorstep, so to speak. I found him angled against the lamp post outside our office, around three o'clock one Saturday afternoon. He looked tip-top, in new gabardine pants, tall shiny boots and a leather jacket. Scarf around his neck, he reminded me of the advertisements in Red Book Magazine. The girls coming out of our office almost tripped over their feet when they went past him, switching their hips and tittering.

"We'd better get out of here before you get kidnapped by a romantic stenographer." That got a grin out of him.

“Not a keeper in the lot,” he said judiciously. “Bunk, we need to find you a new job.”

“Were you waiting for me?”

“They said you’d be getting off at three o’clock so I hung around. I have something to show you, if you’ve got time.”

“Sure,” I said, following him over to a car that was parked nearby, the sorriest old Reo I’d ever seen, rusted and dented with knock-kneed wheels and a crooked bumper.

“Got her from the junk yard,” he explained. “Fixed it up — it runs okay, most of the time. Some day I’ll buy me a real humdinger of a car. Lately, though, I been putting my money into something else.” He did love to be mysterious. I was puzzled, I had pictured him as despondent, even a little suicidal. Wasted sympathy, obviously. Driving briskly away from town with the April breeze flapping the side curtains, he was full of the old excitement.

Turning off on a road heading northward, he said, “You been watching the papers lately? Think we’re going to war?”

It startled me. “Good Lord, no.” I wasn’t taking His name in vain, I meant it prayerfully. “The President won’t do that to us, not after he promised.”

“We’ll see,” Ookey said cryptically. “But I

betcha I'm gonna shoot a gun at one of those Heinies before a year's past."

"You're still thinking of the tramp steamer idea, go to England and sign on with the British Navy?"

He shook his head. "I doubt they have any ships left, the way those krauts sink everything in sight. We should have got into it sooner. Now the enemy's got whole fleets of submarines. North Atlantic is crawling with 'em."

The shipping news had been pretty dismal, all right. The convoys of food and ammunition we were sending across had to run at night without lights, they said, and pray they didn't get torpedoed out of the water. And the pictures from the Front were getting worse all the time. The French soldiers looked muddy and hopeless and kind of dazed. It showed women in the churches praying for a victory. That presented an odd puzzle: I happened to know the Germans were religious people too. They must be asking God to help their side. How could He make a decision like that?

I guess I said something of the sort aloud, because Ookey laughed. "You're still hung up on that folklore. You think there's some beardy old guy looking down and blessing you, or blaming you for having bad thoughts? It's all a fraud."

"God's a fraud?" I repeated, scandalized. "Is that what you believe?"

"I don't think about it much. There's no point in getting worked up over a bunch of fairy tales the old people concocted to keep the younger folks in line. 'Ooooh, be good or you'll go to Hell.' Like saying the boogeyman will get you."

"Jesus Christ isn't a fairy tale. I happen to know He really lived." My mother had a Book of Religions that told the actual history behind the Bible, and it was all true, about the Romans and Pontius Pilate and all.

"Doesn't mean He's floating around in the sky, judging whether you should get promoted or die in an accident with a streetcar. I can tell you personally, He ain't up there." He gave a funny laugh and jerked a thumb at the spread of blue sky overhead, lovely April day, small clouds drifting. "And I'm going to prove it to you."

We had turned off the back road into a broad field of cheat grass and thistles, most of it beaten down by the coming and going of tires, tracks everywhere. One space was cleared down to dirt, a long strip that stretched away from the tall shed where we parked. Corrugated iron, it was big enough to hold a three-ring circus. To one side on a flag pole was hung a fat brown stocking.

"It's called a wind sock," he followed my glance. "So you'll know which way it's blowing." Leading me over to the shed, he rolled back a vast door to reveal a shadowy barn where odd creatures lived — a row of airplanes, fragile, gawky things with big wings and tiny wheels. I'd seen pictures of them in the paper. All too often the caption read: DAREDEVIL TAKES DEATH DIVE. I hoped Ookey wasn't going to try to fly one of the things. It would be a thrill to watch one take off, but terrible to witness the crash.

He had gone straight over to a flying machine with a double wing and two seats, one behind the other. The body, which was shaped like a coffin, looked to be made of a light wooden framework covered by butcher's wrap, the kind you use to make a kite. He smacked it fondly.

"Well, whatcha think of her?"

"Uh — swell. I mean she looks really — nifty."

"Go on, climb in."

"Me? No thanks. I don't know anything about airplanes and I don't want to trespass on somebody else's property. I can see her fine from right here."

"Don't be skittish. Get in the rear seat, put these on." He handed me a pair of goggles and slipped some on himself. "I have to be up front to fly it."

"How do you know — I mean, do you know how to drive this thing?"

He was boosting me up over the side with almost no help from me.

"Been taking lessons for months. I'll show you how it feels to be a bird."

In spite of the big NO writhing inside me, a culmination of a lifetime of cowardice, yet there was a magical lure about the thought of flight. At least you would have one great experience before you died. Ookey was heaving on the propeller, like cranking a car but on a grander scale. The engine caught with a horrendous roar. Grinning joyously he climbed aboard. Above the noise he called back to me, "Just don't spit over the side."

We rolled slowly out onto the long cleared dirt track and began to run down it, picking up speed. I gave a final sad glance at the earth around, the budding trees, the splendid hills. Missouri is a beautiful state in the springtime, I have always loved Missouri . . .

As we speeded up the plane was shuddering so hard I thought it would come apart. I even hoped so. Then suddenly the jarring stopped, the motion became smooth, not even a sense of lift. It was the ground that fell away from us, farther and farther below. The shed, the car, all diminishing to the size of toys, and disappearing behind us, though there was no sense of forward motion now. Hard to tell how fast we were going, except that we were passing over a river — it had to be the Blue River — and those tiny houses were the town of Independence, once the jump-off place for the wagon trains of pioneers. Good, tough men, but all they had to worry about were a few bears and Pawnees. I'd settle for that any time.

Picturing how far I would fall to get back to earth, I was gripping my seat with both hands. Ookey glanced over his shoulder, weird in the leather helmet and goggles, but the grin was familiar. I wished he'd keep his eyes on the road. Then I realized there was no road, nothing for him to run into. I managed to give him a high sign: *This is great.* The wind almost took my hand off.

As we rose higher I began to loosen up. By now it didn't matter what altitude we were when we made the final downward plunge. I had accepted my fate and felt only a morbid sense of enjoyment, like a condemned man eating his last steak. As if to test my nonchalance he put the plane into a bank and came around, heading for our neighborhood. The huge Nelson estate passed under us, the miniature streets of The Plaza. Ookey pointed down and I saw a golf course with tiny figures on it, most of them motionless, staring up at us. Of course he decided to take us lower. We tilted downward going like a sled on ice, the wind zinging the wire struts that held the flimsy wings together. In one part of my mind I wondered: if you didn't dare spit over the side, what would you do if you had to throw up?

Then at the last minute Ookey pulled out of the dive and took us skimming above the golf course, tilting his wings in a rocking gesture, letting out a wild warrior yell. "Ya-a-a-a-a-a-a-ah!"

I found myself screaming along with him. "Ya-a-ah." Mine was at least half in terror.

As we rolled back along the runway to the iron shed I took some deep breaths so that my knees wouldn't shake visibly as I got off. By a miracle I had survived, but I didn't want Ookey to see my overwhelming relief.

"Ain't she sweet?" He kind of sang it, like the words of the song.

"You didn't — ?" I had to clear my throat, which still felt as if cold fingers clutched it. "You didn't buy the thing?"

"Not yet. It took all my cash to pay for the lessons. But some day, oh buddy, will I ever have me an airplane. This was made for me." He smacked the engine cowling with a gloved fist. "Meantime, I figure I just may go over to France and offer to fly some of theirs. They've got a squad of Americans, you know. It's called the Lafayette Escadrille, American flyers who have gone over there to do battle with the Red Baron. He's a German ace, the best they've got. Man, would I like to go up against him."

He made me feel like a piker. I thanked God every day that we were a long way from that filthy war. I wasn't on very solid terms with Him. I'd been neglecting church for a couple of years now, ever since we lost the championship game. I know, it wasn't His fault, but He didn't pull off any miracles for me lately. Now I hoped He wasn't offended that we had trespassed into His sky. *If I stepped over the line, Lord, I apologize.* But somehow I knew there was nobody on the other end listening. Had there ever been, I wondered. Was Ookey right, it was all just fakery that the old timers thought up to help them lay down the law?

One thing the flight had accomplished was to make the earth down here seem more important. Ookey had dropped me off at the streetcar, but I was glad to walk the last blocks home. I needed to feel the ground under my feet, to smell the lilacs, strong and sweet in the front yards along our block. And what was Zoobird doing perched on our front steps?

To see him sit there idly, long hands drooping between his knees, a worried frown puckering his tall brow, I got a nervous twitch inside. He didn't look his usual cheerful self. An odd reflection lay over his face, part excitement, part dread.

"Where've you been?" he demanded. "Gosh-sake, Bernie, you're never around when things happen. I bet you didn't even hear yet?"

"Hear what?"

"The newsboys downtown are hawking extras all over the streets. The President went back on his promise. We're going to go join the fighting over in France. Right now this country is officially at war."

Part Two

Nine

It's hard now to summon up the visions that crowded our minds as we gathered in the Recruiter's Office to offer our lives to the service of our country. I saw myself leading a troop of men up a hill into cannon fire, we were carrying rifles with fixed bayonets, there was a flag, a drum beating somewhere. We were all impeccably clean. The sun was breaking out from behind a cloud. I could almost relate to Ookey's talk about glory.

He was there with us that day. The whole stockyards gang had come over. Pug was telling us about his grandfather who had died with some famous Irish general on the field of battle. I fingered my uncle's medal in my pocket. I couldn't really imagine being dead, but I had to admit it was a possibility, which lent the day a kind of sweet sadness.

Deke was saying his dad had been a gunner on a ship in the Spanish American war.

He hoped we'd get into the Artillery. Fats said the Quartermaster Corps was the place to be, they procured all the food for the Army. He had put on a few pounds this last year running his father's store.

I said, "How's your dad?"

"He's feeling okay lately." Fats shrugged. "He doesn't mind me going off to serve Uncle Sam. He says we won't be there more than a few weeks. The krauts will drop their guns and run up a white flag when they see the United States march in."

Dollars was asking Deke, "Is a rabbi allowed to kill people?" Deke wasn't a rabbi yet, but closing in on it.

"If the Lord commands him to. Read the Bible, all the wars they fought back in the days of Moses and Joshua. They didn't get to the promised land without a few battles, you know." You couldn't stump Deke on the Good Word. "A man's got to fight the forces of evil."

"What about 'Thou shalt not kill?' "

"That's different. That means murdering somebody in cold blood."

I was glad he cleared that up. It had bothered me a little. Whenever I moved beyond the mystical vision of the charge up the hill and got to the part where I had my sights on some German across in the enemy lines the picture got fuzzy. I hoped it never came to that. I was pretty sure that Fats' dad was right: the enemy would take one look at our fresh new troops and lay down their arms. They must be pretty tired of fighting by now.

But suppose it did come to actually shooting at somebody? A whole lot worse than hunting squirrels — my mind flashed back to that day when Ookey had shattered the head off the rooster. I never had gone hunting with him, never had to conquer that innate repugnance that kept me from true manhood. Secretly I knew I was still a coward, but I'd learned to live with it. Might not be so easy if we really saw action in this war. I wished Zoobird were there, I could talk about it to him. But he'd said he was sticking with his job for the time being, maybe he'd join us on his lunch hour.

Which turned out to be a smart move. Ookey had shouldered through the hundreds of guys waiting to sign up and now came back from the Recruiter's desk to report. "Damned Army! You want to join you have to sign up for three years."

None of us was ready for that. We weren't expecting to make the service a lifelong career. Moseying back out into the street, along with most of the other hasty patriots, we tried to absorb our disappointment. I went over to Drovers Bank and informed Zoo that it was all a bust. He was up to his ears in customers. By now they'd made him a Paying Teller and he was counting out cash as fast as his bony fingers could move. People in the waiting line were talking about stocking up on food and water as if the world might come to an end tomorrow.

When I got back to work at the Bag Company orders were running strong. A lot of bags would be needed to send feed over with the horses and mules. The owner of the company looked happy as a king. There's nothing like a stack of invoices to make war positively glorious. I hid behind them, hoping nobody noticed that the erstwhile warrior had returned to his desk.

Of course the situation was corrected rapidly. A week later the papers announced that some new Brigades would be formed, term of enlistment limited to the duration of present hostilities. The gang regrouped, joined this time by Zoobird, and we stormed down to the Recruitment office. Before you could blink we were enlisted in the United States Army, part of Headquarters Company for the 129th Field Artillery, which became at once the best damned outfit in the whole country and we'd collectively punch out anybody who doubted it.

Those early weeks there was no base prepared to receive large numbers of unripe soldiers, so we assembled at the National Guard's drill ground and got taught how to stand at attention. (You never responded to your name with "Here!" It had to be "Yoh!") We learned "Column left" and "About face" and "At ease." Made you feel practically military. Spirits rose. Marching took on a nobility. Except when we had bayonet practice; poking broom handles into sacks of straw — it was hard to take that seriously.

The whole country was in a state of ambivalence. The vision of war was like a violent red flag raised over a nation that had always been rendered in pastels. And yet everyone agreed it was a marvelous thing to rescue the poor British and French who were about done for, and there was no doubt the economy was thriving. Of course the society ladies went on a tear to raise money for the starving French orphans.

"I'm donating five cakes," my mother announced, glassy with emotion. It took me back to the day when Zoobird and I had toted her baked goods down to the Coates House, that long-ago moment when we had learned about jazz music, couple-dancing, and rich people.

Offhand, I said, "What do you hear of Mrs. Forrest these days. How's Belinda?"

Mom stared at me aghast. "What do you know of Belinda Forrest?"

"Oh, we met, some time back, I forget where. Nice kid."

My mother actually turned pale. "Belinda Forrest is one of the city's most popular debutantes, she came out last June. You keep away from her! Those upper-crust people are way over your head, young man."

Which confirmed what I pretty much thought. Mom only wanted to mimic the elite, not really be one. Neither did I, but it was interesting to think that the little girl had cut off her braids and left her snug cocoon to butterfly around at some grand ball, waltzed by rich young men to a thousand dollars' worth of sedate music. Seemed kind of a shame. There was something about the long hair and the bows I had liked. In those days she hadn't seemed to realize that she was privileged.

To my mother I said, "Well, if you run into her tell her I still think about her daffodils." And ducked on out of there before she remembered to start hugging me again. Lately it would come over her: *My son is with the troops. Soon he'll be in the front lines, fighting that awful war!* Hug.

Dad was almost as bad. He'd be up on a ladder painting — he had taken up real estate and was busy renovating old houses. Out of the blue, he would say something like, "Never volunteer for anything in the Army, son. You'll get enough scut work without asking for it. Just keep your head down and your ears open."

Of course he was right. A few weeks later we found that out the hard way. Poor old Pug was the first to make the big mistake. When the Sergeant asked who could handle mules he stepped forward. Got given an order to report to the remount station and we never saw him again. He spent the whole war feeding and watering and grooming and kicking and cussing at the stock. I never realized how much the Artillery depended on mules and horses. They pulled the caissons to which the big howitzers were attached, they hauled the wagons of supplies where trucks couldn't go. Officers rode them and enlisted men groomed them, as we were to find out.

But that came later. In those dog days of summer all we were worried about was our uniforms. None of them fit. I was issued a hat that came clear down over my ears to my nose. My marching shoes were obviously designed for Goliath. Zoobird on the other hand couldn't even get his on. We traded, his hat suited me fine and he was glad for the extra room in the boots for his toes. The Parade Ground was the scene of brisk bargaining. I swapped my huge leather belt for a pair of puttees that Fats said drove him crazy. Not Army issue, they were a gift from his mother — leg coverings that came down over your shoe tops to keep the mud out. He said he'd just have to avoid the mud, he couldn't stand anything tight around his legs. I thought they were spiffy, a fashion statement, like spats. Ookey, of course, managed to look rakish even in his government issued uniform, with his scarf peeking out under the stiff collar and his hat set on a little crooked, for which he was constantly being reprimanded.

He was so good at class work they didn't pick on him much. We all took "skull practice" part of each day, blackboard exercises in geometry and algebra. The reason for that, I found, was to teach you how to pinpoint a spot a thousand yards away so exactly that you could hit it with a shell from a howitzer. Once I got the hang of it the problems came easy, though I never was as fast as Zoobird, who flew through the calculations like a human slide rule. My own talents lay with map making.

I discovered that one day when we went on a field trip to Swope Park. We were instructed to make a rough sketch indicating elevations of a certain high point, and I did a whole three-dimensional drawing of the hill complete with rocks and trees. My work was marked "Excellent" and I nearly bust a couple of buttons off my snappy new uniform.

By late summer the gossip came around that we would soon be bound for Camp Doniphan in Oklahoma near Fort Sill. They had been rushing to set up a whole new encampment for us. I drew an idealized illustration for Mother — of neat rows of tents bisected by well-groomed gravel streets, with a little brook running through it and men crouched there washing their plates after mess. "It's just like a big camping trip," I told her.

Dad glanced over my shoulder. "Be ready to peel a thousand potatoes." I think he was having a hard time accepting my decision to go to war. Of course he realized it was inevitable. To stay home and shirk your duty? Nobody thought of that. Even Zoobird put country first. He had taken his mother on the train down to Joplin to be with her sister. He said he'd told her to try to get over her grief and start a little business with her sewing machine.

My own sister, the incredible Dolly, had taken to grim knitting. She had conceived it her duty to create watch caps for the Navy. "The North Sea is very cold in winter," she informed us tersely, and went at it, dropping stitches and making a mess until Grossmutter took it from her and got it going right again.

I was a little surprised that Ookey didn't join the Navy, he had so much scorn for marching and drilling and formations of all kind. But he went through the motions, and judging from the far-away look in his eyes he was making some sort of plans. I suspected he wanted to bypass the parade ground and get to the action. He kept promising, "It won't be long now. I'm gonna shoot me some Huns."

By then I had become very conscious that I was half German. I thanked heaven my last name was of Welsh origin, in light of the terrible propaganda that now flooded the papers. Wild sketches of babies skewered on the bayonets of bearded, greasy soldiers with evil grins, saliva dripping from their fangs — it was ridiculous. I had aunts and cousins in the old country, I'd seen pictures of them. They were ordinary normal people like me. But the cartoons had an amazing effect on the country. I was shocked at how a few sketches could make the public furious.

Houses bloomed with flags, war benefits were held every weekend. For one of them, a tea dance at the Muehlebach, soldiers were needed for patriotic decoration — our Sergeant passed the word that we would be welcomed. This was the kind of volunteering I didn't mind. Zoo and I pressed our uniforms to a crisp edge, polished our boots and met out on the front lawn, where Dad was waiting with his box camera to take a snap shot. It was a new thing, the Brownie, they called it. "You boys look smart, now hold it . . ."

Even my mother put her stamp of approval on my new military look, no longer afraid I would seem shabby to the society crowd. "Bernard, you remember your manners! There will be some important people there."

No doubt about the aura of money that glowed around that crowd in the lobby of the hotel. Chauffeurs and footmen escorted them in from their cars carrying the donations which would be auctioned off later, all sorts of bric-a-brac of gold and crystal and china. The men were checking their top hats, the women their furs. Tough to be rich in Missouri on a hot September afternoon.

When we went into the ballroom the band was jazzing it up with "Put Your Arms Around Me, Honey." Couples fox-trotted pertly to the music under a banners that proclaimed: GIVE TO THE CAUSE!!

Having lost Zoobird to the dance floor, I wandered over to the table where refreshments were being dispensed. I spied Mrs. Forrest in a classy lilac-colored gown seated at a small desk over to one side, where she was accepting checks and tallying them in a book. Men in business suits had gathered there, exchanging mogul talk — you could see it in their postures, discussing high finance, and how much money they were going to make off the war. I wondered how long it had been since any of them had any fun — just got out there on the floor and danced. About then somebody handed me a cup of punch.

"Well, if it isn't George Bernard Jones." She hadn't cut her hair. It was piled in a tall mass of squirrel-red curls on top of her head. She was inches taller, but the smile hadn't changed, except that it came more easily and had a certain womanly charm.

"Hi, Belinda," I said warmly. "You've grown up when I wasn't looking."

"So have you," she retorted. "You've

turned from a cake-bearer into a soldier. Bravo. Do you like being in the Army?"

"Well — 'like' — I don't know. It's something you have to do, when your country calls you."

Soberly she said, "Of course you do. I'm going to join the Red Cross myself. We're going to be at Union Station to send the boys off with a cup of coffee and a cheer. I wish there were more we could do."

"That's enough," I told her, "to give us inspiration and remind us what we're fighting for." I sounded like a brochure for a Join-The-Army rally. But I've never been great at talking to pretty girls. Truth was, Belinda couldn't be called "pretty" exactly. She was good looking, with strong cheek bones and a firm chin, for a lady. And you'd never forget she was a lady. Even with an apron over her cocktail gown, she looked like true Forrest royalty.

Leaning closer she said, "You once asked me to dance, is the invitation still good?"

"Belinda, it would be my extreme pleasure."

As she untied the strings of the apron, she said, "I hate the name Belinda. Would it be possible for you to call me 'Lindy'?" The flowing silk dress was the color of oak leaves in the fall, it matched her hair and her eyes.

When they met mine there was excitement there and a kind of challenge.

"If you'll call me 'Bernie.' " I felt my breath skip a little as she put her hand on my arm to be led off to the dance floor. "So what have you been doing since I last saw you?" I wondered how a little kid gets transformed into this kind of poised young woman.

"I've been properly finished at a school called Gunston Hall in Washington, D.C." She made a little face, at the school or herself or the nation's capitol, I didn't know which.

"I always wondered what went on at those places," I said, teasing a little. "What exactly gets finished?"

"Mostly our manners." She put on a mock-serious air. "We learn how to hold our spoons correctly while eating soup — you scoop it away from you, that's the secret. We learn how not to yawn when people are incredibly boring. We learn about Rembrandt and Mozart and when we're least expecting it, we learn a little history and literature."

I was glad they hadn't finished off her sense of humor. The band was playing "If You Were the Only Girl in the World," as I took her in hand. I like the waltz, it's the best dance I do, the way you swing your partner around and make her skirts flare. Lindy was adept at it too, her cheeks got pink and her feet flew around me in circles as we whirled. When the music stopped we were both breathless.

"Oh, that was lovely!" She pulled a scrap of lacy handkerchief out of her bodice and blotted the perspiration from her brow.

I turned to find Zoobird coming to join us, escorting his own partner, a big bony girl with long legs, black hair and ruddy cheeks. She couldn't have been one of the elite, more likely their milkmaid, I thought. Dressed in a blue bombazine gown she was fanning herself with a small ivory fan that looked incongruous in her knuckly fist.

"That was some shinny," she was saying. "Cal, I need something to drink."

Zoo was shaking hands with Lindy. "You two were a sight to see," he marveled. "Sure, Miss Belinda, I recall you from the cake sale. Want you to meet Nadine Untermeyer . . ." But by the time he'd turned around she was gone, heading vigorously through the crowd toward the punch bowl. "She's a great dancer," he apologized. "Nice girl, really. Her dad owns the brewery. Excuse me." He hurried after her.

"I'd say Nadine could use a couple of

years at a finishing school," I said, and Lindy gave a marvelous chuckle.

"But she does dance divinely, you have to admit."

"I didn't notice. I was too busy having a good time." The band was starting up the Twelfth Street Rag. I grabbed her and we were off. She was as adept at the foxtrot as the waltz, we matched each other perfectly. That whole afternoon was a golden moment in time, one that came back to give me a lift in days to come when my life was stuck in a lot of mud.

Ten

On September 26th, 1917, our Company was told to be at Union Station by four in the afternoon to head out for Camp Doniphan. I only had a couple of hours to cram some clothes into my duffel bag, leaving a foot locker to be sent later. The gray day was laced with cold wind off the river bottoms. I was shivering as we stood around the drafty yards of the depot where troops were loading, engines chuffing and moving through the switches to hook up to the long lines of cars.

The whole family had come, except for Dolly, who had already left to begin her senior year at M.U. That was fine with me, I wished my mother had a meeting or something to keep her busy too. As it was she had got weepy, sniffling loudly as she reminded me to wash my socks every night. I almost shed a few tears myself when Grossmutter peered up into my face with her old beady eyes and instructed me in a fine spray of German, *"You fight hard, lick the Kaiser good!"*

Dad paced back and forth, glancing upward, as if he were inspecting the station for leaks in the roof. A solid man, strong. I realized I'd never be that strong, he was a rock. Then as our Company was called, he suddenly shucked off his overcoat and draped it around my shoulders.

"Going to be cold, even down in Oklahoma. You'll need a good coat. I can get another one."

I tried to say "Thanks," couldn't, just swallowed, waved and rushed off to join the line of men being herded onto the train. By the boarding steps the conductor kept calling out, "All right, boys, move on, move on." Entering the last car I slung my duffle onto an overhead rack and lunged into the first open seat I saw. I guess Zoobird had been right on my heels, because he settled beside me. Farther up the aisle I heard Fats' big laugh. Deke's voice rose above the chatter.

". . . always been wars, read Isaiah . . ." Answering the inevitable question: Does God really approve of what we're doing?

Right then I didn't want to think about it. The Lord — if there was one — couldn't help us now. Everything was settled, the die cast. With a mighty blast of steam, the engine began to dig in with its massive wheels. As we rolled slowly through the maze of sidings, I stared out the window blankly.

Looking over my shoulder Zoobird said, "Hey, there's the stockyards."

As if he hadn't seen stockyards before in his whole life. We'd all worked over there every day for years. In the stockyards. So where else would they be but exactly where they'd always been? I could have slugged him. Anyway the window was too dirty to see out of, or maybe the rain was falling too hard, I don't know.

Through the night I dozed in my seat as the train moved southward through the darkness, leaving our past lives behind, rocking along crooked tracks through hill country, then smoothing out into a dull clickety-clack across the long sweep of Oklahoma prairies. When day broke an inch at a time next morning we could see the rolling land around us — not Missouri, not any more. Sodden in the rain, it looked worse than Kansas. Once in a while we'd pass some rickety little town of gray clapboard and a few trees around a water tower, a lonely crossing signal dinging away as we bore onward.

At some point food was passed out to us, sandwiches made at the mess car up forward. Oh, Zoobird, I thought sadly, you went and did it. Last evening when the Sergeant had come around asking, Zoo had to go and admit he was a cook.

"Well, shoot, Bernie. I'm bored. I'd rather do dishes than just sit here." He went off whistling.

I didn't pity him quite so much when we got to Fort Sill that afternoon. The kitchen detail got loaded onto a lorry to be driven to Camp Donovan. The rest of us had to hike the four miles carrying our duffle bags. The rain had stopped, but a deep chill was in the air, smelling of winter. Dad's coat was a life saver, but I'd forgotten to bring along gloves, and my hands were raw by the time we reached the encampment.

Our platoon was directed down a muddy avenue that would some day be a street, but it was a mire now. The tents had begun to sag under the night's downpour. No floors in them and they hadn't been trenched. Ookey stood eyeing ours, hands on hips.

"What does this remind you of?" He had been made a Corporal back in Kansas City by random selection, but the choice surprised no one. He just had the look about him of someone who could take charge. Turning to a Second Lieutenant who had come across to check us in he said crisply, "Permission to go find some shovels, sir?" It was almost sarcastic.

The officer wasn't sure how to take it, he was pretty heavily weighted down by those new bars on his shoulders. "Is there a problem?"

Deke had popped inside one of the shelters. His voice came to us distantly. "No cots, no stove, no lamps."

The Lieutenant heard, of course. He said, "Well, carry on as best you can, men." And turned quickly as if he'd been called away to some urgent duty far across the compound.

Ookey muttered to me. "Private Jones, take the troops to the mess hall. I'll be along in a minute."

I led my fellow soldiers in rough formation down the muddy path, then glancing back saw our tent mysteriously fold up on itself and cave in. In a few minutes Ookey joined us, his face poker-straight. Near the makeshift Headquarters building we passed a Captain.

"Sir," Ookey saluted briskly, "reporting a collapsed tent, sir. I'm taking the men to the mess hall." And marched on before the officer could think what to say. It was obvious that this whole Company was pretty green.

The long wooden structure at the far end of the street wasn't labeled, but it smelled of cookery. Inside, we found huge stoves going full blast, one of them presided over by the Zoobird himself, happily cutting onions into a pot that gave off a mouthwatering aroma. Grinning a welcome, he handed me a huge blue enamel coffee pot and everyone grabbed cups.

Ensconced at a broad table near the stoves, we warmed up and watched smugly as the place began to fill with wet soldiers, grousing about the mud, the accommodations, the weather, the Army, the officers. It was a chorus of woe that would become familiar in the next months. Rain had begun to fall again, no question of trying to repair tents in the growing darkness. Everyone slung gear under the mess tables and after dinner was eaten, we bunked down on top. I fell asleep to the distant sound of Zoobird whistling the Merry Widow Waltz as he set out bread for tomorrow morning's breakfast.

In the confusion of that next week, with its whole new routine of drills and guard duty and other frustrations, the mess hall proved to be a haven of normality, the one place we could feel reasonably human. Of course eventually we got the tents up, boards around the bottoms for stiffening, wooden floors laid, tops taut and waterproof. We were issued arms and manuals, there were postings of orders, of demerits for disrespecting the shavetails. More than once I thought back to our camping trip and could see where my discipline had fallen short. It takes an iron hand and a cold heart to form a close-knit unit. Part of that bond, I realized, must be a mutual dislike for our superiors. Lord, how we hated them. I gave up any lingering dreams of leadership and swore I'd never be an officer.

Nor would I ever ask for stable detail. I had always liked horses, the kind that faithfully pull a buggy and never argue. I now found out that there was another whole breed. Shipped in from the far west, herded onto cattle cars and brought straight to our corrals, they were angry, hungry and as thirsty as animals can get. When we were led out to the long double row of beasts they were plunging at the rope line, kicking each other, and whinnying with fury.

"All right, men," our Sergeant told us briskly, "each of you take two of them down to the water tank." Then, "Well, go on, that's an order."

"If that ain't the meanest lookin' bunch of broncs I ever seen —" An awed pronouncement by Slattery, an old hand from the stockyards who had been a cowboy out in Montana. Then, coolly, he waded between the nearest two, gave each of them a kick in the belly, grabbed their ropes and yanked them backward out of the line. I tried to watch the way he did it, held them by the halter up close under their chins, snarling at them to move their unprintable, obscene and profane bones. I knew I'd never match his vocabulary.

Deke strode in fast, his year in the stockyards had made him savvy. He grabbed two and manhandled them, also cursing picturesquely in Yiddish. I don't understand the language, but the horses did. They went with him, at a good pace. Dollars said, "Hoboy," and took the plunge. He too had learned some ropes, he got his out and going. The Sergeant was staring at me like, *Well?*

Yes sir! With inner bugles blowing, I dove between two of the shaggy beasts, untied them, and somehow everything after that went wrong. I had no time to switch my grip to their halters, nor did I need to back them out. They hurtled away from the picket line while I clung desperately to the tail-ends of the lead ropes, as they headed for the smell of water. It was a round tank at the far end of the corral, already well populated with horses drinking their heads off. My charges were at a gallop by now, my feet touching ground every ten feet or so, as I tried to keep a semblance of authority over them. When we reached the solid wall of rumps, my bay went left, the roan veered right, and I was flung up onto the back side of a wildly spotted pinto who kicked at me viciously with both hind feet. I only escaped by skidding under him, I still don't know how I missed being killed. Cautiously I crawled out of the seething mass of horseflesh and into the clear. Seeing more coming, I got up briskly, dusted my hands and sauntered away as if to say, *Well, that little chore's done.*

In the days that followed I had to resort to similar subterfuges, as we were told to groom the mount, brush its tail and never *ever* lift a hand in anger against the creature, even if it's a mule.

"These animals are the lifeblood of the Artillery, and don't you forget it, soldier!" This from a Lieutenant, after he had caught me wielding a curry comb against a thousand pounds of surly mule which had, with ears laid back, tried to sink its teeth in me.

"Private, haven't you ever trimmed a horse's hooves?"

"No, sir." *I didn't work at the stockyards, I didn't learn all that horse etiquette. I should have joined the Infantry.*

"Very well, I'll demonstrate." He beckoned the others over, all us duffers who hadn't finished our assignment. "Give me your tool." He meant a curved knife with a very sharp edge to the inside of the blade. It scared me to death. When you've got the horse's hoof cradled between your knees, one slip could cause you dreadful and permanent damage. It's tricky even getting the subject to lift its foot. The Lieutenant sidled up along the mule's flank, speaking words to soothe. Gently his fingers closed on the powerful ankle, and at that point the beast shot out its hind leg with such velocity it slung the Lieutenant clear across the corral into a pile of sweepings.

He was very young. With a nearly invisible moustache and receding chin, it was difficult to look military, but he did his best. Getting up, he brushed the manure from his uniform. "Well, men, now you know the correct procedure. Carry on." And marched away to the tune of some inner drum that I had to admire.

Of course there came a day, inevitably,

when we had to ride them — not the mules, thank heaven, but the horses were almost as bad. I am sure most of them had never been properly broken, just the rough taken off, as they say, enough to teach them certain tricks. When I would go to saddle my mount it would inflate its lungs, then after I had tightened the cinch as hard as I could it would exhale, leaving the saddle loose. I could swear it snickered at me.

Ookey put an end to that. "Bunk, you're too tender-hearted. What's the matter, you think you're going to hurt that piece of crow-bait? Love of Pete!" He kneed the nag in the gut so hard the wind came out in a *huffff.* Before the horse could take another breath he yanked the cinch tight.

Well, of course, we got through the drill. We learned to ride in formation, and so forth, but it all seemed beside the point to me. The days of scouting the enemy on horseback were over by then. We still practiced the charge, but I thought it must be nostalgia on the part of the aging generals who had once been in the Cavalry. It wasn't until later that I began to appreciate the real value of our remuda. Without those mules we could never have moved the guns through that mud in France. And many a time we had to find ways to communicate with our own forces over terrain which no vehicle could tackle.

We really were preparing for battle, even though it seemed awfully remote, as we sat in a classroom and practiced blackboard lessons on measuring distant heights, calculating an area by its perimeter, the kind of problems I had thought boring in school. There's just so much you can do on paper. I was itching to try out the equations on a genuine target.

ELEVEN

Camp Doniphan had been set up to the east of some low hills — in Oklahoma they took on the aspect of mountains, their tops maybe a thousand feet above ground level. A lot of our classroom projections had centered on capturing an old blockhouse that stood atop the main peak, called Signal Mountain. A remnant of the Indian wars, it was going to be the focus of next week's simulated siege, I learned, as I stood guard duty at Headquarters and overheard the General talking to his aides.

It seemed to me a great chance to get ahead of the other platoons, as I put it to my tent mates that night. "We should go out there on Saturday and scout out the ground before the 'attack.' "

The idea appealed to everybody. Zoobird offered to make sandwiches, Deke and Fats and Dollars were in. Ookey was nowhere to be found. He had taken to disappearing whenever he was off duty. We filled our canteens and added candy bars to our knapsacks. I took along a sketch pad and pencils. As we approached the hills I began to note the contours, gullies, rock formations. When we stopped for lunch I did a complete drawing of the mountain itself, with Zoobird figuring elevations in his peculiar head, using the sun and a compass and a lot of smarts. He was a little disappointed that he would be stuck with the chuck-wagon. But at least he'd been assigned to go along and feed us on the maneuvers.

"Over there, that grove of trees ought to be a good place for the mess tent. Mark it down, Bernie."

It took a couple of hours to make our way up the slope to the blockhouse, just a ruin of fallen timbers now. But it offered a great view of the whole field area below. I could make a map of the terrain with all its hillocks noted, and vulnerable approaches through the dry washes or using ground cover. It was a great carefree day and we came home weary, but elated.

We found two new recruits in our tent, a fellow named Hadley and an Irishman called Mick. They had just come from the horse picket line, where they said another shipment of mustangs had come in.

Mick had got his foot stepped on. "There ought to be some easier way to give a horse a drink."

"There is," Dollars told him seriously. "You give 'em a bottle of strawberry pop and they'll behave like an angel. Ask Bernie."

"Sweet Adeline preferred sarsaparilla." I went on to tell about our invasion of Kansas a few years ago.

"That's a tall tale," Mick snorted disbelief. "Hosses can't drink out of a bottle."

"Sure they can. Like this." I took out my pad of paper and turned to a fresh sheet, cartooning a picture of our Adeline with her hip bones sticking out and her feet planted, holding the bottle delicately in her teeth, head thrown back so the soda could flow down her long throat.

"Well, I'm not saying it couldn't be done," Mick allowed, "but I doubt you'd ever get a hoss to bite on a bottle."

"That's exactly the way it happened. We were all witnesses." Zoobird had joined us. "Good sketch, Bernie. I'd recognize that old mare anywhere." He dumped his duffle near the door of the tent, looking noticeably lower than when he'd left us awhile ago.

"Sorry, I thought there was an empty bunk here."

"We just got transferred over from that new Company," Hadley said.

"You need a bed?" I asked Zoo. "I thought you were supposed to sleep in the barracks behind the mess hall."

"Some barracks. It's a shed big enough for one man, but not two, when one of them's the Master Sergeant head chef." Zoo shook his head. "He can't stand me. Or at least he can't stand my whistling. Doggone, I don't even know I'm doing it, you know?"

"Well, he can't just throw you out," Deke said. "It's illegal and immoral and you ought to take it to a higher officer. Meantime we'll make room for you here somehow."

"Dollars-to-doughnuts we have to get him officially assigned to our tent."

Zoo shook his head. "Don't worry. I'll find a billet."

"No need to look farther," Ookey said, ducking in under the tent flap. "I heard you all jawing, and I've got your problem solved. My bed is free, as of immediately. I just stopped by to say 'So long.' "

"Angels and ministers of grace! He's going AWOL," Deke groaned.

Ookey just grinned. He was so happy it was exuding from him like electricity. "My transfer just came through. I've been working on it for weeks. I'm headed off for Aviation Training Camp. On my way out I will clear it with a certain Sergeant who owes me money for a poker game. I'll see to it that bed is assigned to Private Calvin Fleischman. Meantime, watch your step. Next time you see me I'll be guarding your backsides from way up there." He jerked a thumb at the sky.

After he was gone Zoobird yawned and drifted over to the empty cot. "I better get some shut-eye. I learned that maneuvers are definitely on for Monday morning. I've got to stock up the chuck wagon tomorrow." So he was still on mess duty. I was hoping he'd been relieved of that, too. Stuck off in the kitchen his great talent for calculation was never going to get used. He seemed resigned to it, though. "Let me see that drawing of yours again. I think there's a short cut I could take to get to that grove, give me some time to set up before the foot soldiers arrive."

The others gathered around, looking at my sketches more carefully. Dollars tapped the one of the entire mountain. "That's a good map. Why don't you hang it up so we can get familiar with it before the attack."

So I attached the sheet of paper to the

canvas above my cot and forgot about it. Forgot that Sunday we always had inspection. Right after breakfast a troop of officers came down the line, led by Captain Jennings himself. A tall, severe man with sideburns and a long chin, he was usually only interested in loose buttons or unshined shoes. In and out of every tent they went like raptors hunting prey. When he got to ours he stopped short to stare at my sketch.

"Who drew that?"

"I did, sir." *Shoot, if you must, this guilty head.* For some reason cameras were strictly forbidden in camp. Maybe drawings were, too. I couldn't imagine why the Germans would be interested in rookie troops in the middle of Oklahoma, but orders are orders, and in a flash I saw myself court-martialed. Disgraced for revealing the secret contours of a not-very-high mountain.

"Do you have any others?"

I dug forth my drawing pad and tore the pages out. Leavenworth. That's where they put the Army's criminals.

With my sketches in hand, the Captain turned and stalked out of the tent. The others were gleeful. He hadn't even inspected us. "Do it again next week, Bernie," Dollars said happily. He was always on report for not making his bunk neatly. He just didn't have the knack.

"If you need me to pray for you I will," Deke told me soberly.

"I will do my own praying, thanks," I said in as humorous a tone as I could muster. "In fact, right now I'm off to church." The bus left every Sunday morning for Lawton, where a nice chapel welcomed service men. I felt like a hypocrite. I usually slipped away and went with the other guys to a movie house. Not this day. I had a whole back-log of apologies to make to the Lord, if there was anyone on the other end of the line. It seemed so fruitless to keep praying to an invisible deity, and as for Jesus, if He really was the hand of God He was needed in so many places worse than this, He'd never have time for my problems. But I was in trouble, and even if it was a long shot I was willing to try.

I began while waiting in the line for the bus. *Dear Lord, sorry I haven't been in touch lately. Everything's been moving pretty fast here . . .*

"Private Jones!"

I whirled around to face an unknown Corporal. "Yes, sir."

"You are to report to General Berry this afternoon at oh-fifteen-hundred." Death by firing squad.

As I was saying, Lord . . .

The thing about confessing your sins, it gets boring. It must drive God to distraction listening to all those people admitting they've been wrong. Some say He knows everything we do anyway, why belabor it? I could picture Him sitting up there, watching me like a hawk all these months. *Okay, I'm really sorry, but I'm only human, Sir.* I wondered if that approach would work on the General. I didn't think I'd try it.

By three o'clock that afternoon I was a mass of emotions. By then I had begun to get angry. If they didn't want us to make sketches why did they take us down to Swope Park and encourage us to mark off elevations and so forth? It wasn't fair, but then almost everything about the Army wasn't fair. There was no concept of that word.

All the same, I was rehearsing humility: *I regret the mistake, sir, it won't happen again. It was done in an effort to help my fellow soldiers, some of whom aren't keen on math, to relate the classroom work to actual problems in the field. Sir.*

I walked into the General's office and snapped off my best salute. "Private Jones reporting as ordered, sir."

"Come in, come in." General Berry was

old-Army. It was in the cut of his hair, the droop of his long moustache, the keen blue eyes that had looked into a lot of hot sun. On the desk was spread the sketch I'd done of Signal Mountain, the broad view. "I understand you drew this map."

"Yes, sir."

"How long did it take you?"

"Sir, about a half an hour not counting the coloring. I did the crayon work after we got back to camp."

He shuffled the pages and drew forth the sketch of the terrain on which I had marked possible gun emplacements. "This is all wrong. You've got your cannon too far forward. This salient would draw enfilade fire from up on these heights, and from over here." He tapped the contours I had noted. "It's suicide to try a frontal attack on a well-fortified position above you. That's why you lay siege to it, wear the enemy down by attrition, and attack him as he sallies forth in desperation. We'll cover all that in the maneuvers. But this is a good effort. Actually, what I called you here for —" He opened a drawer of his desk and drew out a genuine battle map, which he spread on top of mine. It was swarming with symbols. "This has got me puzzled." He tapped a circle with zigzags coming out of it in all directions. "It's on a height, but it's not the symbol for a telegraph post. So what the hell could it be?"

I searched frantically for an answer. All those crooked arrows had to mean some sort of communications. "Could it be a — a radio signal station?" I had no idea what I was talking about, but it seemed possible. This was a whole new invention that had been in the papers a lot recently.

"Radio," he repeated the word, intrigued. "Radio. Of course. Lord, how we could have used wireless signals down there along the border when we went after Villa. We had to move so fast there was no way to lay down lines." He put the map away. "Well, it's going to be a different war this time." He tapped my sketches. "Mind if I keep these?"

Would you mind if I fell down and kissed your feet, sir?

"Good. Thank you, Corporal."

"Yes, sir. Except I'm not a Corporal, sir." Complete honesty from now on, I will live a pure life.

The General just nodded as if it were unimportant. But the next time promotions were posted, I was a Corporal.

TWELVE

Christmas seemed to belong to another lifetime, a strange excursion back into childhood, everyone was scrambling to see the list of those chosen for leave. Zoobird didn't get the nod, which caused my holiday spirit to lag. Still saddled with the vindictive Master Sergeant head chef, he hadn't even made Corporal yet. But he was philosophical. There was a dance hall in Lawton with a new Victrola and all the latest records, he said he'd be fine. I personally thought phonograph music sounded tinny, but I was glad he enjoyed it.

"When I'm home," I offered, "I'd be glad to call up Nadine and tell her hello from you."

He got a strange smile and a slight shade of sadness in his birdy eyes. All he said was, "No thanks, Bernie."

So that was over, and I couldn't help being relieved. I'd hate to think of him tied to that girl with her appetite and her rudeness. So of course that left nobody at home for Zoobird. No wonder he didn't care all that much about Christmas. A bunch of the guys who had to stay were planning to go into Lawton some dark night and acquire a Christmas tree from somebody's front yard, decorate it with utensils from the kitchen. Zoo was going to make an imitation plum pudding, using dried prunes. I was almost sorry I was going to miss all that. But elated at the thought of the great welcoming committee that I would find at the station. Even the gray train yards with their dirty patches of snow looked good as we rolled into Kansas City.

It turned out to be only Dad on the platform. He had come over from the Feed Company, said my mother was tied up with a meeting of the Delphians. They were going to put on a cake sale for the benefit of the Russian orphans. The Russians were having a Revolution at the time. There were cartoons in the papers showing the Bolsheviks, and except for their furry hats they looked just like the Huns, brutal and savage and inhuman. In a logical progression of thought, I asked my father, "How's Dolly?"

"She's off at some kind of sorority thing," he said with a sigh. He had never been in favor of her joining the Alpha-Beta-Gammas or whatever their name was. "Bunch of spoiled snoots," he called them. "They're putting on a show for the service men, song-and-dance and you can buy a kiss for a buck. Money's to go to the Red Cross."

"I think I'll skip that one." I'd pay a dollar *not* to kiss my sister. "How's everything at the store?"

"Slow. Most of the beeves go straight off to the Army, they don't keep them in the feedlots any more. Just as well, it was a poor harvest last summer. Anyway, I've got my hands full with real estate. So many guys decide to sell their houses cheap when they go into the services, don't have to pay taxes or upkeep. By spring the war will be over and they'll all be back, getting married, starting up businesses. They'll need a place to live. I'll make a nice profit. You hear anything about peace talks?"

"No sir. I think we're really going to have to send troops over there. I've just been chosen for Officers' Training Camp. We're supposed to ship out in the spring."

"Huh? Well, at least you won't be slogging around the trenches if you're an officer. Good luck on that. How's Zoobird doing? I thought he'd be coming home with you."

"He didn't get leave. Maybe after the first

of the year."

"Too bad. I wanted to talk to him about selling his mother's property. It just stands there vacant — I'd offer him a fair price. When you get back you tell him that."

At the house Grossmutter was elbow-deep in stuffing a goose. She gave me a cross, hasty, loving peck on the cheek and growled at us to get out of her kitchen. Dad went off to see about a bungalow over on Oak Street. Suddenly I was on my own, fiddling around empty rooms. I actually missed camp. Tonight the guys who were left would be playing poker or singing songs to the guitar. Billy Yurt could play any tune ever written. A good bunch of fellows.

I thought of calling Deke. He'd been on the same train with me, but his folks celebrated a different holiday. Hanukkah, he had to spell it for us, didn't have anything to do with Jesus, all about lighting candles and Jewish rituals and so forth. But he was keen on it. He said you need to dedicate yourself to the Lord every once in a while. Christians should do it, too, he said — he was very tolerant of us.

Dedicate myself to do what? I didn't ask him, though, I'd get a whole sermon. The truth was, training to go out and fight a war, kill people if necessary, possibly to die, had made me tougher, both mentally and physically. I wasn't in the mood for any gospel that suggested we turn the other cheek. If somebody threw a punch at me, I was going to give it back to him with interest. I wasn't a darn bit meek, if that's what it took to get blessed. And in the army, you certainly didn't want to be poor in spirit. You'd get extra guard duty every time. In fact I was leaning toward Ookey's premise, that religion was a nice fairytale, but it didn't have anything to do with real life. There was only one thing kept me hanging on: the Lord had finally made me six feet tall. That came out at my last physical.

I felt restless, it was only early afternoon. Dad had left me the car; he had a Ford truck that he used in his real estate renovations. When I got in the old Abbott-Detroit it took me back to younger days, going out to see Ookey on Saturdays. So the car just naturally headed for the farm. All at once I was anxious to know how he had made out in the Aviation Service.

The farmhouse looked deserted, no chickens in the barnyard, no stock in the corral. Too much work for old man Marlowe to handle alone? He was probably long gone, off gambling, maybe in jail by now. I didn't see a vehicle around, but I went up onto the back porch and looked inside. There were dirty dishes on the kitchen table and an empty beer bottle. Nobody answered my knock, so I got in the car and drove slowly over the icy ruts back to the main road.

Tried to think where Ookey might be. He didn't have many friends. On a long shot I decided to drive over to the air strip. And there I found him, sitting on a barrel in the cold sunshine, pitching pebbles at a tin bucket. Alone. I didn't know whether to clap him on the shoulder or kick him in the pants. Pretty elegant pants for Army issue, they fit as if they were tailored for him, and the leather jacket looked expensive. In a spiffy scarf and a helmet with goggles cocked up on top of it, he looked every inch a sky warrior.

"What the Sam-Hill are you doing here?" I squawked as I strode over to him.

"Thought some of the fellows might be hanging out. Guess they're all Christmas shopping." Slight scorn for the idea.

"For crying out loud, you might have called the house."

"I was going to later. Honest." He spun a stone at the bucket, right on the mark. "See you made Corporal."

"By now I thought you'd have bars on your shoulders."

He flashed a proud smile. "I'll get them as soon as I get back to camp. I made it through flight school. January 5th we're shipping out for France." The words were invested with purpose. "No more classroom stuff, technical, maintenance, ground-crew details — I knew all that better than our instructors. I should have just gone on over and joined the Escadrille, I'd have downed a dozen aces by now. I'd teach those Frenchies a few tricks."

"I imagine they've got some of their own, after three years of war."

"Oh, sure. They've had the worst of it for years. When the Fokker came in they lost pilots faster than they could train new ones. Those Germans, you got to hand it to them — they invented a way to fire a machine gun straight ahead through the propeller. The bullets dodge between the blades while they're turning. The French aviators got shredded before they came up with their own version, the Nieuport. It's supposed to be pretty good in the air."

"Doesn't it bother you, the thought of being shot down?"

He shook his head. "What comes, comes. If you do go it's clean and quick. Not like being machine-gunned and left to hang on the barbed wire to bleed to death. That ground war is brutal."

I had heard some stories myself. "We had a couple of French officers advising us. They came from up around Verdun. It's an old fortress they've been fighting over for years. Word is that they have lost over three-hundred thousand men just in that one area, and nobody's won. It's still a battle-ground."

"Trench warfare is a fraud," he said. "It's stupid to keep lobbing artillery at each from opposing positions. Along the whole western front the battle lines haven't moved in months. But the air services will change all that. Get enough planes up there to chase theirs out of the sky, then we drop bombs on their supply lines, demoralize 'em."

"Still it will take artillery to finish the job." We argued back and forth for an hour, tactics, fire power, attrition. At one point I mentioned I had been tagged for OTC myself. "They like the way I can draw maps right out in the field."

Ookey snickered. "You want a map of enemy terrain, give me a camera. I'll make one pass over the lines and bring you back photographs so clear they'll show you where the enemy's latrine is located."

Eventually we got down to the question that had haunted me now for years. "Ever wonder what you'll do when it comes to killing a man, face to face, watch him die?"

Ookey put another rock into the bucket. "Doesn't bother me one damned bit. If he'd just been firing at me, I hope I do put him away. It's no good to have doubts, Bunk. Remember the time I did the tightrope walk across the ravine?"

I wasn't likely to forget that. We had been out hunting birds' eggs and came to a steep dry wash with a bottom full of rocks. It was going to be a hard climb down, and even tougher to get up the other side. As we considered the problem, Ookey spotted a telegraph wire strung across a few hundred feet away. He gave that crazy laugh and climbed the pole, starting across the wire. But it wasn't taut, it swung a little and he didn't have a long stick to give him balance. Halfway over he tilted and fell, grabbing the wire at the last minute. Forty feet above the rocks, he hung there, face working, sweat pouring off him as he swung across the rest of the way hand-over-hand. When he made it to the far side he crowed with laughter and slid down the pole triumphant. Of course his hands were so stiff he couldn't climb a tree for a week.

"That was a close one," he admitted now. "I was scared stiff. But if I had started doubting, I'd be dead. You have to be your own hero." That word again.

"You ever pray a little?" I said it lightly, but it was looming on my mind. Would it be a show of weakness to say, *Lord, I would like some help passing OTC, I hear it's tough?*

Ookey brushed that off with a grunt. "Anybody who prays to a mythical God to help him out of a scrape is still writing letters to Santa Claus. You got nobody but yourself to depend on, and the sooner you believe that the longer you'll live."

I left him sitting there, I don't think he really expected anyone to open the hangar, it just was a place he felt comfortable. I understood it, even. My house, my neighborhood, Kansas City, all of it was foreign country where I had once lived, but no longer felt at home. Bored and impatient to get back to the real world of the Army, I tried to think what could give me a boost into the Christmas mood. Or who.

She rose before my mind's eye as if she'd heard my call and answered. Lindy. By now she was probably swamped with the attentions of every eligible bachelor left in Kansas City. There was no chance that she'd be available for a date, I thought, but I gave her phone number to the operator.

"Bernie! How good to hear from you. Of

course, I'd love to go out." Genuine delight in her aristocratic little voice. "What time?"

You could have bowled me over. My mother, too. When I mentioned I had a date with Belinda Forrest that evening she spilled her coffee all over the table cloth. "You're going over to the Forrest's mansion?"

"Sure. I have to pick her up for the movie."

"What movie!" She looked horrified. She thought motion pictures were vulgar. "Oh, the Forrests would never approve of their daughter in one of those cheap places."

"No, no, we're going to a big theater. They're showing 'The Birth of a Nation.' "

Dad frowned at that. "Pretty tough show, they say. Very violent. It's about the Civil War, not exactly suitable for a young girl."

"Lindy's the one who picked it out," I told them flatly. "May I borrow the car?"

Of course he didn't object. As he followed me out, he even stuck a twenty-dollar bill in my hand. "Take her to the Muehlebach afterward. We don't want her to think we're poor." So Mom's longing to be elite had rubbed off on him, too.

By now, after mingling with a lot of fellows from all walks of life, I had noticed everyone looks alike in an Army uniform. I wasn't ready to kowtow to the Forrests or anyone else. Besides, their home wasn't really a "mansion." Just a big Victorian building set on a large lot with a curving driveway that had a certain look of elegance. Where the money showed was inside.

The door was opened by a maid. The foyer had a parquet floor and was ornamented by several marble statues. One nymph was especially noticeable, very classy with only a few draperies and nice breasts. I was trying not to eye it too closely when Lindy came running down the stairs and forget about marble. This was one lovely warm living woman, her own fundamentals concealed beneath a blue satin dress that draped from the shoulders to a few inches above her shins. It looked like the latest fashion, no bustle, no ruffles.

The details of that date are sketchy. I was strangely affected by the whole thing — the unknown girl, the darkness of the theater, the thrilling piano music that accompanied the grim motion picture. It was tough, all right, the battle scenes so realistic I got a little worried. But Lindy was transfixed. Her eyes never left the screen, and if she held tight to my hand it wasn't from shock. Strong hand for a girl.

Afterwards we went to the hotel for coffee and pastry. In an elegant little drawing room people were having late-night suppers, many of the men in uniform, a small orchestra playing. Lindy nibbled her sweetmeat soberly, still enthralled by the picture.

"This war is going to be different, isn't it?" she appealed to me. "We have hospital trucks to bring the wounded off the battlefield. A friend of mine is a nurse, she hopes to go over with the Red Cross and help at the field stations. There'll be plenty of food and all that, with modern trains to bring it to the troops?"

"Oh, yes," I said firmly, not having the faintest idea how the commissary worked. "All the modern comforts, I'm sure."

Those complicated brown eyes looked relieved, and I was secretly ashamed that I had never thought about the worries women would have, stuck here at home while we men went off to battle. I had refused to think about the darker side of warfare, but Lindy was willing to face the grim details.

"I wish I could go. Women could be useful to the Army," she told me sternly. "I took stenography when I was off at school. I can do typewriting and run a telephone switchboard. I've joined the Red Cross volunteers, you know. We meet the trains every day to cheer the troops along. And when the wounded start to come back we'll be there to give them comfort and aid them in getting in touch with their families."

I didn't really want to think in terms of the wounded. "How do your parents feel about that?"

"Father doesn't like it a bit. But I believe my mother is a little proud of me," she said shyly. "I told them: Women have a lot of inner strength! We're not just ornamental."

Strange talk from a girl, I thought, and added mentally, *You can give me aid and comfort any time.* It was a wonderful evening, and Lindy seemed to enjoy it too, because when I asked her for another date, she couldn't wait to say "Yes." I suppose a lot of her gentlemen friends were off with their families somewhere.

I hardly remember having Christmas with my folks. Before I knew it I was on my way back to Oklahoma, and happier than I'd been in years.

THIRTEEN

By the second week of Officers Training Camp I seriously considered dropping my gun. At six a.m. on a January morning, as you stood in drill formation out on the parade ground with the temperature skewering the thermometer at zero, ears freezing, fingers numb, it would have been easy to bungle the "Present Arms" and just let go of the rifle. I had to wrap my arms around it and hug it to me, before straightening it out, but everybody was doing the same thing and nobody got called down. It was pretty obvious that this part of the drill wasn't going to happen out in the middle of a battlefield. All the same, it was part of the manual and if you dropped your rifle you were dismissed immediately back to your outfit.

Sometimes I wouldn't have minded. Except for Deke, who had also made OTC, I hadn't seen the gang since Christmas. I heard that Dollars had transferred to the Quartermaster Corps. Our group was getting pulled apart. Zoobird was still stuck in the mess hall, but I never got over there. Our barracks were two miles away from the main camp. We had our own mess, our own routine, which began at 5:45 in the morning and proceeded through hours of rigorous drill, target practice, grenade practice, bayonet practice, then marching at 120 steps a minute, increasing to 140, which pretty much finished us off. Afternoons we spent in classroom instruction. Field problems, assignments to solve, oral exams — only half of us would make it through, we were told. There were times when I questioned the need for all this suffering. And then, slowly, I began to understand. There had to be a turning point when unprepared recruits would grow up, forego the horseplay and take the war seriously. To turn into soldiers.

After that I began to take a pride in it. I started to respect my instructors. One, a French captain, had been through three years on the Front and been wounded, seconded to our Army as a teacher. Because he was quite short we called him "High Pockets," but we never called him Gimpy. There was a sadness about him that went deeper than mere personal grief. He had faced the guns and seen friends die, had watched his country wrecked, a whole generation of young Frenchmen decimated. For all his polite smile, he was in mourning.

Our Company Captain was battle-worn, too, and impatient. A grizzled veteran, he had been judged too old for active duty overseas, but he knew more about the practical side of warfare than all the young West Pointers. When he found out I had been a bookkeeper he assigned me to records, which meant I was relieved of guard duty. We got along well, and toward the end of our training he even arranged for me to have that rarest of blessings, an afternoon off. I needed it.

By that last week of camp I was beginning to worry that I wouldn't pass the finals. The math was brutal. Problems in Gunnery and Ballistics were made tougher by the need for rapid calculation. Our tests were timed, we had to think fast. High school had never taught this art. I needed Zoobird.

Back in our old stamping grounds I found him still in the kitchen, red-faced after another skirmish with the head chef. The seamy old goat was in a constant bad mood. He looked ready to take a swipe at me when I handed him the note from the C.O. ordering him to give Zoobird the rest of the day off. We sat down at the mess table and in a matter of hours the Bird showed me amazing shortcuts, tricks of mental arithmetic, easy ways to solve tough problems. He had a gift for making calculations look like a game. I went back to the barracks with my confidence bolstered.

Now all I had to do was get through the final field review without falling off my horse. It was to be a simulated military action, followed by a mock charge, galloping a full battery down the field and setting up the guns. We had even been allotted ten rounds of blank cartridges to fire from our three howitzers. The first time you hear real artillery fire it makes your breath catch in your lungs, the ground jarring underfoot, the smell of powder. Everyone was so infused with the reality of it all, over in the reviewing stands one of the younger officers jumped up and fell off the top row of seats. The arrival of the ambulance gave the whole day a touch of realism.

In the aftermath we all felt let-down, with grades due to be posted the following morning, commissions awarded and assignments made. I almost hoped I had flunked — new officers are never sent back to their original units. It was deemed too awkward for them to have to order around the enlisted men who had been their buddies. I missed my old tent mates, and by now I knew that Headquarters Company was the center of action. So I had mixed feelings as they began to read the list of names, the Captain standing before us on the stage of the assembly hall. Distantly it registered on me: Deke had passed. "Lieutenant Daoud Markowitz." They mispronounced his name. He was assigned to the Corps of Engineers. There followed several others that I knew to be a lot smarter than I was in the math department. And then . . .

"Lieutenant George Bernard Jones is assigned to Headquarters Company, 129th Field Artillery, General Berry's staff."

For an instant it didn't sink in. I thought: I am an officer in the United States Army. Then the word "staff" registered. I wasn't going to be shunted off to some new unit.

Outside in the distance church bells were chiming. It was Easter morning, 1918. And God had come through for me in a big way. At that moment I guess I believed in Him. In a fluster of embarrassment I looked upward and said inwardly, *Thank you, Sir.*

I look back now on that moment and it occurs to me that for all the tough training, I was still pretty much a dumb kid.

■ ■ ■ ■

The word went out that we would be leaving at once for France. I never thought it would come to this, really. But when I reported to General Berry's office that next morning he wasted no time. Showing me to a small office nearby he said, "Lieutenant Jones, I have a special assignment for you." I envisioned maps, real battle maps with gun emplacements, barrage plans. I pictured the General and me studying the terrain, I was showing him a clever deployment of his long guns . . .

"The people over in OTC were impressed with your bookkeeping talent," he went on. "So I'm putting you in charge of baggage on our trip overseas. It's not a very glamorous assignment, but it will be a bigger challenge than you think. To make sure the men's personal luggage gets there in good order — that's one thing. But you will also have to see to packing up the stable tack and the equipment from the mess hall. We can't expect any facilities over there waiting for us. You'll have to inventory hundreds of items, see that they're crated, loaded onto lorries here, then a train, followed by a ship, unloaded in England, reloaded for our trip across the Channel. Don't ask me why we can't just go directly to France, I'm not informed on that. The reason I'm going into this detail is, I don't want you to take the job lightly. You may choose an enlisted man to help you, but you will be responsible."

"Yes, *sir!*" The assignment didn't thrill me, but I enjoyed the prospect of stealing a good cook from a certain obnoxious Master Sergeant in the Mess Hall. My first act as an officer, it gave me a great sense of power to write out the order. In less than an hour, Zoobird appeared in the door of my office, dressed in his best uniform. Joy lit his long face as he snapped off a salute that would have impressed President Wilson.

"Private Fleischman reporting for duty, sir!"

"The pleasure's all mine — Corporal."

I kicked the door shut and for a few minutes we had a reunion as enthusiastic as it was quiet. He confided that he'd be glad if he never saw a spatula again, and I told him how much his help had enabled me to pass those finals. Best of all, he was tickled at the prospect of our lengthy tedious assignment.

"This is better than the Bank," he said. "What we got to do is set up our own system, color code everything. Red tags for the officers' baggage, and blue for the enlisted men. Green for the stable tack, yellow for the kitchen equipment which they might need to get at somewhere along the way. We'll have to find out so we know what order to stack things in the hold of the ship. Maybe a separate color for stuff like the coffee pots . . ."

I left him rummaging happily in the drawer of the desk for a notebook. I didn't doubt that he'd keep track of every pencil and shoelace.

My own job, I figured, was to get our itinerary, be prepared for each cargo switch, find out at which points the men would need to retrieve their baggage. I had a notion if any of their footlockers went missing the blame would fall on the shoulders of one sorry Lieutenant Jones.

By May 10th the trucks began to roll out of Camp Doniphan bound for France, and I was relieved that I knew every item in them, thanks to Zoobird's system. I had arranged the order of loading, from lorry onto the train, last on, first off. At the dock in Hoboken, the same thing happened in reverse. After a couple of days on the hectic waterfront of New Jersey we had it all stowed aboard the good ship *Ceramic,* a 20,000 ton Australian merchant vessel that had been converted into a troop transport.

Unit after unit they filed on board, answered roll call and went below decks. As darkness fell no lights were permitted, troop movements were like magnets to the German submarines. But we could go up on deck so long as we didn't smoke. I wanted a glimpse of New York. So far there had only been distant fragments seen between the docks, of tall buildings, square and dull against the gray sky. But now as night came on they turned glorious with a million windows, festoons of lights across the bridges, the Statue of Liberty rising in majesty above the harbor, the silent mystery of other blacked-out liners moving on the tide. Everything seemed so huge, bigger than I'd ever imagined — I was never so aware that we were one heck of a long way from Kansas City.

FOURTEEN

The guys were all laying bets on the exact moment we would catch sight of England, so of course we arrived in the pitch black of night. The threat of enemy submarines was even greater here, everyone was pretty tense by then. I was just glad to see the bulking dark silhouettes of the warehouses along the docks of Liverpool. When the sun did come up — at least there was an easing of the deep clouds to let a thin light through — we might have been back in Hoboken. The shipping looked a lot the same, the harbor full of freighters, tugs, naval craft and garbage.

The dock workers seemed a "jolly lot," and helped me with the task of unloading. I couldn't understand much of what they said, but they knew how to handle cargo. We transferred everything straight onto the big lorries lined up to take the stuff across England to the Channel. I envisioned a journey like the one we'd traveled from Oklahoma to New Jersey; it was hard to conceive that it would only take a few hours to cross an entire country.

In fact nothing about England was like my scrapbook of mental images that ranged from Oliver Twist to Tess of the Durbervilles, all moors and cliffs and heaths. As we trundled along on a small train across the countryside we passed neat villages set in rolling hills so green it almost hurt your eyes. If the Native returned here he would have been met at the depot by swarms of pretty pink-cheeked girls begging cigarettes.

"Cheerio, you blokes!"

"Down with the Kaiser."

They didn't look haunted. I had read about the bombings that had flattened parts of the cities, but out here in the farmlands it all seemed untouched. The train tracks were almost hidden by deep meadows, which were as well kept as our lawns at home. The only thing wrong — I had to search for it, as we passed another railway station — there were no men anywhere. Not on the platforms or on the road or the streets, as if a terrible Pied Piper had marched off with them. I didn't see a male over about twelve or under the age of fifty.

The same thing was true in Southampton,

where we finally left the cars. Here was the shabbiness I had expected from Dickens, the dogged faces of people who had lived lean for a long time, full of a harried impatience, even a little resentment of a company of healthy looking boys all fresh from another country. They didn't do a lot of cheering. It was more a case of "What kept you so long?"

"Real Englishmen," Zoobird marveled. "I wish we had a chance to talk to them."

No time for chatting, though. We went straight to work supervising the transfer of those piles of baggage onto another ship, a smaller one, that would take us across the Channel. I hoped. It looked more like a ferry than an ocean-going vessel, and when we finally shoved off it was so heavy the portholes were awash.

Most of us stayed on deck. That passage lived up to its reputation, almost everybody got seasick. I didn't, the deep chill had my stomach in its frozen clutches. And I had taken Zoobird's advice, not to eat before we left. Those who had dug in at mess were sorry, numerous times that night in the darkness and fog. I tried not to look over the side. The sea had an oily quality in the white haze. I was relieved when we finally bumped solidly against the dock at Le-

Havre. I wish I had a nickel for every doughboy who uttered those immortal words.

"Lafayette, we are here."

When day broke over the land we saw we were in another dirty crowded seaport bristling with docks, jammed with ships, fishing boats and more naval vessels. But what most of us focused on lay beyond — a long, long hill that rose from the harbor. The official rest camp was at the top. Men could be seen trudging painfully up it, carrying their gear, moving slowly. I'd heard about that hill, but I didn't realize how steep it would be. No car ever made could have driven it in high gear.

Zoobird nudged me. "What do you say we tend to the baggage first."

I was glad to agree. We spent the whole day loading it all on another train, this time with an eye to the officers' personal equipment, which we made sure was on top. The next stop would be our final destination, presumably. By the time it was done to Zoobird's satisfaction the sun was wallowing in the sullen chop of the Channel. It must have been eight p.m. by then. Europe lies in a latitude so much farther north we were still in broad daylight. Chores over, pitching seas done with, I was suddenly ravenous.

All we'd had to eat from time to time was a quick bite grabbed from a makeshift canteen set up near the docks by the Red Cross. I thought of Lindy. What a marvel it would be, to walk over to that aid station and see her face there. But the tables were serviced by men, medical corpsmen to judge by their insignia. The food tasted as if it had been prepared days ago. Sandwiches, cookies, what I needed was something hot in my belly.

Zoobird looked up at the long slope and sighed. "Wonder if there's a mess hall up there?" Some men were coming back down — two officers veered toward the train tracks where we stood. I recognized one from OTC, Hobby Carter, a gunnery man. Odd-looking fellow, no hair on him at all, not even eyebrows. We learned later that he'd had scarlet fever when he was a kid, and his hair never grew back. When he saw me he headed over. Introduced us to Abe Peters, a Captain in charge of one of our batteries, a tall handsome Irishman, but he presented a strange silhouette. On his back he seemed to be carrying an oblong box, under his rubber poncho.

"Good to see you guys."

"How's it going?"

"We were about to head up the hill," I

said. "Any food up there?"

"Don't bother," Abe advised with a shudder. "Nothing to eat, and the huts aren't fit for a pig. Place hasn't been cleaned since the days of Charlemagne. I think some of his cooties are still kicking around up there."

"The bedbugs are so bold," Hobby added, "they don't even wait for you to go to bed. They attack your ankles where you stand. We came down to find somewhere else to sleep tonight."

It only took me a minute to consider the situation solemnly. "Corporal Fleischman," I said, "it seems to me we need to post a heavy guard over these boxcars. They're full of government issue, who knows what kind of thievery you get on the docks. I say we need about four people to stand watch over them. Or rather, to lie in watch. No need to overdo it."

Zoobird came back, "Lieutenant, sir, I agree, sir."

Hobby nodded soberly. "It's a tough job, but I volunteer."

"Don't we need somebody's permission?" Abe looked around at the confusion of the railroad yards.

"Yep," I said. "We need it to be cleared by the Officer in Charge of Luggage, which is me. Now let's go find a place to eat before I fall on my face."

"What I wouldn't give for some ham and eggs," Hobby sighed.

The frontage street that ran along the docks was lined with saloons and halls where women cavorted to the sound of accordion music. We followed our noses to a café down the block from which emanated a wonderful aroma of stew. There was a sign on the door which needed no translation: *Officiers.*

Zoobird drooped a little. "That's okay. You guys go on, I'll find some place to grab a bite."

"No!" I told him. "We're sticking together." Taking off my Army field jacket I draped it across his unbarred shoulders and Hobby whipped off his cap with its Captain's insignia, leaving his bald head shining in the lamplight. The cap stood up too high on the Bird's wild crest of hair, but we put on our most official faces as we marched into the canteen..

Talk came to a sudden hush, eyes turned. I gave the room a snappy salute, which the others copied. It was like a dare, for those Frenchmen to object to a quartette of young whippersnappers who had come a thousand miles to save their butts. The Gallic faces were boldly cut, long planes and big noses, features so similar they spoke of generations of undiluted lineage, unlike the polyglot features on the faces of America, where a half-dozen heritages are mingled in one man. Their dark eyes were wary, a defensive tenseness in their postures, the way dogs get when faced with an unknown pack of mutts.

Hobby was perusing a small handbook, titled "Dictionary of French Phrases," and found one. "Bon soor, amees. Jay fam. Avay-voo a table?"

The thin lips of our hosts began to twitch. The proprietor came forward, an old man in a dirty apron. In real French he said something and led us over to an empty booth.

"Where'd you get that booklet?" Zoobird muttered. "I'd like to have one of those."

"Kids on the street were selling them as we disembarked. One franc. I think that's about a quarter, American." Hobby frowned at the book and then the menu. "Got it." Turning to the proprietor he said, "Noo-sommes les oofs."

That did it. The entire room went up in laughter. I knew enough smattering of French to understand: Hobby had just said "We are eggs."

"I want ham with mine." Abe Peters took

the phrase book. After a minute he said, "Cochon?"

I did it the easy way. Pointing to a man nearby who was digging into a plate of beef stew I said, "Whatever he's having." Zoobird made a me-too gesture. By then everyone in the room was involved. They went into hysterics when the old boy brought Abe a plate of pigs' feet, which looked as though some pig had recently used them.

We finally were served plates of slumgullion and a loaf of heavy rough black bread that tasted wonderful after it was softened up in the gravy. Then I committed the biggest blunder yet. "Avay-voo any water?"

It baffled them.

"To drink." I pantomimed and pointed to it in the phrase book.

"De l'eau? Pour boire?" They didn't grasp the concept at all. In the months I was in France water was never provided at table. Maybe the supply wasn't sanitary, but for whatever reason everyone drank wine. Even the children. I never liked *vin rouge* much, but I got used to it. And it made for convivial spirits.

Several of the Frenchmen were enlarging on the humorous Americans to the chuckles of their comrades. I said to the others, "These fellows think we're a bunch of clowns. How can we make a good impression on behalf of the United States Army?"

"Maybe we should sing the Star Spangled Banner?" Zoobird suggested.

"I've got a better idea. I never saw a crowd yet that I couldn't soften up with my box." Peters had hung his poncho on the back of his chair, in a way that still shielded the object beneath. Now he took it forth, a handsome five-string banjo. "What this place needs is some good old U. S. music." And he launched into the Turkey in the Straw.

It was incredible how the atmosphere was transformed. A current of delight ran through those somber Frenchmen, as if they were transported away from the heavy echoes of battle. They began to clap their hands to the driving rhythm, that insistent fifth string with its dissonant twang, sad and sassy. Peters went straight on into the Artilleryman's song and we belted out the words at the top of our voices.

"Over hill, over dale, we will hit the
dusty trail,
As the caissons go rolling along."

The listeners were pounding their tables in time, smiling now with no trace of contempt.

But the capper was Peters' mellow rendition of Roses of Picardy. He strummed it softly with a running obligato — the man was a master of his instrument. I saw several hardened officers wipe away tears. One whipped out a harmonica and joined in with a masterful tremolo. Later I learned that the French are not ashamed to be sentimental, and after all those years of war they had a lot to be nostalgic about.

When we got up to leave the proprietor wouldn't let us pay for the meal. People came over to shake our hands. Zoobird sought out the man with the mouth organ and tried to convey a question. "Where can I buy one of those?"

Everyone joined in to translate and the man smiled through his tears and presented the harmonica to Zoobird with such an air of ceremony it rose above all refusal. The Bird gave him an equally solemn bow, dug down in his pocket and got out his high-jump medal. It was big as a silver dollar and decorated with a laurel wreath. When he bestowed it on the harmonica player, the Frenchmen launched into The Marseillaise.

For some reason that evening brought home to me the reality of this war like nothing else had. All at once it became about people, about loss and desperation and pride. As we walked back through the cobblestone streets a bell was ringing, and when I glanced down a side street I saw a flock, mostly women, heading for a small church. I got an odd notion — that if I could have gone with them maybe I would have found God in person waiting there. I shook it off as a result of all that *vin rouge.*

When we reached the train yards again Hobby was saying, "That's the best beef I ever tasted, and I worked in the stockyards in St. Louis. I thought I knew all the breeds, but they must have different varieties over here. I asked the waiter and he said something that sounded like 'cheval.' "

Zoobird nudged me silently and jerked a thumb at the train standing on the tracks, waiting to be loaded with the troops tomorrow. A line of cars that were part passenger, part boxcar, they bore markings on each: *40 HOMMES & 8 CHEVEAUX.* These would be the famous forty-and-eights we had heard about, designed to hold forty men and eight — horses.

I swallowed hard. "Cheval?" I muttered.

"Yep," he said. "I knew it all along. I've eaten horse-meat before."

We didn't mention it to the others, but from that day forth I never again ordered roast beef in France.

FIFTEEN

That next morning when we viewed the conditions of the troop cars, with men crowding on, filling every inch, we all four elected to continue "guarding" the luggage. From the open door of the box car we had our first real look at France, a long look, trundling through miles of woodlands so dense I was amazed. I had pictured Europe as being stripped of trees after all the centuries of burning firewood and building houses. But they had preserved those forests as if they were sacred. In fact, I learned later, you had to get a permit to cut down even a sapling.

The cities used coal from the northern provinces for heating, but out in the rural districts they used dried cow dung, except in their cook stoves, where they hoarded each stick of kindling as if it were gold. I thought of the carelessness with which people back home were cutting down whole stands of trees. Ohio had no more of the great forests, and Missouri was half farmland or pasture, except for the Ozarks. They were still pretty wild, but not like this countryside.

We had plenty of time to absorb it. The train only moved about twenty miles an hour, but the day passed easily with Peters playing his banjo and Zoobird accompanying on the harmonica. He didn't know how to play it, of course. He had one chord for breathing in and another for blowing out.

"You should get somebody to give you lessons," Hobby suggested.

"Nah," Zoo insisted. "I'm getting the hang of it."

I didn't know whether to laugh or cry. You ought to learn the mouth organ when you're about six. It's like shooting marbles, the older you get you think about it too much. But Zoobird was happy, his face shining with concentration. To help, or to camouflage how awful it was, I began to sing along.

" 'Oh, I come from Alabama with my banjo on my knee . . .' " The others joined in and we managed to startle the French birds flitting through the woods with sounds that were sour and sweet and ancient, accompanied by the racket of wheels and an occasional toot from the pea-whistle on the antique steam engine up front.

In the villages we passed, women gathered to watch us go by like any farm folk back home, maybe a little more primitive in their clothes. The girls wore scarves tied over their heads and the children wore wooden clogs. The earth was deeply muddy, in fact it was still raining from time to time. Toward the end of the second day we chugged to a halt at a rail head where a multitude of tracks came together flanked by huge train sheds and warehouses.

As the troops began to file off the cars Hobby and Abe went to join their units while Zoobird and I waited by the baggage car for further orders, which were soon forthcoming. An aide came over and saluted me.

"General Berry wants you to bring the officers' gear and join him at our new Headquarters. That lorry is assigned to you, Lieutenant."

Thanks to Zoobird's color code it took us no time at all to load the truck. Leaving him to keep an eye on the rest of the carload I climbed into the front seat with the driver, an aging Frenchman in a shabby uniform. We trundled along a dirt road so deeply rutted the vehicle swayed from side to side, but it managed to plow its way through.

Then all at once the woods opened out onto a scene from a fairy tale.

On a slope a few miles away stood a castle towering above acres of manicured grounds, a palace of turrets and balconies, with high arching windows. The driver turned down the long entrance drive. As he pulled up at the ornate entryway he announced, with only the slightest touch of superiority, "Chateau D'Ronceroy."

I felt a little guilty, sight-seeing, when the General was waiting for his bags, but I tried to take in all the details of the place so that I could write my mother about it. It looked exactly like a picture from one of her travel books. It wasn't until several enlisted officers came forth to help with the baggage that it dawned on me — this was my destination. Nothing like this had entered my head as part of fighting a war.

The great hall I walked into was bigger than our entire house at home, with a fireplace you could stand in without ducking. The walls were covered with tapestries the size of our living room rug, and huge paintings of noble Frenchmen, or women in royal gowns with little dogs curled up at their feet. The relics scattered around were from another time, swords and shields and a suit of armor that looked so real you wondered if there was an old knight inside it.

"But that's not all," I wrote Mom next morning. "You should see my bedroom. It's all gold and mirrors, these little gold chairs and skimpy tables. Nothing skimpy about the bed, it's big enough to park a car in, with a hand-carved head board and a pile of six or seven feather mattresses. It's how they keep warm in winter, so I was told. Depending on how cold the room is, they get in between number two and three, or they can go deeper. Of course it's warm these days. I slept on top of the whole lot, needed a good running jump to get up there. Later I found out they have little step-stools. The one thing they don't have is bathrooms. There are lots of chamber pots, but no tubs or showers. I have an idea they don't take many baths, they just put on a lot of perfume."

Pausing, I glanced at my watch and jumped up to finish dressing. I had only seen the General briefly after I arrived yesterday. He had asked me to join him at eight hundred hours in the morning and it lacked only fifteen minutes. I wasn't going to get much breakfast. As I hastily shaved I was startled at my own image in the elegant little mirror. I seemed to have acquired a different look, thinner and tougher, and I had started a moustache, though that didn't bear scrutiny right now. I tied my boots and ran down the great staircase — only to get lost. Hallways branched off everywhere, but I followed the scent of hot bread and found a vast dining hall, where a heavily carved banquet table was piled with food. The General was there ahead of me.

"Good morning, Lieutenant. Be sure and have plenty of breakfast, then come to my office."

A half hour later when I located the room where he had set up Headquarters I saw new orders posted and scanned them in anticipation. The members of his staff had been assigned permanent duties: Operations Officer, Intelligence Officer, Munitions Officer . . . my name wasn't there. Swallowing some hurt feelings, I knocked at the office door.

"Come on in, Lieutenant." The General was filling his pipe. He looked more than ever like a retired judge, the drooping moustache, the world-weary eyes. His uniform jacket was draped over the back of the chair — the day was warming up, getting humid. "I want to congratulate you on the job you did with the baggage."

"Thank you, sir, but I owe a lot to the

man I had helping me. His name is Cal Fleischman. He's only a Private, but I made him a Corporal. I don't know whether I'm allowed to do that, sir. Maybe you could make it official. He's a brilliant man, used to work in a bank and has math far beyond mine. He got stuck in the mess hall at Camp Doniphan and never had a chance to show what he could do." I could see I was losing his attention.

"Very good, well noted." General Berry was fingering some papers. "Then he can finish the inventory for you? Good. Because you have a new assignment."

"Yes sir?"

"It's going to take a while for us to move forward to our next deployment, which right now has to remain a secret. We'll be standing by here, probably for weeks. So it seemed an ideal time for you to get some advanced training. There's a class in Intelligence work at the American Artillery Headquarters in Bar-sur-Aube. You'll be taught advanced tactics by officers who have seen first-hand battle situations. You'll be going into the field. I want you to get a sense of the war as the French have been conducting it, working with men who have been solving artillery problems for years. It will be valuable after we are deployed. You can pass along whatever you learn to the rest of the men."

At the thought of more schoolwork, my spirits sagged. The General gave me a fatherly smile. "Don't fret, Bernie, I won't forget you. In fact, I envy you, probably be going up to the Front, see some real action. Good luck, son." He shook my hand.

The Front. When people spoke that word their tone of voice gave it a capital letter. There were front lines, stations up-front, and so forth, but the Front was referred to with a kind of dread, as of Hell itself. As I found myself on a train rolling northward my stomach felt queasy. The food at the Chateau had been wonderfully fresh, best breakfast I'd had in months, but I'd eaten too much, or else things were moving too fast. I'd been looking to a few days to get my legs, so to speak. Instead, here I was being rattled along on a northbound train taking me into new, chillier country, where the rain outside looked cold and the little towns more threadbare.

Looking down the aisle of the coach at my fellow passengers I found not one face that I recognized. I got out my letters — the mail had caught up to us at the Chateau. I had only glanced at them hastily this morning. Now, moving through an unknown world, I held them like gold, and read them all again. Lindy had written me three and in each she had enclosed a pack of chewing gum, taken apart and the sticks laid flat. It tasted great, settled my stomach like nothing else could. Or maybe it was her handwriting, which was strong for a girl, no finishing-school formalities. She wrote as if we were having a conversation.

"I got my Red Cross uniform the other day. It makes me look like a nurse, with a little white cap and veil. Who knows, maybe I will get some practical nursing to do. Even now, men are coming through bound for home. They've been in some training accident or they're sick with lung fever. Anyway, they all seem glad to have a friendly hand and a smile."

Her smile. I closed my eyes and — I couldn't see her. I suddenly realized I had never gotten a photo of her. It just about wrecked me. I couldn't remember exactly what she looked like. But in the writing I could almost hear her voice. "Anyway, seeing the young men off makes me feel I am doing a little bit for the war. It helps me feel in touch with you, out there in the danger zone. Please take care. I say a prayer for you every night."

Nobody had ever done that before. Did it

mean — ? I had to back off from that thought. It's easy to read too much into a casual friendship, any of the guys would tell you that. It's a woman's nature to love the man she's with. Lindy probably had a dozen beaux. And praying is easy, it doesn't cost a cent.

Beyond the window now I saw a different kind of French countryside, stubbled fields dotted with hayricks, and in the distance a windmill. It looked exactly like the ones pictured in "Hans Brinker," one of my favorite boyhood books. But that had been set in Holland. I hoped the train hadn't gone astray by mistake. If it did, I'd never know. The signs I saw along the tracks as we came through the small cities were all unrecognizable. I'd never felt so alone in my life.

I was even tempted to stroll up and join the poker game going on at the front of the car. Different outfit, I'd be a stranger there too. Somebody won a pot and the rest of them groaned. They too were looking out the windows.

"Where on earth are we?"

"God only knows."

If He did, I wished He would tell me. If He was up there, I kept coming back to that. Sinking into a mire of gloom, I felt weak and wondered if I was afraid? Not really, not scared of the war. I still thought it would be over before we saw any action. When the Germans learned of the thousands of us pouring into the fight, how could they face us? No, it wasn't fear.

So what, then? I wished I could talk to someone. Which is probably why people pray, I thought, but that wasn't for me. I never made up a real formal type prayer in my life, and judging by the ones our preacher gave, it was the kind of thing you don't try if you don't know how.

But I wouldn't mind talking to the Lord, the way I used to before Ookey made me feel stupid and childish for believing. If I were to try it now I'd feel like a complete hypocrite. Anyhow, what would I say? *I don't feel too well, so please don't let me come down with something here, when there isn't an Army medic within a hundred miles.* That really made me feel silly. When you think how many thousands of people are in worse shape than me, I should shut up and firm up. And I would, if I only knew what the heck was wrong with me.

At that point a strange thing happened. Answers began to pop into my brain as if it were a blackboard and Somebody was writing on it.

I am homesick.

I miss my father.

I miss Missouri.

I miss our car.

I miss my room and the red blanket on the bed.

I miss my outfit and Zoobird.

I even miss his harmonica.

I miss Ookey.

That surprised me a little, but right then his sneer and his cold self-assurance would have been bracing. He would certainly never moon around about being alone. I could see him again that day, pitching stones at a bucket, perfectly at ease with himself. It must be the greatest gift in the world, and yet I didn't envy him. Maybe it wasn't too bad to have a bunch of friends you miss. They'd be waiting when I got back from wherever this train was taking me. Who would ever meet Ookey at the station?

I settled back and let the motion lull me into a drowse. I guess it was a good hard sleep, because I slept through Paris. I roused up once when it was dark outside. We were in a giant railroad station. Then drifting off I slept again until it was morning and the conductor was shaking me awake.

"Bar-sur-Aube, Monsieur."

I followed the crowd to a line of automobiles, one of them bearing a little American flag with the symbol of the Artillery on it. A touring car, it was already crowded with officers from various units, Americans and a couple of officers in foreign uniforms. I wedged myself into the rear seat next to a pudgy little Britisher with a small neat moustache which he kept touching as if to make sure it was still there.

The school actually was in a small town nearby called Luneville. When we arrived we were escorted to a kind of barracks, where we were assigned quarters, two to a room. It seemed that the Englishman and I would be billeted together for the next few weeks. As we stowed our gear clearly introductions were in order. He clicked his heels at me and raised his cap to reveal a straight brush of ruddy hair.

"Angus McIntyre," he said, "of his Majesty's . . ." There followed a string of identifications, units, divisions, armies with ancient names, I can't remember them all.

But I did my best to match him. "George Bernard Jones, Second Lieutenant, Headquarters Company, 129th Field Artillery, 60th Brigade, 35th Division, First Army of the United States of America. Glad to meet you."

Sixteen

From the window of our cubbyhole on the second floor I could see rooftops nearby that showed damage. It dawned on me that the holes must have been made by bombs. But we were not that near the Front, I thought, so it must be from some time past when war had come this way. And then one of our hosts, a young French officer, stopped by to warn us.

"The Bosch send their planes over *parfois.* When you hear the sirens, *marchez vit* — run to the *abri.*" He took me down the stairway and showed me: across from the back door was an air raid shelter a few feet away. Angus scorned the idea as if it were unmanly. I couldn't understand that. England had been bombed so ferociously its cities were honeycombed with shelters.

I told him mildly, "I don't see anything cowardly about not wanting to get hit by shrapnel."

"That's because your country hasn't any experience with the lower classes." He was brimming with so much knowledge it simply had to be imparted to the untaught. As he expounded on warfare and the psychology of the primitive mind, the necessity for looking calm and well-groomed at all times before the troops, it came out that he had served his entire career in India and had only just returned, to be sent directly to the Front. The British, he informed me, would be leading some fresh offensive, using us Yanks as reserves, of course. Meanwhile it was important to put on a good show for the natives.

I tried to tolerate his posturing with basic American civility, and actually I found there were things I could learn from the guy. Not just about India — in a few hours I knew more about the Raj than I would ever need. But he had studied other histories, most lately the long animosity between Germany and France. He knew every campaign from Caesar on. He could talk about Huns when they were savages roaming across Europe with Attila. He could trace them right on up through Prussia to the time of Bismarck who fought Austria and France and grabbed territory to create a German nation by killing off anyone who stood in his way. Now

Kaiser Wilhelm had taken over, even more greedy to acquire territory, so he told me. We would be walking in the footsteps of a million dead men.

Angus was not the cheeriest buddy to live with, but at least I wasn't totally in the dark when we would have conversations around the dinner table in the officers' mess, those evenings. They were a lot more interesting than the classroom work, which was pretty much the same as I had gone through in OTC. But when the instructors got talking about real battlefield problems we all listened and learned.

The discussion right then was about an engagement that had occurred a few weeks earlier at a spot between Rheims and Soissons, designated as Chateau Thierry. I gathered that the French and British had taken a terrible beating in that area and were ready to pull back when the American troops arrived on the scene. Our First and Second Divisions and a Brigade of the Seventh Marines had been sent in to plug the line long enough for an orderly retreat. It was the first time our boys had ever taken part in a war, and they had waded in with such vigor that, before anyone was ready for it, they had broken the German salient and hurled them back to their original lines and then some. They had wanted to keep driving forward, but the high command had called a halt, and that's where the argument arose. Even the veterans were divided — half of them thought the Americans should have been allowed to press on, and the others warned that such a rapid advance couldn't be supported and would collapse into a disaster.

"Once you have them on the run you should keep the heat on."

"But my dear fellow, high spirits can get you into a proper pickle. The cooler view is to move more cautiously, allow reinforcements to come up."

At that point Angus rose and made a stirring speech about the valor of standing tall and firm when others all about are losing their heads. One of his fellow British officers took me aside afterward and said, "That chap is suffering from a case of nerves. Try to talk him down, will you?"

And another whispered fiercely, "And tell him to stow that demmed pipe!"

"He's okay," I told them. "The pipe is beyond my control."

It really did smell terrible. It stank of rotten fruit, the reason being that Angus had picked up a pear out of a nearby orchard on his way here and put it in the can to keep the tobacco moist. By now it was sickening. So was his condescension. When we got back to the barracks that night he lectured me on the fact that Americans had no respect for the elements of command. They should have instantly deferred to the French generals and waited for the British troops to arrive before pressing their offensive. I didn't think it would be kind to remind him that the English had pretty much shot their wad. And the pipe was making me gag, so I left hastily, saying I thought I'd take a stroll around town.

Luneville, I saw as I walked, had sustained a fair amount of shelling. Several homes had been reduced to rubble, and there were signs of fire damage. And yet the citizens seemed in good spirits, gathering in a café where there was laughter and plenty of *vin rouge.* I thought of our night in LeHavre and missed Zoobird acutely. I hoped they hadn't stuck him in the kitchen again.

As I headed back to the barracks I was startled by the ear-splitting sound of the siren blasting — it was right over my head. Breaking into a trot I sniffed the air anxiously. Sirens were used to warn of a gas attack and I didn't even have a gas mask. Then I heard a drone overhead, spotlights thrust up into the darkness, searching to find the enemy in their beams, fixing on an illusive little fighter plane. For the first time I heard the sound of guns nearby, anti-aircraft pumping shells upward at that silvery fish playing dodgeball with the lights. I had forgotten I might be in danger, but stood fixed watching the show.

In a few minutes other planes came flickering into view, wheeling in and out of the brilliance, turning cartwheels in a ghostly sort of dance. Abruptly it was over. They were gone, where I don't know. It was too late to seek the air raid shelter. As I got back to the barracks I saw women coming out of it, clutching their night robes. They had obviously made a dash to cover, but they didn't look panicked. I was the only one with heart racing. For the first time I had heard the guns of war.

I will remember Luneville for that, and for other things, not the least of which was the shower room. After months of trying to keep clean with only a washbasin and sponge, I made a marvelous discovery out in back of the barracks. It was just a wooden stall with a make-shift rig — a jerry can with holes in it set on a scaffold and filled with water that could be released by a jerk on the string. I'd bet some doughboy set that up, and I was grateful. The deluge was cold, but the morning was warm and I was singing when the woman came in carrying an armload of towels. In a complete fluster, I slipped on the soap and went down in a heap, from which I scrambled to gather my nudity into a protective crouch. The old girl, sturdy and red-cheeked and arthritic, came over cheerfully to help me up. The people in France, I found out over time, are casual about the human body. They have no false modesty. They have seen it all and who cares? It was a point of view I admired, but never did quite accept.

That was only the beginning of a new phase of my education. Our instructor that morning announced that the book phase of our learning was over. We were all going into the field (in pairs, of course) to witness the artillery in action and bring back our observations to share with the others. Angus and I were assigned to a staff car driven by a French soldier, of what rank I never was sure. All I knew was that he was more of a madman than Ookey.

Gripping the wheel of the touring car, he took us tearing across the countryside on a rutted road that flung us about from side to side and had chuckholes in it to lift us off our seats — I actually bumped my head on the canvas top of the vehicle. Crow-hopping and slithering through the mud, we must have been doing forty-five miles an hour.

Angus kept muttering through his teeth, "Slow down, you idiot, are you trying to get us killed?"

Death didn't seem out of the question. The land around us had begun to look blighted. Here was the real edge of the war zone, I thought, blasted trees and wrecked fences, farmhouses with half their walls gone. As we swerved wildly around a large crater in the road the Frenchman glanced over his shoulder.

"C'est nouveau," he explained apologetically. By then I had begun to pick up a smattering of the language. He meant it was a new hole.

It dawned on me. "A new bomb hole? Where is — *ou est Le Front?*"

He pointed northwest. *"Quatre kilometres."* And held up four fingers.

A little over two miles. Angus went pale. "Can't you drive this old crate any faster, you idiot?"

Now we joined another road with deep tire tracks that indicated heavy traffic and soon pulled into a broad cleared area where crates of war materiél were stacked on a loading dock. The Frenchman parked beside it and got out, beckoning us to follow. As we descended into a kind of ditch, Angus said in a high-pitched voice, "Ah. The trenches. We are now in the trenches."

"I think this is just a communications crosscut," I told him. "It's straight, you notice? The forward trenches are curved or zigzag to cut down on the damage that any one shell can inflict." We had learned that back in OTC. This was too neat, sunk a good eight feet deep with a board walk along the bottom.

In a few minutes we came to the real thing. Turning at a right angle we followed a crooked ditch with damaged sides, gaping breeches that had obviously been made by shellfire, and no board walk. Our boots sank up to the ankles in deep mud, which stank of blood and decaying flesh. The French had to bury thousands of their dead out on the battlefield close to their own lines. With so many odors, including the more recent ones, of sweat and garbage and lack of sanitation, you felt as if you were inhaling pure pestilence. And yet the soldiers of France had grown immersed to it. Men crouched stoically in their cubbyholes, dug out of the walls of the passages, smoking or snoozing or waiting with blank eyes.

This then was the Front.

And beyond it the killing fields. When I

raised my head a scant couple of inches I could see out over no-man's land, criss-crossed by barbed wire, littered with debris, empty tin cans, broken bottles, dead rats. Maybe not all dead — out there in the offal something moved. I had to grit my teeth and pretend I was Ookey, blasé to the ugliness of battle. But then he would be above all this. Up in his plane he would never have to contend with the underbelly of war. In a curious flash of insight, I wondered if he could handle it.

Angus was certainly having a hard time. He looked as if he might throw up at any minute. Only that British pride kept him going as we followed our guide through a complex network of trenches. We were getting closer to the enemy lines, by my inner calculation, when abruptly we found our destination. A large dugout, six feet square, it was built up on the forward side of the trench to overlook the wasteland beyond and protected by a mound of earth. The forward side was pierced by a small lookout hole which widened outward to give a broad view of the enemy's position.

Two French officers were on duty, one looking through a telescope mounted on a circular base which had calibrations marked on it. The other was seated nearby at a table with a notebook. Beside him on the wall was a stop watch. They greeted us without much warmth until I produced a package of cigarettes which I had stuck in my pocket at the last minute, thinking they might help to establish good international relations. It broke the ice and they began to explain what they were doing, though they spoke so fast I couldn't pick up a word.

McIntyre, it turned out, had some French. He translated: "This is a forward observation post. Their job is to locate the enemy's gun emplacements. When they observe a muzzle blast through the telescope the gauge on the base gives them the angle, and they start timing the shot to get the distance. When they hear the shell explode they immediately phone the next nearest post which has also made calculations. By triangulation they pinpoint the gun's position and direct fire onto it. Pretty much the way we practiced it in class."

Yes, we had learned all that, but seeing it in action was a little different. It occurs to you: suppose the burst of the shell was only ten feet away from your post? Well, no need to worry, you wouldn't be around to care. That little heap of earth banked around the dugout didn't seem very formidable, and the enemy was closer than I'd dreamed.

When I took my turn looking through the telescope I could see a German soldier over on the far side of no-man's land, sitting on a parapet a thousand yards away — that was some telescope. He was cleaning the mud off his boots.

The enemy. That man sitting over there, with the same fears, smelling the same death odors. He suddenly disappeared from view, ducked down in a trench and a moment later, not far away the puff of gunfire went up.

"Hey, come look!" I stepped aside and let the Frenchman take the telescope. He rattled off some figures to his buddy who started the stop watch. In a few seconds we felt a jarring explosion, not too near, maybe a hundred yards or so away. Before he could pick it up, the phone rang. Another station was reporting — the man in charge of the pad jotted down their figures and did some rapid math. The first officer was already ringing up the nearest battery, snapping off coordinates. Standing back then, he motioned to me to take another look. Far out across no-man's land a big spray of earth went up where our shell had hit. No way to tell whether it had taken out the enemy gun.

Angus took a turn with the telescope too. He was still pale, his upper lip very stiff indeed. Our field trip so far had left him a little rattled. I had an idea that all his soldiering over in India hadn't prepared him for violence the way my younger days had. There wasn't a lot of gentility in our school yard. We had fierce fights even when we were still in knee pants. And later on came the hard knocks on the basketball court, the close calls with farmers' shotguns back in our days of raiding birds' nests, the brushes with the dicks when we would ride the couplings of the freights down in the train yards. All of that had taught me the feel of the adrenaline rush. It was good and it was bad. You kind of drank the excitement, but the hangover can leave you shaky.

I was glad I could eat with good spirit when a courier brought us some sandwiches and a couple of bottles of *vin rouge.* I began to realize we were expected to spend the night here. There were two bunks over to one side. We took turns on them, but I was too keyed up to sleep. I wanted to have a look through that telescope now that it was dark. Very dense clouds had moved in and stifled the sky. I let the glass move slowly across the land, turning it with screws like a micrometer. Not a light showed anywhere.

Around four o'clock a subtle change came, as if veils were being withdrawn. The sun never rose, there was just a shift in the grays. I enjoyed the dawn through the telescope. The two Frenchmen were asleep. Angus was hunkered down in the corner staring at his pipe (they had made it amply clear that only cigarettes were allowed, a rule they probably created on the spot.) I was about to offer the telescope to him when I saw a puff of smoke far out in the twilight.

"Venny eecy," I hollered, and one of the Frenchmen was by my side in seconds. He started the stop watch even as he called out the numbers. I wrote them down with the other officer looking over my shoulder.

"Bon, bon."

When we heard the explosion nearby we looked at the time and they cranked up the field telephone. In a few minutes one of our batteries answered. They let me look, again — out on the horizon a great blast lit up the sky, maybe a whole stockpile of ammunition. I was thrilled for an instant. The sense of power was overwhelming. Then I wondered, *how many men went up with it?* I felt guilty about my own elation, and the Frenchman nodded at me with a grim smile.

"Mais oui," he said softly.

Seventeen

It had been a long twenty hours that we spent in that post. When the driver came to collect us next morning Angus almost embraced him. Europeans do quite a bit of embracing, I learned, but the poilu backed off fast and motioned for us to come with him.

"Vit, vit."

As we left the dugout the French officers were back at their duty with the telescope, and I realized they were not going to be relieved any time soon. There weren't enough men for such frills. It was their position to hold. That sobered me as much as anything else on the field trip — the reality of hanging on, hour after grim hour, for days on end with nothing gained. No victory in sight. No hope.

There was little cannon fire that morning, but the guide rushed us through the trenches and back off the line by way of another crosscut. Another field car was waiting. At a different supply point near a railroad siding we passed a row of tanks. I had seen pictures of them, huge armored vehicles. They were an experimental weapon being tried out to see whether they could traverse the maze of trenches and barbed wire to get to the enemy's lines, but I would hate to be shut up inside one of them. Beyond the clearing we entered more dense woods, driving at breakneck speed as if we were late for an appointment. And in fact that turned out to be the case.

At one o'clock we arrived at a broad open area that had been bulldozed down to raw dirt, on the far side of which stood a great tin shed and a pole with a windsock. At least I knew what this installation was. I said to Angus, "An airstrip. Where they keep their war planes, that's a runway for them to take off and land."

"Very interesting. The use of aircraft, I mean. Such a strange way to fight a war. A bunch of dinky little flying machines. I suppose they drop the bombs out the windows." He was stretching his cramped limbs after our ride. But the guide was urging us to follow him.

It all became obvious when we went into the hangar. There, among the parked planes, a table was set, apparently in our honor. The French pilots came forth and greeted us enthusiastically, shaking hands, babbling in their melodic language. I recognized the breed — they all looked like blood kin of Ookey's, the damn-it-all grin, the cockiness, the racy spirit.

We were gathered together to feast, and what a meal. Best food I'd had in France so far, lamb stew, fresh-baked bread, homemade spaghetti and newly harvested yellow squash, served by a hefty Frenchwoman who was plainly their unofficial mother. Her green apple pie was so much like Grossmutter's my throat clogged up and I had a hard time eating it.

Like most Frenchmen the pilots were loquacious, and fortunately one of them spoke English. He translated back and forth so that we could converse, though it was awkward. Angus was trying to explain to them the British attitudes as taught at some place called Sandhurst. Our hosts tolerated him, but barely. When I could put a word in I asked, "Is there an American air field anywhere nearby? One of my best friends is an Army aviator."

They brightened immediately. "Yes," the translator said, "there are several. The most large is up near Verdun, many flyers, we have heard. We do not yet run into them."

Another said something in which I caught the word *"envieux."*

"We all would like to be up there," their buddy explained. "That's where the action will soon be." And when the others got nervous and hushed him, he added quickly, "It is the grand secret, please do not repeat. Come, let us have some songs."

"Aujourd'hui," another said, "it is to celebrate, *non?*"

"I say," Angus looked puzzled, "I wasn't aware of a national holiday."

They eyed him in a kind of pity. The translator said, "We toast ourselves that we are alive." They raised their wine glasses. We had finished off several bottles of the stuff, but they showed no sign that they were the least bit tipsy, unless there was a slight mellowness in their voices as they broke into a rousing rendition of "Mademoiselle from Armentiéres."

When the phone on the wall rang they fell silent, alert, then eager as the leader of the squadron nodded and gave them the high sign. Running for their gear, they began to don helmets and goggles. Some went to roll back the doors of the hangar and others seized on the light planes and began to run them out into the field where mechanics were gathering to start the engines. The only one left behind was our host, the translator, a Captain with a recent scar on his left cheek and a huge bandage on his ankle. When I glanced at it he nodded ruefully.

"I am temporarily sitting on the bench, is it? *Oui.* I got myself shot yesterday."

The planes had begun to roll down the strip one after the other. A thin sunlight had broken through to brighten the scene — I could see the craft better. Battered, their thin skins pocked by bullet holes in a spray pattern, bits of wings torn off, they looked a lot more rickety than the one in which Ookey had given me my skyward initiation last year. It seemed another lifetime.

"Pity." Angus spoke up beside me as we watched them rise and disappear into the glare of the sky. "We were scheduled to go up in one of the blasted things this afternoon."

"Perhaps we will be able to send you aloft in the balloon." Our Captain suppressed a smile, making a little fun to see poor Angus squirm. But they did actually have a balloon. He took us to inspect it, a massive pile of rags that had been stitched together unevenly, by hand. To one side was a wicker basket that would hang beneath it to carry the observer. When the wind was right, he told us, they could send it far out over the enemy lines.

I shrank at the thought, but I could see that it made sense. "Do you take photos from up there?"

"It has been tried, but the movement of the balloon in the breeze, it makes difficulty." He teetered his hand. "Also they are shooting, you know. That is why she is so patched up. Many times the balloon is shot down."

"Oh, I say," Angus protested. "What happens to the chap on board?"

"Ah, he must disembark over the side. See here." He showed us a bucket stuck to the outside of the gondola. It was mounted upside-down. "In it is the parachute. You clip the rope on and jump, the parachute she is drawn out of the case. Float to earth, and hope the sniper down below is off his aim, eh?" He clapped an arm around Angus's braced shoulders and laughed. "No, we will not go up there today."

So it looked as though there would still be need for a map-maker on the ground when we launched the forthcoming campaign. I suddenly wished I were back with the outfit. If the fighting was going to be around Verdun, the Regiment would be moving out. I hoped they wouldn't lose track of me, stuck off here in the backwaters of the war.

We had returned to the hangar now. The planes weren't back yet, and I wondered if maybe they had been sent on a false alarm. The Front seemed inactive today, the sound of cannonade so distant it could have been summer thunder. Then separating from that remote grumble came a drone of engines, like mosquitoes buzzing from the gray sky where clouds had closed over again.

One after the other they appeared, first just a slit of wings and then taking shape, dropping lower, wavering as they reached to touch down. The Captain was counting under his breath, "*. . . deux, trois, quatre, cinque . . .*"

Six had gone up. I turned to ask, but his face told the story. Then at the last minute another plane came sliding sideways out of the overcast, staggering, tilting precariously. As the pilot skidded it onto the runway it swung in a circle, one wing dragging the earth, but he managed to bring it to a stop without wrecking it.

We all ran toward it, the Captain hobbling behind, muttering thanks in his own language. I think their word for God is *Dieu.* Helping the pilot from the cockpit they were pummeling him.

"C'est bien, mon vieux!"

"Raoul, il est le mieux!"

"Jolly good show," Angus piped up, staring at the blood running down the man's leg. He had received a wound in the thigh, but he was able to walk with the others into the hangar. Our driver pulled us aside, reminding us that we were due back in Luneville for supper. I think it was his own supper he was concerned with.

But they did have a grand repast laid out that evening. After our banquet with the pilots I didn't have much appetite, so I ate little and soon excused myself to go to my room. I had a lot to think about. This first real brush with war had left me with a bunch of questions. And a sense of impending disaster, which was natural enough, I just hadn't expected it to feel so personal. For the first time I really did believe that I might die. And if I did shouldn't I be on better terms with the Keeper of the Gates upstairs?

Where was Heaven, anyway? Certainly not in our earthly sky, as Ookey had once proved. But then I'd never believed it was right overhead. Just a massive Somewhere. And I doubted if an old angel named Gabriel stood by actual gates and refused to let people in. I had a hunch you had to earn the entrance fee in life. Afterward you'd never find it. Especially if you were a disbeliever like Ookey. I had to ask myself: what if he was wrong? That would leave him out in the cold. And it came to me: Hell isn't flames, it's ice. Terrible numbing boring ice where you float naked in the frigid water forever. When I thought of doubting the existence of the Lord, that was the feeling I got inside. Having been very cold and near to frost-bite several times, I thought: I'll take fire rather than that. Living is heat, passion, desire. Love. Love . . . ?

I wondered what that would feel like, but there was no time to ponder the question. Angus had left the party early too. He came in looking limp, saw me and straightened up. Taking a seat at the desk in the corner he said briskly, "Bit of ugly business today. But we must get used to that. It's a bloody affair, this war."

Weren't all wars bloody? I wanted to ask, but for once he wasn't in the mood to lecture. Opening his kit he got out a picture, set it on the little desk and took up a pad and pencil. Pens were hard to carry with you, they made a crease in your uniform pocket and they were always out of ink. We all had learned to write our letters home in pencil.

I came to look over his shoulder at the

snapshot. A girl with tight golden curls framing a very plain, bony face, but she had a sweet smile. And the baby was cute as a bug. "I didn't know you were married."

"Yes, we said our vows two years ago." For once his voice wasn't self-important. "Angeline, her name is. The boy is Wilford. They're back in Delhi. Her father's a Regimental Commander." Then he added, "He'd be interested in this field trip of ours."

"But she's the one who needs to know you're all right."

He nodded and set himself to write. I went back to my bunk. The two hard days were catching up to me. I was suddenly so weary I could hardly keep my eyes open, just flopped on top the blanket with my clothes still on.

"Bernard, old chap, that's not the way to get a good night's sleep. We were taught early on that it's important to do it properly, nightshirt and all, helps you rest, build back your strength to fight again tomorrow."

"Yes, but how about the bombs? There might be another air raid, and I don't want to run for the abri in my underwear." I was mostly kidding him. I really intended to get in bed later. Right then I just needed to flatten out and loosen my collar and relax.

"Well, at least see to your muddy shoes, man. Officers must maintain the civilities even in trying times. The servants, the enlisted men, all depend on your example."

I glanced at his boots and damned if he hadn't shined them before we all went to supper. I wondered distantly what sort of place India was, that they had to put on airs for their own servants. I'd seen pictures of India. My mother studied it one year, elephants and tigers . . . I drifted off into a place where I played marbles with a bunch of monkeys, who were actually pretty good at the game. They wanted my taw and kept trying to steal it, but I hung on and began to win. Each time I hit one of their glassies it would explode, which made a siren go off and all the monkeys started screeching . . .

"Bosch! Bosch!"

The words spiked through to my inner brain. Fighting my way up out of the depths of sleep I was only half awake as I floundered toward the door in the darkness. Blackout, all lights had to be extinguished when the sirens went off, and now I heard more bomb blasts, not too far away. I went rattling down the back stairs full-speed and hurled myself across the ten-foot gap between the barracks and the shelter, into the soft arms of those already gathered there.

In the inky dark they set me upright and took me into their huddle. The explosions sounded as if they were coming nearer. And then the unseen people around me stiffened, as an ominous sound grew — the sinister whistle of a falling shell, dropping almost on top of us. The terrible burst sent us sprawling to the ground. In blind confusion we sorted ourselves out, unseen fellow-travelers in a world of chaos. Ears ringing, heart flopping unevenly, I tried to get oriented.

"That one was close," a man's hushed voice nearby.

We could hear planes up there now, the keening noise of a battle going on overhead, while below, the anti-aircraft guns began to fire. I crawled over to the door to look out and a woman yanked me back, as shards of shell casings began to fall around us like metal rain. Those few minutes were as intense as anything I had ever known in my life. I was gasping for breath as if I'd been in a hard race, by the time the engagement broke off and the planes faded into the far-flung reaches of the sky.

"C'est fini." The man lit a lantern, which flared to reveal his face, shadowy and ancient as a prophet's. A string of white hair lay across his baldness. To the others, all

women, he said something in French. I think it was a joke about their scanty attire.

"Vieux crapaud!" Their laughter sounded shaky. By the thin light I could see they were wearing bathrobes and slippers. There is no etiquette in a bomb shelter. The thought flipped a switch in my brain.

"Angus?" I called.

He wasn't there, must have stayed in the room, I thought. Pretty risky. That one bomb had been a very near miss. The old man leading the way up to ground level halted at the doorway. Then stepped forward to bend over a prostrate figure that lay between the barracks and the shelter. I went to his side and stuck, as if I'd had a blow to the chest that knocked the wind out of me.

"Il est mort."

Angus lay stretched on his back, his moustache as neat as ever, his uniform clean — he had taken long enough to dress like an officer and a gentleman. Too long. He had arrived just in time for that shower of anti-aircraft debris. A chunk of shrapnel protruded from a terrible wound in his neck. Blood had flowed everywhere, over his coat, his jodhpurs, over those freshly polished boots.

EIGHTEEN

I hadn't even liked the guy. So why was his death like a screw in my gut? Sharp edges of anger kept twisting inside me, a kind of rage that I had never felt before. I was glad I had blown up that gun over on the enemy's lines. I wanted to do more. It would have felt great to get behind a howitzer and aim it myself, straight at the heart of the dirty "Bosch." At home the sneer-word for Germans was "kraut," but the French lent a special fury to their epithet. And now I shared it. Plus a lot of frustration, a sense of impotence.

I had written a letter to his wife; it seemed the least I could do. "I was with him when he died" — a minor lie — "and his last thoughts were of you." Which was no lie at all. I wished I had encouraged him to talk about his family, but the truth was that poor Angus was remote from us, a self-important, superior know-it-all who would never have shared his private side with a Yank. No matter, he still didn't deserve to be wiped out.

Cold . . . I couldn't seem to get warm, though it was August by then, full summer outside the train windows. I was in a compartment with a half-dozen other soldiers on the way to the unseen, unmentioned, but ever-looming new offensive. Our orders had come in, the classroom was done with. The 129th had already moved up to Gerardmer. I hoped they would wait for me there. I wanted to get out and push the train to go faster.

It trundled along at a snail's pace through a ragged countryside that had been devastated by war, though not recently. Farmers had repaired their barns, a few cows roamed the pitted fields. The small towns were ruined, but people still lived in the blasted buildings. They baked their bread and raised their pitiful kitchen crops, sold them at the street markets. As we crawled past they waved, but they were too exhausted to cheer. The war was a long way from over and they knew it. The Germans had not folded just because the United States entered the fighting.

It would take more troops, many more. I could see thirty or forty cars trailing behind us, as we went around a curve on precarious tracks, where workmen labored to repair the damage dealt by the bombs. They hardly paused to witness our passing. The sense of urgency in the air was unmistakable. We were headed for a great battle, we all knew it. Through the long night I hardly slept, just sat there shivering, more sure than ever that Hell was a frozen place in the heart.

In the morning when we stopped for the engine to take on water, as I stood on the platform and stretched my cramped limbs I heard a distant rumble, like thunder. The sky was cloudless for once, sun shining, birds calling in the fields. So it was artillery fire and I was grimly glad that we would soon be in the midst of it. *Let's get this damned war over with!*

At noon, when we reached the railhead and poured off the train we could hear it more distinctly, the separate grunts of the mortars, the bigger growl of the howitzers, once in a while a massive *krump,* which I took to be one of the French long guns, the 220's. I looked around for transportation and saw a familiar face.

"Hey, Hobby! How goes it?"

"Bernie! Welcome back." His lashless eyes crinkled with delight. "You're just the man I want to see. I've been told you are a legend in the matter of getting the officers' gear to them, all the way from Doniphan to Ronceroy and not a single piece missing. Now I can't even find the baggage car. I could use some help." He started off through the growing crowd.

"Where's Cal Fleischman?" I asked, following him. "He's the one who was a whiz at inventory."

"Who? Oh, the skinny fellow with the harmonica? I haven't seen him lately. But he's bound to be here somewhere. The 129th is on the move." He mopped his shining naked head with a large red neckerchief. "Looks like the whole 35th Division, for that matter. Hey, they're unloading luggage over there." Men were slinging foot-lockers off a car, hurrying, as another train waited down the track to move onto the siding. About then a Corporal intercepted us.

"Captain Carter, sir, have you seen Lieutenant Jones?"

"He's right here in person," Hobby jerked a thumb at me, as he rushed off to join the mob around the baggage car.

I called after him. "Look for the red tags. What is it Corporal?"

The boy was so new his uniform still had the original creases in it. Saluting, he said, "Sir, I have been instructed to bring you straight to Headquarters." So the General hadn't forgotten me. I slung my duffle over my shoulder and followed him.

It was a short drive to the new camp, where they were putting up barracks out of raw green wood. I wondered how they had persuaded the French to part with some of their lumber. The forests were dense around us here, and just above the treetops I could see distant heights, which accounted for the chill in the air.

The Corporal had parked in front of the largest of the buildings which bore a hand-lettered sign over the door:

ADMINISTRATION

I found General Berry in a familiar posture, bent over a table in his office, studying a large map. As if we had talked only an hour ago, he glanced up and said, "Good, Lieutenant, maybe you can unscramble these contour lines."

It must be a very steep mountainous region, for the elevations came close together in a complicated tangle. "If we color them in groups, so that each elevation stands out more sharply —"

The General got the idea at once. "Good." He rolled the map up and handed it to me. "Fix it up as soon as you get settled. I'd like to have it by the end of the day tomorrow. Bernie, it's good to have you back. Sit down. Tell me about the Front."

"It was very — interesting," I said, for lack of any possible word that might cover the complexity of emotions I was feeling by then.

I got out my notebook and detailed the operations of the forward observation post. I described the aerodrome, the balloon. "They told me they had tried to photograph the enemy lines, but it was hard to do with the balloon swinging around in the breeze."

"Yes, aerial pictures will be useful in the future, but for right now we're going to have to do our own cartography. The French maps are focused on defensive warfare, they've been in this stalemate so long. To mount an offensive we need new charts to help us plan a staged advance. We need to pinpoint forward objectives."

"I noticed some mountains to the north, sir."

"Yes, the Vosges. But those will be someone else's problem. Our orders are to move on up close to Verdun, so don't unpack your bags. Meantime get some rest, young man. You look bone-weary."

I hadn't done anything to earn his concern, but I didn't tell him that. He was the one with deep lines around his eyes. I saluted and left, to search for my assigned room, which was A-19 according to the orders posted on the Headquarters bulletin board. Officers Barracks A was a long narrow building that still smelled of pine sap and sawdust. Down the middle was a corridor flanked by two rows of close-set doors — small rooms, but private at least. And from far along the hallway came a sound that dragged me bodily out of the hole I had been in for days, the drawling cry of a harmonica badly played.

Oh, I come from Alabama . . .

You could even make out the tune — he had improved significantly since I left. Zoobird, what in tarnation are you doing, trespassing in officer country? When I burst in without knocking, the lanky figure on the Army cot rose in the air like a startled pheasant. The crest of hair stood straight up and his beaky face split in a grin so wide he could have swallowed the mouth organ whole.

"Bernie! You made it! I was scared the Army had lost you somewhere." As he pumped my hand I took in the proud glint of bars on his shoulders.

Snapping off my best salute I said, "Lieutenant Fleischman. Looks like congratulations are in order."

"Just got 'em last week. They ordered the OTC at Nancy: graduate those guys and send 'em back to their units."

"Officers Training Camp over here? I didn't know they had one."

"Yep, they keep needing more of us. It was the strangest thing. The day you left for Bar-sur-Aube, when I went in to present the completed inventory to General Berry he already had my orders cut. Said we did a good job on the move, only how did he know? He hadn't even checked my figures. Anyway, I was off on the next train to Nancy. Gosh, it seems like a long time ago. Did you ever see the Front?"

After a long hour of gab about that we got to the gossip. "What's been happening to the rest of the gang?"

"Pug's at the remount station in Paris. Dollars ran into him last time he went there to check on supplies. He's in the Quartermaster Corps now, you know. Deke transferred to the Corps of Engineers. He couldn't do the math on the big guns, but he's great on reading blueprints. He's out there somewhere helping build this camp. We're only here temporarily but there'll be a permanent contingent billeted here. This is a railhead for ammunition and supplies.

The sector we're heading for is a fifty-mile stretch between Rheims and Verdun."

"There's an American aerodrome up at Verdun. You hear anything about Ookey?"

He shook his head. "But I have some bad news about Fats. He's in the guardhouse, went AWOL. His father had another heart attack and he wanted to go home. Instead of applying through the Red Cross, he just hitched his way back to LeHavre, going to try to jump a merchant ship. They caught him. I'm afraid he's headed for Leavenworth."

That was too bad. He never was a brilliant thinker, but this was a fool's play. "Somehow, I thought if any of us was arrested it would be the Ook. I figured by now he'd either be a jailbird or a hero."

Zoobird considered his harmonica judiciously. "Well, I reckon he'll probably be the first to bring home a medal."

Which isn't the same thing, of course. I knew what he meant.

"You never did care much for Ookey, did you?" I said. Every time I would suggest to Zoo that we go out to the farm he'd find something else urgent that he needed to do. "I grant you he's a show-off. But you have to admit he's not afraid of anything on earth."

"Or elsewhere," he said cryptically. "Thing about that is, if you're never scared how can you tell that you're brave? We used to go visit the field hospital in Nancy, try to get first-hand information about the Front. Bernie, they've got hundreds of French soldiers in there, arms and legs blown off, lungs rotted with poison gas. Some of them have got the shakes from too much shelling, stuff we haven't even gone through yet. They're not what Ookey would call heroes; they just went out there and laid their lives on the line. They've got courage, and I call that better than a ribbon."

It jolted me back to my own lifelong misgivings — that secret question I never had answered. *Am I a yellow-belly?* Such a basic fear that I was pretty sure it contained its own answer. You ought not to have to worry about the thing.

It was always there in the corner of my mind, these days as we idled around camp and waited for the Generals to lay their plans. I still wanted to fire those big guns at the dirty Bosch who had killed Angus. But it's one thing to shoot at someone out of sight across no-man's land, and another to follow orders onto the field of battle with the bullets flying. I had to admit, I hoped I'd never have to do that. *Yellow-belly.*

It occurred to me that I ought to pray. Whether God was genuine or not, it wouldn't hurt to hedge my bets. But when I tried, the lines were down. I didn't feel any connection the way I used to, or thought I did, when I would mention to Him that I wished He'd help me figure out women or would He please help me pass the OTC tests. After what I had seen out there on the edge of a battlefield, I just couldn't picture a God who would sit off in heaven and let this war happen.

And, then, as if a door to a room had come ajar, something prompted me to speak up the way I used to: *Lord, please let this offensive be the one that ends the fighting.* I felt a little sheepish, because the room was probably empty.

Meanwhile, we sang. In the recreation hall they had built a low stage at one end so the officers could look out over the heads of the men as they gave their morning briefing. Afternoons, we made it our own. Abe Peters would start off with his banjo, while a fellow named Jameson played a very hot piano. Hobby converted a cook kettle to act as a drum and Zoobird was always in attendance with his mouth organ. I was usually the vocalist, leading them into the "Dark-town Strutters Ball," or "Waiting for the Robert

E. Lee." We yelled and stamped and played as if we were auditioning for a Tin Pan Alley musical. For a while we managed to push back the ominous burden of our expectations.

Another rescuing moment was mail call. The post had finally caught up with us. I got three letters from Dad, one from my mother, and four from Lindy, which I opened first. I knew there would be chewing gum sticks in them. Five to a letter, enough to go around the whole group who had gathered in the mess hall. They promptly voted her our mascot.

"Come on, Bernie, read to us. All the lovey-dovey stuff."

"She doesn't write mush. She's a very smart girl."

"Don't be a worm, share a little. I didn't get any mail this time."

"Me neither. Go on, I'd like to hear what a girl sounds like!"

Under siege I gave in, partially. "Okay, she says she liked my last letter. 'I love your little drawings.' I put sketches in, because I don't write very well. I can't describe things like these old villages and the way people dress. So I drew her some pictures."

But the truth was, I couldn't write sweet-talk. I kept thinking how many guys must be sending her letters, all of them a lot better educated than me, probably knew exactly how to say they missed a girl and wished they could dance with her once in a while.

"What else does she say? Come on, Bernie."

"She writes, 'What do you think of President Wilson's statement that he won't make peace with a country unless it has an elected government? I thought the Germans always had dictators. Does that mean there'll be no end to the war until they overthrow the Kaiser?' Like I told you, she's a very intelligent young lady." She made me feel backward. I didn't know anything about the German government.

"If that's the kind of letter she sends," one of the guys said snidely, "you're doing something wrong."

"No," Deke spoke up in my defense. "A woman's got to think serious thoughts. My mother and my sisters pray all the time about the war getting over."

"Well, you can tell 'em to quit worrying," another man said. "We'll make those Heinies want peace so bad they'll crawl through the barbed wire and lick our shoes to get it."

"Don't mind these idiots," Zoobird said

impatiently. "What else is going on back home?"

"She says she's still working at the Red Cross booth in Union Station. 'Men are being sent back from France now with the influenza. It's a terrible disease, it spreads so fast. It's getting to be a whole epidemic.' "

"I heard that too," Abe Peters said. "My cousin had it, he's in the Marines. He said that at Chateau Thierry there were more men in the field hospital with the flu than with wounds. A lot of them actually died."

"Isn't the flu like a bad cold?"

"No, more like pneumonia, I guess. My sister had it last spring," said another. "You run a high fever, that's what kills you."

As they gabbed on, I finished my letters. Dad's were brisk and full of optimism. My mother told me to look for some fancy cathedral if I ever got to Rheims. I hated to tell her, but the Heinies had been lobbing bombs all over that city. There probably wasn't anything left to admire. "Mostly," I said, "everybody asks me when the war will be over."

"Well, we should hear something soon," Abe said. "The General's off in a meeting of all the top dogs, trying to coordinate the offensive. I understand —" At that point he was interrupted by a commotion going on outside in the yard.

Somebody said, "It's a courier."

He had just come in on foot, a young Corporal in a brand-new uniform that was now a wreck, covered with dirt and stinking like a barn yard. "The Detachment is moving out." He felt the front of his tunic as if making sure the orders were safe. "I've got to find the C.O. But you can take my word: the General will be back late tonight and tomorrow we'll be on the march."

We followed him over to Headquarters where he delivered his letter, then looked around at us. "Is there a shower anywhere?"

That was met with a laugh. "You sure need one. What happened to you? You smell like a pile of cowdung."

In the smeared face a grin appeared. "Gee, sir, you put your finger right on it. I was told to make good time, y'see, and my car got stuck in the mud a couple of miles from here, so I took off on foot across a field. All at once I hear an enemy plane, you know those Fokkers, they make that odd noise. So I ducked under the nearest haystack, only it turned out to be — uh — fertilizer. He circled around, I had to dig in deeper. I'd still be stuck there if it wasn't for an American fighter plane that came along and went for him. They had a real dog fight up there, chasing each other, doing loop-the-loops. Then our guy hit the Heinie's gas tank, I guess, because the plane's tail caught fire and he went down in a long trail of smoke into the forest not a mile from here."

A Captain who had been listening turned to one of the enlisted men.

"Get a detail out there, the enemy pilot might still be alive. I'd like to interrogate him."

I asked the Corporal, "Was there anything special about the aircraft that saved you?"

"Just that it was one helluva good pilot. He flew back over me and wiggled his wings. I heard this yell, as if he was cheering, you know?"

"A sort of Ya-a-a-ah?" I suggested.

"Yes, sir. Just like that."

I gave Zoobird a look. "I think we just found Ookey."

We went off to pack our gear for the big move tomorrow, but a half hour later someone knocked.

A private looked in. "Sir, they'd like to see you over at Headquarters."

When I reported I found that they had indeed picked up the young German airman, not too badly injured. He had brought his plane down in a grove of trees.

"I understand you have a fluency in German, Lieutenant?" the Captain asked. "Good. See if you can get him to answer our questions."

The terrible "Heinie" turned out to be a battered kid, probably no more than fifteen, the down of adolescence was still on his cheeks. He stared around at us in open terror until I spoke to him in colloquial German. It helped him find his tongue. He pleaded in a spate of words for us to inform his parents that he was alive. I took his name and address without making any promises. But when I asked the location of the air field, it dawned on him that this was enemy country and he shut his mouth tight. Wouldn't spill a word. I was kind of proud of him. I had to wonder if I'd show that kind of dignity if I were captured.

"All right, that's all we can do," the Captain turned away. "They'll question him some more at the prisoners' compound."

But I managed a private word with the boy. In German I asked, *"Could you describe the pilot who shot you down?"*

He gave me a rueful smile. *"Ach, Ja! We all know him. The one with the nose of his plane painted black. We call him Der Teufel".*

The Devil. Who needs a medal when you

have earned a really mean nickname? As always, the surge of envy racked me.

Nineteen

Finally, the offensive.

Under cover of darkness we moved, in long columns on foot and by lorry and horseback and mule-drawn caissons and supply wagons, in all 600,000 men. The shadowy roads were glutted with traffic. A hushed urgency hung like invisible smoke across the French countryside those nights, until dawn when the troops went to ground and lay quiet. For five days the American forces advanced like a creature with tentacles, deploying across the thirty-mile stretch of the Front, positioning their guns until the line was crowded with every caliber, hub-to-hub, from Rheims to Verdun, all of it done under a numbing steady cold rain. We were in September now, and the skies were sullen with clouds.

Our own Brigade, the 60th, consisted of 5600 men and 5000 horses. Our fire power included twelve American batteries of four

75's each, plus nine French batteries that had been attached to us for the fight, six batteries of 155 mm howitzers, six batteries of French mortars, three batteries of French long guns and two of their massive 220's. All this was crammed into a 2-1/2 kilometer sector facing Vauquois Hill, a well-known landmark rising above the Argonne forest. We were told that the French called it "Dead Man's Hill." They had lost over thirty thousand men trying to take it.

Headquarters for the 129th was set up in a farm house near a crossroads called Grange-le-Compt. I have since seen it spelled Grange-le-Conte, but we were using French maps at that time. General Berry had commandeered the place because of its central location, and the family who lived there resented being evicted. As we gathered in the big kitchen one of the younger kids said rudely in French that we would never win.

General Berry knew the language and in courtly terms he told them they would be compensated for the use of their house. He said he was aware of the inconvenience, but suggested they would probably not prefer to have the Huns for guests. Glumly they withdrew to stay with neighbors. As the staff gathered, grim-faced officers spread a large map on the table. It showed the topography we faced.

"Gentlemen," the General said, "our ultimate objective is to take the railhead at Sedan — here. It's the staging area for the entire German front. All forces of the 35th Division will eventually converge on that. Our sector includes this patch of woods on the left. It's a particularly impenetrable stretch of forest. In front of us is Vauquois Hill and to the right, toward the north you'll see three ridges, Montfaucon, Romagne and Cunel. The German positions are heavily fortified. Up on Vauquois they have dug deep underground to provide living quarters for their troops. They've got plenty of supplies, plus a tram railroad that can deliver them anywhere in the complex in a matter of minutes. So our job will not be easy."

Vauquois didn't appear all that ominous. I had walked out along the trenches to take a look when we first got here. No great elevation, not a steep climb, it was a long barren slope like any no-man's land, ripped clean of vegetation, crossed by ragged segments of barbed wire. This had been torn by shells, but it could still make the advance difficult. Toward the top I could see the contours of machine-gun nests, and there would be a row of artillery somewhere under the brow of the hill. To think of thousands of hidden German soldiers waiting up there took an effort of imagination. It lay so quiet.

"Our offensive," the General went on, "has been carried out in such secrecy we believe the enemy has no idea what's about to happen. The Hun thinks he is facing weary French troops. Instead he will find out how Americans fight."

A tangible thrill went through the little huddle around the table, battle fever.

"I want you to make plans for a great attack, beginning with a three-hour demolition barrage. It will begin on September 26th, three days from now. By then the First Corps, the Fifth and the Third will all be in place. Guns along a thirty-mile front will commence firing simultaneously, and for five hours we will pour everything we've got onto the enemy's lines. A *feu d'enfer,* as Napoleon called it — a rain of Hell. Then at daybreak the Infantry will move forward under cover of a rolling barrage. Our guns are crucial to this attack. The enemy will not be driven off their hilltop easily, we'll need to take out their batteries. But also it's important for the forward observers to make sure our troops don't run into our own cannonade. Communications will be a problem. The Engineers will do their best to keep the field telephones operational, but if the lines are blasted out you must use messengers, good old moccasin telegraph, as we called it in Mexico. Try to prepare for all contingencies. Make your plans, Gentlemen."

I don't remember sleeping for the next twenty-four hours, though we had been assigned billets upstairs in the farmhouse where the attic was partitioned into bedrooms. We did eat well. The Army sent in mess personnel to see to our meals, but within hours the farmer's wife returned to take over. I guess she couldn't stand to see her kitchen in the hands of others. A dumpy, capable woman she actually became tolerant of us, especially after we dug into her *omelette* with such gusto. After a while the woman's daughter came back to the farm to help her mother, a girl named Marietta. Buxom, homely, nose too big and teeth rather crooked, but she was female and the men flirted with her shamelessly.

Mostly, though, we worked our heads off and by sundown on the 24th were able to present the General with our best version of a battle plan. We had marked out areas where ammunition could be stored for swift transfer to the Batteries. We had indicated communications centers and where the lines should be strung. The main connecting roads were marked off in red, with alternate routes in blue. We had indicated gun emplacements, howitzers alternating with the mortars, which had a shorter trajectory, so that we could blanket an area in depth. The French 220's we positioned where they could cover the far side of the hill, shooting over the heads of our own troops as we moved forward. (It never occurred to any of us that we wouldn't advance.)

General Berry bent over to study the maps. Then, without looking up, he said, "Get some rest, fellows, you've earned it."

Under a dormer window in the attic my bed was just a pile of straw with ticking over it, but I never saw a more welcome sight. I don't even remember lying down — for awhile I was dead to the world. How long? I had no idea. When I finally woke the whole place felt empty. Four-twenty in the afternoon. Which afternoon? I couldn't believe I had slept around the clock. Groggy, I went down to the kitchen and helped myself to a bowl of *potage* from the kettle. French farm households all have a black iron vessel on the back of the stove where a marvelous indeterminate stew simmers, day-in day-out, a pot into which they throw every scrap of left-overs, peelings from the potatoes, stems from the greens, the bones of the roast. Nothing goes to waste. I never tasted anything better than that meal.

Feeling overstuffed, I wandered out into the farmyard to find the area full of parked lorries, trucks, wagons, and men slumping on their footlockers, sleeping, playing cards, gossiping, smoking, scribbling on tablets, letters home no doubt, love letters, just-in-case letters that they could leave stowed in their duffel bags. Some read their Bibles while others sat silently to one side, day-dreaming, praying maybe. Waiting. A sense of impending action was in the air.

Beyond were corrals full of animals and a tall barn. Looking for Zoobird I wandered that way. Near the hen-house I saw Abe Peters in the middle of a small bunch of doughboys, playing his banjo quietly. No loud twanging fifth string, it would have jarred on the raw nerves that were a tangible presence. One of the men was feeding crumbs of black bread to a scrawny chicken that snatched them as if it were starving. Only one chicken? I hoped our Commissary was filling the Madam's kitchen with groceries courtesy of the Army.

Hobby was not too far off, sitting in the sun — a thin phenomena in those gray days. With his back propped against a watering trough, he was reading from a book. I couldn't help wondering what could be that important and when I went over, he looked up with an absent smile.

"Les Fleurs de France", he said. "I can't find zinnias in here."

In the barn I passed a few horses in the stalls, the General's favorite, a tall chestnut, and two or three others that the officers had taken a liking for. I hadn't ridden a horse since training days, but there was something comforting about them. They were so unaware, so innocent, munching their oats. One raised its head, giving me a snort of greeting as I passed, the way a dog will wag its tail.

And then in the distance I heard the low breathing of the harmonica. The tune could have been anything, Zoobird only played accompaniment, and though he had added another chord to his original two, it was impossible to tell what the moody sounds meant. He was directing them at an old sow who lay comfortably in a mud hole nearby and seemed to be listening. I liked that sow, all these animals, drowsing when the world was about to explode. I came away softly, I wouldn't want to invade a man's privacy.

Going back inside I sat down at the big dining table and took out my notepad and pencil. "Dear Lindy. I think we're about to head into the biggest battle of the war. I . . ." At that point I got stuck. I had meant to say "I'm looking forward to it." But the truth was more like "I'm scared stiff," an admission I dreaded to make. I wadded up the scrap of paper and threw it in the stove.

What the fellows had said that day when I read them excerpts from Lindy's letters — it still bothered me. *If she writes you stuff like that you're doing something wrong.* In all our correspondence she had never ventured to get personal and neither had I. Too shy, too inept, too uncertain of where we stood. If anywhere. Lindy was so much above me when it came to understanding world politics and history, she made me feel foolish. I could imagine her other men-friends, off at Harvard or Yale, some day going to be lawyers, judges like her father. Maybe even the Governor of the State. Beside them, my letters must seem pretty shallow. When she didn't go all sentimental it was probably because she really didn't feel that way about me. I was just another boy marched off into danger whom she was trying to cheer up, part of the war effort.

I wished there were somebody I could talk to. It even occurred to me that there was — Somebody. At least there used to be. Now, I had too many doubts, questions that couldn't be answered. *Deke keeps talking about good and evil, but what's good about this war? And if it's evil what am I doing here? It must be right to fight for your country, but this isn't my country. I don't have a cause, like the boys in the Civil War, those men in Birth of a Nation. Here, if we die, it doesn't prove anything, does it?* I wasn't really expecting an answer.

When Zoobird caught up with me I was sitting on a rail of the horse corral trying to drum up a conversation with a large bony dapple-gray mustang, all scuffs and scars and one blue eye. I could picture it running wild across the West, dodging mountain cats and bears. I was discussing Indians when Zoo climbed up beside me.

"I guess this is it, huh?" He glanced around at the muted activity of the yards where men were gathering, shucking off the doldrums, bunching in readiness for the order to form their battalions.

"Zoo," I said, "did you ever go to church?"

"Uh-uh. The company frowned on it — the mine bosses, they figured it put rebellious thoughts into the heads of the workers. They wanted the guys to think of the company president as God. But my mother said they couldn't make rules about what you believe. She used to read the Bible out loud all the time."

"I tried that once," I admitted, "I couldn't get past the old-fashioned language. All the begets and begats and who cares, you know?"

"Yeah. Mom understood that. She said there's a lot of history in the Book that you don't need to worry about, who the old rulers were and their sons and such. That's for people like Deke. But there are a few things in there that really help you figure out your life, and that's what she wanted me to remember."

"Like what?"

"Like Moses and the Ten Commandments. Or Noah and the ark, saving all those beasts. I liked the story of Jonah and the whale, which has to do with being obedient. Mainly I remember the one about the seasons and reasons. She put it in a poem, helps you to memorize a thing." He tipped his head back and recited.

" 'For everything there is a reason
And a time for every season.
A time to be born, a time to die.
A time to laugh and a time to cry.'

Let me think . . ."

I puzzled over it. "What did your mother

want you to learn from that?"

"I'm not sure, but it gives me a good feeling — that everything is happening right on time. Maybe not my time, but the Lord's time, you know? In other words, it's all supposed to be. And in a while it will change, so you got to take it as it comes and have faith. Like the poem goes on:

'There's a time to love and a time to hate,
A time to be single, a time to mate.
A time to tear up, then mend what you tore,
A time of peace and a time of war.' "

He looked at me, marveling. "I never paid much attention to that last line until now. I guess it means there's a good reason we're over here."

I thought it was dumb. It made me kind of angry, as if I didn't have the say-so over my own life. I said, "Ookey claims that God is a fraud, just a trick to get you to do what everybody wants you to. Your folks, the church, the schools, they all try to shove you around as if you didn't have a brain."

Zoobird studied the harmonica in his hand. "Poor guy," he said at last, "it must be tough not to have a mother. And his dad isn't much help either. How's he ever going to grow up?"

That startled me. Ookey had always been the most mature person I knew. He was born knowing more about life than I ever would. I even resented him for it, I had to admit. So why didn't Zoobird realize that? "Well, *he* certainly isn't confused about why we're in this war. He's already up there a thousand feet high, doing battle with the Bosch and winning."

"Oh, well, yeah. Sure, Bernie, I know he's your friend. Hey, let's go see where we'll be stationed. I hope we'll get a forward observation post. I'd like to put it to use, all that stuff you learned at Luneville."

General Berry was waiting for us in a large dugout near the trenches which would be the Brigade Post of Command. He was handing out assignments — ours was a French position called "Les Cotes de Fornimont" which seemed pretty ornate for a mud hut. About a mile from the command post, it was dug into the side of a hill on the forward side, with a roof of timbers mounded with sod and earth. On the rear it was a flimsy construction of boards with a door that opened into a connecting trench. We found a stove and a bunk and a telephone. Instead of a telescope we had binoculars mounted on a calibrated stand that served to pinpoint the exact coordinates of a burst out on the battlefield. We took turns checking it out. The German guns had started up their usual evening fireworks. They had a tendency to keep firing at one spot, and so long as it wasn't hurting anybody we had orders to let them do it. Kept them happy and we didn't give away any of our own guns' positions.

The word was to lie low, those last hours before the attack. Zoobird looked sadly at his silent harmonica. When one of our Captains dropped by to check up on us, he stuck it in his pocket hastily. "Sorry, sir, I know I'm not supposed to make any noise."

"Wait a minute, son. Don't put that away. Go ahead and play. If the enemy has forward scouts out there in no-man's land they'll report back that everything is peaceful along our lines. I think I'll pass the word to the others, sing some songs, laugh a little. They'll never suspect we're going to hit them with Armageddon at midnight."

After he'd gone, I said, half kidding, "What's an Armageddon?"

Zoo looked shocked. "You really ought to read at least *some* of the Bible. That's about the end of the world, Book of Revelations. That's where they separate the sinners from the saints on judgment day."

I had a feeling we weren't going to have

to wait that long. Just six hours to kill, a phrase that was taking on new meaning. Zoobird was warming up his mouth harp, he needed somebody to give him the tune. I took a breath and sang. " 'It's a long way to Tipperary . . .' " I had no idea where Tipperary was, but by now it had come to symbolize *home.*

As dusk came on I lit a small coal fire in the potbelly stove. Outside the air felt thick, as if we were under heavy cloud cover. The sky was pitch-dark, but in the trenches that led forward to the line I could hear men moving into position. When I glanced at Zoobird I saw the same kind of dread in his face that I was feeling.

"Well," I said bluffly, "what d'you think. Is it our 'time to die'?"

He shook his head. "The Lord told me I wasn't going to get killed."

"He *what?* When did He start talking to you?"

"All my life. Mom said, if you ever want to know something just ask, and then listen real hard. So I did. On the way over here, walking along the connecting trench, I asked Him: *Am I going to get shot?* And He said *No.* Flat-out."

"Like a voice coming out of the air?"

"Oh, shoot, Bernie, of course not. It's in

your head, what you say, what He says. Sometimes when you have a problem He puts the answer in your brain."

My mind flashed back to a moment on the train going to Bar-sur-Aube when I suddenly realized what was wrong with me. It had come out of the blue and quieted my heart. Could that have been — ? I got so confused I said, "Okay, let's do 'Bye-bye, Blackbird.' " From there we went on to "I Love You Truly," and Zoo got sad and sweet with his instrument, making it wail. Then he knocked it out and stuck it in his pocket.

"Bernie," he said, "tell me about your girl. She sounds like a real keeper. Those letters she writes are great. She talks about important stuff. She doesn't feel she has to be silly, like most girls. I don't know why they think we won't like them if they don't giggle a lot."

"She's very smart," I told him. "A lot smarter than I am. She's way ahead of me, reading up on the news and European history and all that. She even studied French when she was off at school."

"Well, shoot, you could catch up with her any time you want. You got those offers from universities."

"They don't hold over, Zoo. Now nobody's going to give me a free ride to college, even if I wanted one."

"I never did understand why you didn't go, right after High."

"Didn't seem important. Maybe it seemed too easy, to sit around some classroom when I have my whole life to live? I wanted to get started, you know, make some money, get experience. Like you did in the Bank."

Slowly he said, "I would have given my eyebrows and toenails to go to Mizzoo. It was a really great scholarship. Mom tried to insist, but she was ailing and I couldn't bear to leave her alone. Reminds me —" He fumbled inside his uniform jacket and came out with an envelope. "Will you keep this for me, just in case?"

"What is it?"

"My last will and testament. I got a fellow at the Bank to help me draw it up before I left. My account amounts to a couple of hundred dollars, with interest accruing every day. If anything happened I'd want my mother to get it."

"Aw cripes, Zoo. You're not going to get killed, the Lord said so."

"He didn't include stuff like accidents. I could get run over by a truck. Please, Bernie."

Feeling sore, I stuck it in my pocket. "Doggone you, now it means I've got to write one, too." I took the notepad by the lookout window. Rapidly I scrawled, "I, George Bernard Jones, do hereby leave all my worldly possessions to my sister, Dolly." She was the neediest person I knew, and she always did want my red Indian blanket. I signed my name. Zoobird borrowed the pencil and wrote on the bottom: "Witnessed by Calvin Fleischman, September 25th, 1918, Argonne Sector in France." He folded it and put it away in his pocket.

After that he withdrew. I sensed it more than saw it, he got all inward and unfocused, standing at the lookout window pretending to survey the Hill. I went to lie down on the bunk, no chance of sleeping, of course. Perfect time to get in touch with the Almighty, see if I could. Just as an experiment I tried it: *Hey, Lord, if you're up there, am I going to buy the farm in this battle?* No answer. Of course. Zoobird had to be imagining it, making up what he wanted to hear. He knew it wasn't anything you could count on or why did he give me his will?

Even if there was a God, there were too many people trying to get hold of him at once tonight. Out there in the trenches they were praying. I could feel the petitions like a current of fear all flowing together through the night. I was swimming in a river of spent prayers . . . it was taking me to a waterfall, a big cataclysm of a waterfall . . .

The crash threw me off the bunk, onto the floor. I floundered there, holding onto the ground which was shaking under my hands and knees. The noise was beyond what the ears could absorb, this was a concussion of the heart. The battle of the Argonne was on.

TWENTY

The shuddering chaos of that wall of artillery sent vibrations through the earth and everything on it, a turbulence that left you deaf and blind and helpless, like a celluloid toy bobbing in the water under Niagara Falls. Nothing was stable. The quaking went on and on, a pulsing of destruction that rattled our minds down to the core. Thought was fragmented: the cot had tipped over — the notepad was on the floor — my boots were untied. The stove — I squirmed to look, but it still stood upright, anchored by the stovepipe.

Zoobird was getting his bearings, too. He had picked up the binoculars and was peering out the window. Was it possible that the enemy was returning fire? In the midst of that Hell? Suddenly he hit the timer and reached for the phone. In seconds he was rattling off coordinates.

It dawned on me: I was supposed to be

over there on the notepad making calculations. So how did he do it in his head? It seemed an interesting question. And then I got my brain straight and began to gather my parts together. Getting to my feet, I joined him at the window. I had to cling to the wall as a huge detonation rocked us, notable even in that terrible melee of noise. We had fired one of the French 220's. I looked through the peek hole just in time to see the hit, high on Vauquois Hill, a brilliant explosion of flame hung with the fragments of a German howitzer that seemed to float in mid-air. Zoo had called that shot.

I gave him a thumbs-up and positioned myself at the table beside him. When he gave me the coordinates I did the calculations in one part of my mind, while another part was asking *How do you get shell-shock? From your own guns? I thought it was from the enemy's fire, but this is worse. Isn't it?* He had to raise his voice for me to hear, pinpointing an enemy position. I set the timer. Only, how could they man a gun with this barrage blanketing the top of the Hill? I could picture it churning up the dirt deeper and deeper, right on down to those bunkers where the Bosch crouched, holding their ears, holding onto their sanity by a thread. German boys, like me. In a throe of disgust

I hated this war and what I was doing.

As dawn came on I glanced at my watch: 5:35. Leaving Zoobird on his own, I went to the rear door of our dugout. I wanted to see this advance, this moment in history. Along the trenches they were on the move, shadowy figures swarming over the parapets, running forward at a crouch, a rippling of bodies like a tide surging up the Hill. Ahead of them our howitzers laid down a protective curtain of fire, and yet on those heights I saw the stutter of the Bosch machine guns still blazing away. At least some of the enemy had survived our pounding and was able to pour return fire at our troops. With sickening perversity I was almost proud of them up there, so much courage, so much heart. *If there was a God he wouldn't let this happen to good men.* But my thoughts were in slow motion, my mind muddy with that terrible racket.

Meanwhile Zoobird was calmly manning the observation post as if it were the window of the Paying Teller at the Stockmans Bank. He didn't blink when a bomb landed so close to us it threw dirt against the rear structure of the dugout. But when he tried to use the phone he got mad. "Damn it, that one cut the lines. And right now we have to get word back to the Command

Post: our barrage needs to accelerate the pace. Our boys are about to run into our own cannon fire."

When I was a little slow to understand he said sharply, "Bernie, somebody's got to run back to headquarters!"

"Me?" I protested, "Why me?"

"Because I can hold this post alone and you can't," he snapped. "I can do the math in my head, I don't need the notebook. But I need a phone. Bernie, don't pull rank on me now."

I plunged out into the connecting trench and ran into the war. From there on, things come back to me in fragments.

Yellow belly, what's the matter? Afraid you'll get hit by a mortar round? Don't want to die, you poor simp! Out of the sky, that ominous whistling arrowhead of sound that precedes a falling shell . . . I dive into the nearest shell hole . . . mud. The blast is only yards away, shrapnel cutting the air overhead, showers of earth, chips of bark off the trees falling around me. I get up, belly heaving, and run on.

I'm at the Command Post, winded, bedraggled. The General says, "Yes, Lieutenant?" Turns to his phone, a few curt orders for some linemen to get out to Fornimont and repair the wires. "Engineers are on their way, but they're stretched thin. The lines are out to Battery C too, and we need to get them this message right away. Lieutenant, get over there as fast as you can and alert their C.O. that the barrage needs to be stepped up. Tell them to increase the range to a rate of a hundred yards every four minutes. Check out the map, their position is to our left . . ."

I know that. Positioning the batteries was part of our job. I even know a shortcut.

Roads clogged with heavy traffic, hub-deep in mud, but there's a railroad track . . . damaged road bed, crooked rails, *I've been running on the tracks since I was knee-high.* Rails good, they cut straight through the forest, they don't get muddy. But it's harder to run when you're deaf. The noise is so overwhelming it's like black smoke, a barrier that you have to force your way through. My whole head is ringing, couldn't get any worse, and then something slams me to the ground like a hammer, almost took off my face.

Am I dead? As I fight to get my senses back, trying to breathe again, I hear distant voices.

"Cease fire!" Pound of feet running over, hands, a familiar face. "For God's sake, it's Bernie Jones." Hobby helps me to my feet, shaking his head. "You almost ran right in front of my guns."

I have found Battery C. They were placed down behind the railroad embankment, a whole line of 75's. When I get my breath I tell him about the need to alter his barrage. He turns away at once and gives orders down the line. The woods are so thick here you couldn't see the Hill, but they had their coordinates already figured to an inch. All they had to do was change the elevation of their guns and step up the timing. He comes back to me frowning.

Hard to frown when you don't have eyebrows.

He mops sweat off his bald head. "Need you to deliver a message back to the General from me . . ." *distant small voice encased by the thunder of the guns.* "We have enemy fire over on our left flank. The German batteries are beginning to get our range. But we can't take them out because of the order not to fire outside our own sector. I tried to reach the 127th, but our lines are all blown to Hell."

"I'll see that General Berry passes the word along."

"Thanks. And Bernie, don't take the railroad back. I'm expecting return fire from the Hill . . . path over there will lead you to a good road. See you later."

Just a dirt trail that had been widened by the hauling of caissons, it was choppy with mule tracks, foot traffic. But those guns are in place now and I have the road to myself. Follow it to a clearing that's obviously a staging point. Trucks standing everywhere, a couple turned over by some big shell burst. Getting used to the weight of the noise . . . living with it. Over to one side, thirty yards away, a small group of guys is gathered around an empty oil drum in which they have built a fire. The smell of coffee is like a magnet . . . *sell my soul for a cup of java right now . . .*

Out of the thunder overhead a whistling. I stop in my tracks, nowhere to hide. Then a blinding flash leaves the far side of the clearing bare as the palm of your hand. The oil drum is spinning across the earth like a mad thing. A shard of metal rips the arm of my uniform and bounds away, looks like a torn tin cup. A lot of stuff falling now, parts of — it looked like a boot, with something in it. Not ten feet away. I close my eyes and run.

The Command Post is crammed with people, all agog, trying to get a look at somebody, a General, who is speaking to our officers. He seems somehow familiar, short, tough, neat white moustache, gun-metal blue eyes under stubby brows. Focusing on me . . . a battlefield look.

"What is it, Lieutenant?"

"Sir, Battery C is being enfiladed by enemy shells coming from the left. Their Captain is hamstrung by orders not to fire outside his own sector." I am over at the map, pointing out the area.

General Pershing is beside me, studying it. "Mmmm, yes. Well, to Hell with orders. Go back and tell them to blow the Bosch out of there."

By then I know him, of course, and a great gulp rises in my throat as I snap off my best salute all muddy and spangled with other men's blood. Before I can go, General Berry stops me.

"I'll send a runner with that message, Lieutenant. I need you here."

"Lieutenant Fleischman is all alone over at Fornimont, sir." At least I remember that, about time, too. Night's coming on now.

The General nods. "I've sent him a couple of men to act as runners. He'll just have to hold the post alone a while longer."

I am on the floor, propped in a corner of the Command Post, which is almost empty. I must have dozed off. Did I want a sandwich, somebody asks. The thought of food makes me sick. My belly is knotted up like a fist, and I can't stand the aroma of coffee.

When I rouse and look around Pershing is gone. It feels like morning, and General Berry is still at his desk, talking on the field telephone. "Well, let me know, as soon as you find out." He puts it down and we are having a conversation as if I'd never left his side. "Lieutenant, I need to know conditions up on the Hill. Our men took it yesterday afternoon, but we haven't had time to lay down lines. I need for you to go up there and scout our positions. Take a couple of runners to bring back messages. Make a map, as accurately as you can, of where we can put our batteries when we move forward. Try to assess where the Germans are by now and let me know what's going on out toward Montfaucon. The right flank of the drive seems to be held up there. Our left flank, over in that dense forest, is totally bogged down. We can't advance much farther until I get more information. But be careful, son, the enemy is proving to be tough. They are trying to take the Hill back. Keep your head down."

Vauquois Hill. This is Vauquois.

Thin daylight, raining again, everything misty, I am just as glad. I don't want to look at the blighted landscape as I press on up the Hill under the ever-present noise of the guns. Shell holes all around me, but I am once removed from them. It's like a scene in a movie, windrows of dead bodies, a few men crouched in a kind of stunned paralysis, staring up as I pass. . . .

Cigarette? Sorry. I did have a pack of cigarettes yesterday or was it two days ago, must have lost them. Never mind, don't smoke, coach says it ruins your wind.

An arm. Somebody's going to miss that. *Dear God . . .* If He's there He sees all this, He even tolerates it. "A time of peace and a time of war." *Zoobird, how y' doing?*

More dead bodies, twenty, twenty-five, machine-gun nest right ahead, silent now. *Thanks guys, I owe you one . . .* I glance back at my messengers, a couple of Infantry enlisted men. Volunteers. Hazardous duty, they stepped forward, brave boys, but one of them is vomiting. The other limps.

"Sprained my ankle, sir."

"I understand. Go on back. Wait a minute, take this with you." I scribble a few words describing conditions from where I stand.

Deep mud, difficult to get batteries up the Hill. Still vigorous fighting. Hard to tell toward Montfaucon what's happening. Down in the Forest there's too much smoke. I hand it to him. "Give that to General Berry."

The left flank is a seething inferno of cannon fire, through which I can hear the rattle of small arms, the chatter of a machine gun. Hobby must be in the thick of it down there. Some of the enemy batteries are lobbing shells our way. One hits about fifty yards to my left, I observe. I don't seem able to feel anything, it's as if I'm in a box.

Top of the hill, it doesn't look like the top. A lot of the ragged crest is blasted away, but I find men on the far side, standing around, waiting orders. Sitting in the German dugouts, smoking, playing cards. Fools don't seem to realize that the Germans didn't fortify the back side of their trenches. They're sitting ducks. Me, too, but I can't think about that. I look for a dry place to get out my tablet and draw a map for the General. From this elevation I can see the battleground like a great diarama. I make a quick sketch, shielding the page with my body . . .

Where's that messenger?

And then I see something that snaps me back to normal. In the fading afternoon light, across a hundred yards of wasteland, it is the old Bird himself. The familiar gawky shape is standing tall, half-shielded by a German revetment as he peers through the glasses at the flashes of the enemy's mortars. Even brought along his calibrated stand. I see him make a note, which he hands to a runner. On the hillside below engineers are rushing to lay a line up to the crest, but they duck every time a round hits nearby. Not Zoobird. Calm, efficient, he stands there like the commander of a ship. Like a man. What does it take to make you a man?

I start across to him, then halt. This is no time for chitchat. Need to get that map back to Headquarters. My volunteer has finally caught up with me.

"Bunker down there." He points at some steps, his voice almost lost in the awful whistle of incoming fire. Takes the map and starts running back down the hill.

I find a room hollowed out of the earth, bunks, tables, a stove where men are cooking up some bully beef. I shake my head at their offer, *couldn't eat. But I need to get off these shaky knees for a minute.*

It's another morning, I guess. I hope the volunteer made it back. If so, it didn't help much, I guess, the firing continues as fast and furious as ever. Our guns firing over my head, theirs answering. Targeting the hilltop. The constant percussion jars the walls and floor of the bunker. Tarpaper fastened to the ceiling keeps the dirt from raining down.

Damn, that one was close!

Fire is out in the stove. Where is everybody? Advancing? Or retreating? I climb the stairs to find myself in a heavy fog that's part cordite. On the left I can hear the unrelenting crump of artillery, ours, theirs. Quiet off to the north. *Did we take Montfaucon?*

I start across the ridge, going to look for Zoobird, when a man rises like a ghost from a dugout and stops me. "Lieutenant, aren't you on General Berry's staff?"

"Yes, sir." This guy is a Major.

"I need you to take a message back to him. The 77th is in trouble over in those damnable woods. They seem to have lost track of an entire battalion. And we're at a stalemate over below the ridge at Montfaucon. We need a new battle plan . . . just finished writing a detailed report. I think we should send in some of the reserves, especially over there in the forest." He handed me a folded sheet of paper. "It's easier going downhill," he adds with a grim weary smile.

It's still raining, hear it coming down steadily on the canvas roof of the Command Post. Hard to tell the time of day by the sky, and my watch has stopped long since. Never made to get this wet. Uniform soaked, skin raw underneath . . . I think of that arm lying out on the hillside and I don't mind the discomfort at all. General Berry is tireless, the guy must have learned it in the Mexican War — how to live without sleep. He and a couple of other Generals are stepping away from the map now, made their decision.

"Lieutenant Jones. I've got a job for you. We need to meet with the other Commanders and lay out new strategy. What I want you to do is to go over to Division Headquarters. They've set up a post over in Cheppy, but we're closer to the action. I am requesting that they come here, so that when we decide on orders they can be sent out along the line fast. I want you to get on over there and tell them to join us for a conference tomorrow morning at first light. And Bernie, take a horse. The roads are so glutted with traffic you'll never make it in a staff car."

Over in the corrals I see a familiar face, scuffed and bony and one blue eye, the dapple-gray mustang. "Hi, Traveler." Robert E. Lee called his horse Traveler. The warmth of horseflesh is companionable. I begin to feel something inside, something approaching human, I guess.

I throw on a saddle and we make our way out to the main road, which is a skidding, slipping, wheel-spinning mess of lorries and bogged-down ammunition trucks. I hope we are a safe distance from the shells, which are falling not too far away.

Cheppy. On the map it was about five miles north. We are never going to get there. The horse has ten pounds of mud caked on each foot. He is plodding heavily with all his skinny strength, but we are never going to make it this way. I leave the road and try to take to the forest, which isn't as deep as on the left flank, but it's tangled with deadfall and underbrush. Traveler can hardly scramble over it. Horse was a bad idea.

I can make it on foot faster than this.

Pulling the saddle and bridle off the beast, I slapped him. "Go home. Good luck, guy."

The mustang looked at me with that wall eye. *You too.*

A battered little village, torn houses, collapsed buildings. The war has surged over Cheppy more than once, but now it's somewhere in the distance. Just a roar in the sky, vibrations in the air that will not fade for the next thousand years. I walk down a ghost street and find the city hall. It is empty, the clock on the wall stands at seven. In the evening? I'd better hurry, find these Division Commanders, Generals, whoever, alert them to the meeting over at our headquarters. I stand there stuck, staring at the calendar on the wall, which has not been turned since last July.

A feeling of desperation prods me into action, I rush into the street. Sound of voices coming from a café down the block. Accordion music. On a battlefield? In the dim light of the eating house a bunch has gathered around a dinner table, bottles of *vin rouge* in plenty. American officers of different ranks, singing "My Wild Irish Rose."

I don't know how to get their attention, but eventually somebody sees me waiting, like grim death on the edge of their gaiety. I tell them in my best official voice that I have an urgent message for their Commanding Officer. Eruption of laughter, very funny, ease up a bit, buddy, the war will still be there tomorrow. It's bedtime, go find a bunk somewhere.

Fury boils up in me. I mean, there's a dead arm lying out there, a whole battalion missing in the Argonne forest, a one-man observation post up on Vauquois trying to silence all the guns of the German Army single-handed. I call them cowards, I call them lazy pigs and rat-stupid and every name I can think of, while they sit belching and grinning as if I were insane. Which I am — I could be court-martialed for an outburst like that.

Shaking with reaction I am back out in the street. At that point, if I were a believer I'd think the Lord took a hand. Shells begin to drop on the town. I duck into a concrete building nearby to wait it out and get back my composure, and as I watch, from the restaurant bursts the crowd of drunken sots I'd just addressed so fluently. Flustered and panicky now, they run off in all directions. One headed for a large shell hole, but the cook beats him to it. The chef from the restaurant, complete with a tall white hat, he plunges into the hole first, waving a huge black-iron frying pan so fiercely, the officer scuttles away. The frying pan, I see now, is the cook's armor. He holds it over his head as bits of shrapnel are sprayed from the sky. When the shelling finally stops I go over and help the man out of the hole and shake his hand.

Almost dark by then, I am getting desperate. Breaking into a trot, I head for a building down the street that shows the Stars and Stripes. As I reach it, I run straight into a familiar figure, and for a minute I am on my way to the tree house.

"Dollars! Thank God." Well, it *might* be the Lord that threw us together. "I thought you were off in Paris living the good life. Aren't you still in the Quartermaster Corps?"

He shakes my hand enthusiastically. Seems older, wearing the insignia of a Captain, but mostly it's the look in his eyes. Another shell shakes the town and he draws me back inside the building, which is serving as Division Headquarters. Downstairs is a basement room with maps on the wall and telephones.

"At least somebody cares that there's a war on." I tell him about the fools in the café.

He gives a curt laugh. "Every outfit has a few slackers who disgrace it. Don't worry, Bernie, I will see that the top brass gets word about your meeting. In fact I'll do it right now. Meantime why don't you put your head down over there on the cot. You look bush-whacked."

Couldn't lie still. Or maybe I slept for a while, I don't know. My next image is a dark side street where I find a hole-in-the-wall bar. *Could use a glass of wine.* And a piece of pie. The bartender's wife made it, he insists that I eat it, cries a few tears. We are very good friends. I try to eat the pie.

Another bar, half-dozen doughboys, all of us dirty, no sense of rank here. They are discussing some guy I didn't know.

"You remember how he used to talk on and on about getting to the battlefield, the joy of combat?"

"Wouldn't shut up."

"Yeah, well that first day we moved on Montfaucon, into the face of their artillery, he kept lagging behind, excuses, got tangled in some barbed wire and couldn't seem to get out of it. Funny, funny." Nobody was laughing including the story teller. "Got to shaking so hard they had to cart him off in an ambulance."

"Field hospital's full of them, I hear. Shell shock."

"Gut-shock. Too many guys thought the war was going to be some kind of a picnic."

Including me. But not Ookey, he knew it was a fight to the death. I wondered if he was happy now, get his teeth into the enemy.

Mostly, I didn't think anything.

Another day. I need to get back to my unit. Big conference, was that today? I must have slept through the morning, because the sun is straight overhead, trying to burn through the clouds when I step out into the streets of Cheppy. Artillery only a distant presence now, but the town is still jammed with traffic. Going north, it feels as though the war is moving this way.

I try to take the road back, by staying high on the sides away from the deep mud ruts, but I keep slipping. Better off yesterday in the woods, climbing over the deadfall. Pick your way and you can make some time in between the patches of heavy growth. There are shell holes here too and shattered tree trunks. The forest looks as though a madman smashed it with a hammer.

The day is humid, airless, buzzing with flies. A sickly swarm of them hovers over something up ahead. And as I reach it everything hits me like a physical blow, the cruelty and pointlessness and stupidity of this war. To destroy an innocent bystander like Traveler? Lying there with a hole blown in him and his guts spilling out onto the ground, his blue eye is wide open, but lifeless. Can't blink the flies away . . .

Damn You! What harm did that old nag ever do? I hurled the words upward at Somebody I was never going to believe in again. *You really are a fraud!*

Twenty-One

The man lies sprawled face-down in the forest, sobbing. He has soiled his pants. His helmet lies on the ground nearby, I pick it up and set it on his exposed rump. He scrambles up, in shame and rage, tears streaming.

"Hey," I say, "I was just thinking about the shrapnel."

He pulls out his service revolver and kills me. I don't know where to go. I'm lying there dead and I don't know where to go. Or who can help me find out. Lost, lost, lost, lost . . .

Someone was shaking me awake. "Bernie. Come on, get up."

My eyes are glued shut. I rub them until they come unstuck, enough for me to recognize Zoobird standing over me. Dimly, I thought, *he looks so clean.* His uniform was pressed, his hair neatly plastered. It was as if there had never been a battle.

"Wake up, Buddy, the General wants to see us."

"Can't. Got to get some sleep."

"You've been sacked out for eighteen hours. You're okay, you just need to get up and have a shave and then come on downstairs." He hovered, waiting to make sure I understood.

We were in my cubbyhole up in the attic. "How'd I get here?"

"I found you yesterday afternoon. You were in the stable, explaining to the horses that somebody named Traveler wasn't coming back. Hey, don't worry, we all went a little crazy after eleven days on the battle line."

"Eleven — ?"

"Actually twelve. The reason we didn't stand down with the rest of the Brigade is that they asked us to support a new deployment of troops coming onto the line. Don't you remember? Replacements moved in, you were running orders back and forth — I'd catch sight of you in the distance some times." He was hauling me to my feet, dragging me over to the wash basin. "I put a bucket of hot water over here."

It just dawned on me: I was naked.

"I gave your clothes to Marietta to wash." Something about the way he said her name.

I looked at him, really looked for the first time. He had a balmy kind of happiness about him . . . *Marietta? Zoobird, you didn't.*

"Go on, scrub up. You stink." He punched me and went out.

He was right about one thing: I reeked of sweat and horse manure and mud, and I needed a chamber pot quickly. The dregs of memory clung to my mind, visions of barbed wire hung with bodies, some of them still moving, the rain and the mud and . . .

Beyond the window — it seemed impossible — the sun was out and birds were calling. Some French version of a meadowlark.

Above the wash basin hung a square of mirror, slightly tacky with age. Or did I really look like that? The guy staring at me with bleak old eyes had a beard. I never had much chin hair before. This was a half-inch of gray stubble that was coarse as a steel brush. The sight unnerved me. I went at it with a razor, as if I could shave off the days of brutal reality and get back to the clean young skin of innocence. But nothing was going to flush the darkness from those murky eyes. They were raw with inner images, as though I had looked into Hell fires, and I had.

Dressed in my extra uniform, which was reasonably clean, I headed for the stairs and the smell of food. Coffee. I wondered if I would ever again be able to drink it, and knew grimly that I'd better start right now. I didn't really want to eat, but my stomach was so empty it had lost its sense of hunger and was starting to cramp.

In the kitchen General Berry was tucking into a big breakfast at the huge wooden table, with Madam hovering solicitously, all smiles now that we had actually done it, driven back the Bosch. But if the battle was over why did I still hear the distant rumbling of artillery?

" 'Morning, Lieutenant." The General waved me to a seat opposite him. "Glad to see you among the living. You looked half-dead when Lieutenant Fleischman brought you in here yesterday."

"Thank you, ma'am," I tried to smile at the husky woman setting a small feast before me. "Did we — ?" Sausage, I have always loved sausage. "Did we — uh — achieve our objectives, sir?" Obviously the war was going on, nobody was ever going to win it.

"We drove the enemy back a few kilometers, which is more than the French have been able to do. The Hun held us up for twenty-four hours at Montfaucon, which gave them time to reinforce the other ridges.

Five Corps and Three Corps are attacking Romagne and Cunel right now. Over on the Meuse there's some heavy fighting, but our outfit is headed in a different direction. We have orders for Verdun. That's where the next big offensive will take place."

Again? We have to do this all over again?

Two officers had come in to report to the General, one I didn't know, the other was Hobby Carter. His bald face a sickly wax color, he went to pour some coffee without so much as a look at the rest of us. When he brought it to the table it was as if he were sleepwalking.

"Hey, Hobby," I said. "How's it going?"

Blankly he looked at me, my face finally registered. He said, "Abe Peters bought the farm." The lashless eyes watered and he lowered his head to the coffee cup.

Some others came in then, more walking dead. Conversation was awkward, as if we were all enclosed in our own private horrors, unable to speak naturally. It took Zoobird to bring a shaft of normality to the kitchen. In a clop of boots he breezed in, glowing, as if he'd polished his face with a chamois.

" 'Morning all. *Bon Jour, Mére Beatrice.*"

Madam beamed at him as if he were a prince.

Zoo, what did you do? Ask her for Marietta's hand in marriage?

He came to join us at the table where the General had begun to set out our immediate plan of action. "Verdun is likely to be tough. We'll start deploying northward as soon as we can make the necessary arrangements. I want Bernie and Cal to go up there and secure billets for the officers. Battery Commanders will coordinate with our support personnel to move onto the line in stages, as expeditiously as possible. It will take a couple of weeks, but I'd say we should be ready to launch a new attack by the first of November."

The assembled officers stood silent, visibly staggered by the prospect of another offensive so soon. A month? To recover from the Argonne? The General gave us a grim smile.

"You men are to be congratulated. You have turned this Regiment, which was not even made up of regular Army troops, into a well-coordinated fighting corps, one that is now entrusted to spearhead a big push which may just end this war. Now that you've had your baptism of fire, the next campaign will be easier. Take it from an old-timer." His face was tight with pride. It lifted our spirits like nothing else could have.

After he had left us I sat and watched Zoobird put away a half-dozen eggs with ham and black bread hot from the oven. Madam filled his coffee cup again.

"Merci, mille fois, c'est trés bien." And when she had gone off to feed the chickens he gave me a sheepish glance. "Her daughter is teaching me French."

"Since when?"

"Well, actually since day before yesterday. I was pulled off the line, so I came back here . . ."

"Weren't even tired, huh?"

"I was worn out. But in a different way. While you were dashing around drawing maps and doing the General's liaison work, I was stuck in one observation post or another, peering through those binoculars. My eyes felt like shoe buttons. I was laced up so tight I could hardly breathe. So when I got back I sat down over there by the hearth and began to play my joy-box. And Marietta came and sat beside me, sang the old French songs. Did you know the French use the same chords that we do? Anyhow — *Bon jour, Marietta.*"

The girl had come lightly down the steep steps from the garret carrying an armload of bedding. Mine, I would guess. Giving us a snaggle-tooth smile, she headed out for the big wash tub in the yard. Over her shoulder she said something pert in French and Zoobird laughed like an idiot.

Yes, you sang songs with her and then you went upstairs and . . .

The truth was written all over his big simple face, a sort of smug infatuation. "She's a very affectionate girl."

"Aren't you worried about Madam?"

"That's the interesting part." Zoobird explained seriously, "Marietta says her mother wants her to learn about — life. You know. And the men around here are gone, the ones her own age. She'll never be married, probably, it's sad. I was glad to help out." He smeared a heavy coat of butter on another slice of black bread.

When we presented ourselves at the Headquarters building we found the General standing before the big map on the wall. He was studying the upper right-hand sector that was labeled in heavy black print:

VERDUN

By now I had heard enough of its bloody history to get the shivers at sight of the name. More than just a town and a couple of forts, it was a symbol for some of the most bitterly contested ground in Europe.

Going back to earlier wars, it had changed hands between the Germans and French many times. A legion of ghosts walked its perimeters.

When we joined the General he, as usual, addressed us as if we'd been there all along. "Here is the small town of Sommedieu." He tapped a spot on the map. "We'll set up our Headquarters there. What I want you boys to do is take a car and go over, pick out some good rooms for the staff and yourselves. Save the best for me, of course."

It dawned: the General was in high spirits. He was never one to joke around, but he must be pleased with the way the Argonne had been fought.

"Once that's done," he added, "take it easy for a few days. After a battle you need to replenish."

Replenish what? Our bodies, our minds? Our souls . . ? *No, I will not think about that again ever.*

As we drove northward, my heart sank at the thought of hauling the entire Division another twenty kilometers northward, lock, stock and barrel. New battle plans, figure out gun emplacements, set up supply depots. Brace yourself for more death and destruction. It made me sick, but then I wasn't a true soldier and never would be. I still doubted what kind of guts I would show if faced with the need to shoot an enemy in person. *Yellow-belly.* The snicker still showed up once in a while. For some reason those days of slogging around the battlefield hadn't proven anything. I'd just done what I was ordered to do. I hadn't thrown myself on a grenade or charged a machine-gun nest, had I?

The General had mentioned that he had put both of us in for a promotion to First Lieutenant, which was nice. But if it meant the war was going on and on forever, I'd decline the honor.

Sommedieu was around eight miles from Grange-le-Compt, just far enough to have escaped the worst of the cannon fire. The town was relatively intact compared to Cheppy and some of the other villages we'd left. Finding quarters presented no problem. The Mayor would be honored to have the General take rooms in his house, including some nice billets for his staff above the stable. We settled that and then I went looking for a place to bunk that didn't smell of horses. My emotions had got all tangled up in the heat of battle, so that now even the sorriest nag made me want to bawl like a baby.

Zoo and I decided on lodgings above a

bakery a half-block away from the *Mairie* where Headquarters would be set up. It was a single large dormer room up under the eaves. Our mattresses were made of corn shucks, but by then we weren't fussy.

It felt good to be free of orders for a while, just to roam the crooked cobblestone streets and wander into a café. Above the door a hand-painted sign proclaimed this to be the *Chez Paris.* The name was a touch of irony. There were only two tables in the place, the décor was shabby and the floor unswept, but the smell of roast duckling made such considerations irrelevant.

"Avec des pommes de terre," Zoobird added to the girl who took our order.

"Zoo! Are you considering becoming a Frenchman?"

Dreamily he said, "The thought has crossed my mind."

"Is Marietta that good?"

He looked offended. "Trouble with you, Bernie, you've never been in love."

"How do you know? What do you know about me?" I can't say why his offhand words had pricked so sharply. I felt kind of betrayed. As if he had moved on to some more mature plane of existence that I would never reach.

"You've got a point," he admitted slowly.

"What do any of us know about each other's deeper side."

I wouldn't have admitted it to anyone on earth, but I doubted that I had one. At least not very deep.

"So tell me," he went on. "What do you see yourself doing after the war?"

"I haven't really thought about it." Which was a lie. Sometimes I couldn't think of anything else. I hated the idea of going back to the Bag Company. And the prospect of a family, wife, kids, obligations, worries over money — the whole subject made me shudder. How do you ever take on that kind of responsibility?

As we were finishing our meal the door opened and a foursome of officers walked in. Pilots — you couldn't miss the clues, the leather jackets, polished boots, goggles shoved on top of tight leather helmets. The scarves at the throat, the strut — it took me back to the aerodrome at Luneville. But these fellows wore the insignia of the American Air Service.

We gave them the brotherly salute and as they settled into chairs around the table next to us Zoobird said, "How's the war in your neck of the woods?"

"Can't complain," one said. Friendly, though you sensed they held themselves aloof, as a breed apart. "We were just discussing your Generals. Wish they'd make better use of our planes."

"In what way?" I asked.

"Let us drop some bombs on your objective, soften it up. More effective than Artillery."

"Well-l-l now, I doubt that," Zoo drawled, which meant his back was up. "Toss a little firecracker out of a moving aircraft, you'd be lucky if it hits within a hundred feet of some spot below."

And the argument was on.

"Come the next battle we'll just have to show you. You'll be fighting up in our sector," one said. And when the others tried to hush him he added carelessly, "Well, the Army is moving this way. Isn't that why you guys are up here?"

"We're on leave," Zoo said quickly.

And I said, "Where's your aerodrome, anyhow?"

"About ten kilometers north of Verdun."

"We've got a buddy in the Air Service. Ever hear of Luke Marlowe?"

They exchanged glances. "Yeah, we know Marlowe."

"He's from our neighborhood in Kansas City. Is he still as crazy as ever? We used to call him 'Ookey.' "

They hesitated. You don't criticize a fellow pilot. One of them said, "We call him 'Scattershot.' "

I flashed on a mental image of Ookey holding that shotgun, blasting a hole in the ceiling of his bedroom. "You mean he doesn't hit his targets?"

"Oh no, he's a dead-eye shooter. It's just —"

One of the others said, "He tends to go off in all directions."

"Not exactly hampered by obedience to orders. But then we pilots are an independent breed, y'know."

One fellow, a redhead who reminded me of Pug with his fierce Irish jaw, said, "Nothing wrong with a little initiative. So the guy is a maverick, he's one hell of a flier."

Zoobird said dryly, "If you're going to take part in a coordinated campaign like the Argonne you need discipline. You can't stray off on your own."

"Marlowe just can't stand seeing an enemy plane run away into the clouds." They all laughed. "The dogfights he's had, it's a wonder he's alive. Like the other day he ran into a stray Fokker, it was onto him like a hawk on a jackrabbit. But Marlowe's got tricks of his own, did a barrel roll with his tail on fire and still managed to blast the

Heinie out of the air before he brought his plane down bellyflop in a cornfield. Nosed over, but he got out with only a busted arm. He's a survivor."

"Will he be going home then?" I asked.

"Oh no. They couldn't even keep him in the Field Hospital. He won't let a busted wing stop him, not with a new offensive coming up. We'll need every man we've got. They better finish this war pretty soon or there won't be anyone left to fight on either side."

Zoo got up restlessly. "Let's go check out this little burg, see if they have any dance halls?"

"They got one in Nancy," an airman said.

I paid our tab. "If you see Marlowe tell him a couple of friends from the 129th are going to be around here for a while."

As I followed Zoobird down the street he was whistling, irritated music.

"Yeah," I said, "I don't care for the type either. They walk like they just appointed themselves President of Everything."

"They've got big mouths," he said. "Who knows who might be listening, all that talk about the new offensive?"

"Well, it's going to be pretty obvious in a day or two," I told him. "When the caissons start moving in."

"Maybe they'll bring 'em up by night. Anyway, it doesn't hurt to keep shut about it. They ought to know that, but they're too busy being heroes."

There it was again, the word seemed to rise up and taunt me whenever I had thoughts of Ookey. "Well, you got to admit, it takes a special kind of courage to go up in a plane and trade bullets with the enemy at one thousand feet in the sky."

"More than the doughboy I saw who walked up to a Bosch machine-gun nest and wiped it out with a grenade? Miracle he didn't get killed. Six of his buddies did. All part of the job. Nobody gave them a medal, to get one of those you have to be noticed. Which is why those fliers blow hard. You remember how Ookey always made sure there was an audience for his stunts?"

"That may be." I don't know why I came to his defense. Everything Zoobird said was true. "But if you've really got the guts it isn't showing off."

"For my money," the Bird spoke slowly, "the hero is the man who stands up to danger when there's no glory in it, when nobody's watching. Somebody who makes the tough decisions, stands by them, never forgets his obligations to his buddies. Did I ever thank you for putting in a good word for me with the General? I know that's why he sent me to OTC. I really appreciate it."

The change of subject got me a little flustered. "Shoot," I said, "I didn't do you any favor. If you were a cook you'd never have got stuck out there in no-man's land getting your ears shot off."

He laughed. "I said a few prayers, believe me."

In a while I asked him. "Zoo, can you still believe in God after what we saw out there?"

His blue eyes went wide and baffled. "God didn't make the war. Men did."

"But you think it's okay that He lets it go on?"

"Once there's evil turned loose on the world, you have to fight it to a finish. What else?" He shrugged his bony shoulders and got out his harmonica.

Twenty-Two

Another mail call, and this time I was the goat — not a letter to my name. I knew it must be because of a hitch in the system, some truck probably blown up and with it my lifeline to home. I knew they hadn't all forgotten me. Dad had been very faithful, a letter every two weeks. Mom had gone to writing just once in a while. Said she was pretty busy as Treasurer of the Delphians. The thought of those ladies far off in Kansas City, Missouri, in another land across a broad ocean was so outlandish when you tried to superimpose it on the bleak landscape of France, it felt almost comical. Of course the one I really missed was the envelope that smelled faintly of Spearmint. Lindy's elegant handwriting was always like a magical touch to remind me of more gracious days. But I had to remind myself that I was only one of many that she tried to cheer up. Her letters, like the chewing gum, were only a temporary cure for the blues. And now not even that.

Leaving the others in the mess hall to read their messages, jealous of their private smiles, I left the camp. Our Regiment had set up in some old French barracks a quarter mile from town. When I reached the office in Headquarters, where Zoobird was supposed to be on duty, I found only a couple of enlisted men sitting around, jawing about the Argonne and what they had been through. I was about to leave when General Berry came in.

"Bernie. Good. I was just looking for you."

"Where's Zoo— I mean Lieutenant Fleischman?"

"I sent him off to establish our observation posts. There are a number of well-built dugouts used by the French in earlier times that should do. But we need to have telephone lines run out to them, and we've got to find men who have mathematical background to man them. I turned it all over to Lieutenant Fleischman."

"Yes sir. He's good with those binoculars." *And I am jealous. Of the Bird?* I tried to shake it off, ashamed of myself.

"Now I have a job for you," the General was going on. "Major Howe has been ordered back to the States for reasons of health. His lungs have been bad ever since he got caught in a gas attack over on the Somme."

I didn't know Howe. He had joined the General's staff while I was off at Luneville. "Sorry to hear it, sir."

"Yes, well, the point is I need a younger stronger man to head up my Intelligence Department. I want some accurate reconnaissance of the enemy's positions before we can start to plan a new attack. He's out there in force." The General walked over to the map on the wall, put his hand on a large area to the north of us, about a fifteen-mile front. "I suggest that you pick out some volunteers for a scouting party and go out there tonight — they predict that it's going to be cloudy, which is fortunate. Wear camouflage, black your faces, keep your heads down, but get me some coordinates if you can. Without killing yourself, understood?"

"Yes, sir!" I snapped the words off with enthusiasm, partly because fear has its element of thrill. But mostly I relished the thought that I had been chosen to carry out an important assignment that involved forming a detail on my own. I could almost hear Ookey's derisive taunt: *Lead on, O Leader.*

As we gathered at the mess hall for lunch later Zoobird joined me, shining with delight. "Heard you were made head of Intelligence. Hey, Bernie, nice work."

"Oh, shoot, it's just a little reconnaissance party."

"So count me in."

"You've got other duties, don't you?"

"Well, yeah, I have to teach some new troops the joys of flash-ranging."

"Don't worry, I can handle this alone."

He gave me an odd look. "Of course you can. Nobody better. Bring us back some coordinates on the Heinies' positions. If they're deep in those woods we'll have a hard time pinpointing them, can't see the muzzle flash. And try to find out where the boxcars are coming from."

Every evening the Germans would send over a few bombs to annoy us in our new position, 220 mm shells that dropped without warning or pattern. They didn't do much damage, but a nine-inch explosive shakes the earth and rattles the nerves. Our nerves were very near the surface those days.

And I didn't kid myself, the scouting trip was going to be a dicey venture. After lunch I made my announcement. Banging my cup on the table, I said, "Gentlemen —" Trying for the grave tone of authority borrowed from General Berry. "I am asking for volunteers to go out on a dangerous mission tonight, a vital intelligence operation which must remain secret for the moment." I figured that would whet their curiosity at least. "Anyone interested, please stay behind after lunch. We'll discuss our strategy." That should make them feel like Pershing himself. Mainly I didn't want to embarrass anybody by asking for a show of hands, or the "step forward" routine, which makes the rest of the troops look like cowards. I just hoped a few would remain at the tables as the rest left.

Finishing my chow, I took my plate out to the kitchen where the K.P. detail was washing dishes. When I got back I found several dozen men still lounging around the tables. I wished they'd finish their grub and go on off. It was only when I saw they weren't eating that I realized — these were all volunteers. Thirty seven of them.

One of them, a brash black-haired kid who reminded me of Ookey, said, "So what's the story, Loot? We gonna hunt for buried treasure?"

For a Private to speak like that to an officer back in the days of Doniphan would have been unthinkable. I supposed I didn't present a very imposing personal appearance, but maybe for this assignment that was good. I gathered them around me at one of the long tables and described what our objective would be. With so much available talent I decided on the spot to send out three scouting parties, ten men each. When I warned of the danger, I expected some to renege. A couple did, one because he couldn't see well in the dark and the other because he had a cough that was uncontrollable at times and might give us away. The rest stuck with me, a motley bunch, mostly raw recruits, a few veterans of Vauquois Hill. Those I appointed squad leaders and told them all to gather on the north side of camp at seven that evening.

As darkness deepened into night we blacked our faces and threw rain gear over our uniforms. The rubber ponchos disappeared into the shadows as we split up and made our way forward toward no-man's land. Taking the northernmost route, which was nearest the old forts, I made mental notes along the way, of shattered tree stumps, a crumpled stone wall, a ravine. We deployed into it silently, picking our way through the rubble of many years of war until we reached a barricade of splintered wood, bricks, debris that had to be manmade. We must be getting close to enemy lines, I figured. Passing the signal to the others to hold up, I crawled quietly up the bank of the ravine onto a barren muddy stretch where nothing lived. Quiet as a church. Or a barnyard, I could hear the distant sound of geese squawking. As I was about to motion the men forward a burst of machine-gun fire sent me scrambling back down into the ditch.

It had come from a spot a hundred yards ahead, a long random spate of bullets that raked the land blindly. I guessed they hadn't seen us, but that some tripwire around that barricade had warned them of our presence. Go back and regroup — I didn't know what else to do, but you can't argue with a spray of hot lead. I ignominiously withdrew my troops. As we trudged back to camp I asked for suggestions as to how we had given ourselves away. Nobody offered an answer.

It was small comfort that the other squads reported similar difficulties. As soon as they got near their objectives some forward signal set off the machine-gunners.

When I reported unhappily to General Berry I said, "The fellows want to go out there with a sack of grenades and try to take the tommyguns down."

He shook his head. "We can't start the offensive on our own. Let me give it some thought."

Back at our room as I sheepishly recounted our night's adventures to Zoobird he began pacing the long attic, sort of bouncing off the walls. He had been in a state ever since we moved up to Sommedieu. I thought it just might have to do with Marietta. But that was his business, and the Intelligence Department was mine.

"Don't worry about it," I instructed him. "We're not going out again any time soon. The General said it's not worth risking our lives."

He came to a stop in front of me. "Listen. Maybe there were too many of you. Thirty guys wandering around out there? What you need is one good man, and I volunteer."

I was open to suggestions. "You could be right, but if anyone goes it'll be me."

"Okay. We'll both go. You scout north and I'll head south."

Once more: so much for my skills of leadership. But it did make a certain amount of sense, so I took it to the General and after some reluctance he okayed it.

Actually it felt good to have the Bird with me as we ventured out silently that night. Even shoe-black hadn't dimmed his excitement as we crawled across deadly flats under the thick dark sky. At the ravine I pointed: *I'm going that way.* He jerked a thumb toward the south and was gone noiselessly into the heavy night. I couldn't even hear his steps.

My own sounded loud in the crackle of dead brush down in the ditch I was following. Stopping well short of the barricade this time, I crawled up onto the flat, taking a long detour around it. Once a dog barked way over in the outskirts of Verdun. I wondered how a dog could still be alive in this war-stripped land. Bird's nest: *I spy.* That's what we used to say on our hunts, to establish our rights to any eggs found. Night bird cawed, back toward Sommedieu, and off to the left I heard those barnyard geese. I lay down on my belly and wriggled forward . . .

A tremendous blast of machine-gun fire tore the underbrush just above my head. Thank all my lucky stars he was aiming high, about where a man's knees would be. With the sputter of muzzle-flash still flickering I inched backward. I didn't think suicide would be in the Army's best interests, not to mention mine. This time I didn't even feel like a coward. You have to be realistic about bullets.

When I was halfway back to camp I heard another distant crackle of tommyguns off to the south. *Zoobird, don't you dare get yourself shot! I know you think your Lord's out there protecting you, but don't count on it.*

My fears got stronger when I reached Headquarters and found one of the General's aides there alone, transcribing some notes.

"Where's Lieutenant Fleischman?" I asked.

He stared at my smeared face. "Bernie? Is that you?"

"I'm looking for —"

"Haven't seen him. Sorry."

I hurried back to the attic, but it was empty. *Zoobird, if you went and got yourself killed I'll never forgive you.*

At four fifteen in the morning I heard the clump of boots on the stairs. Zoobird, looking horrible. His clothes were mired, he had lost his poncho and was soaking wet, so it must be raining again. Hair plastered flat against his head, he looked murderous as a vulture. For the first time I noticed how long his neck was, Adam's apple the size of a wing-nut. It worked up and down, as if he were swallowing some very bitter pill.

"Well, I found your problem," he said, glowering. "It's geese. The Bosch have got them tethered around a big pond out there halfway across no-man's land. Minute anybody comes within a quarter of a mile they start squawking. That's how the Heinie gunners were ready for you."

"I'll be damned. I did hear some sort of racket in the distance —"

"Oh, I knew you'd take credit for it. I knew you'd claim you figured it all out yourself."

"Actually I didn't. What the Sam Hill is wrong with you? Where have you been all night anyway?" The geese alarm had gone off hours ago.

"Did the mail come?" He scowled at the letter I held in my hand.

"No. I didn't get any this time, so I was rereading one of the earlier ones from Lindy."

"The chewing-gum girl," he sneered. "Fancy handwriting, I'll bet she went to one of those ritzy schools."

"Yeah," I said. "She's way over my head, I know that. Asks what do I think of President Wilson's Fourteen Points. Whatever that is." I was just talking to fill in, while I tried to determine what was eating my best friend alive from the inside-out.

"If you don't go to college," he said darkly, "you'll never keep up with her. Or is that important? Did you decide to be a lone wolf for life, maybe bum around the world with

Ookey and go to Hell in a handbasket?"

Zoobird is trying to pick a fight with me.

Helpfully, I said, "Well shoot, why don't you go to college yourself after all this is over? How's your mom? Is she doing okay down in Joplin? Don't have to worry about her any more, you should send in your application to MU. They'd still remember you from basketball, get a nice scholarship. Unless all you want is to work in the bank all your life."

"Are you calling me dumb?"

"No, I think you were the one handing out the insults. Implying I will end up a bum."

"No, no, you and Ookey, you're going to be copperplate heroes. You think it takes a piece of metal to prove you're a man."

If he's bound to fight I will help him along. "Well, that's better than pinning your hopes to a cheeky little French girl."

He came at me in a rush. We shoved and wrestled and pushed. I held him off while his long arms flailed wildly. It was like getting hit with a barrage of rabbits. As he seemed to be getting tired I grappled with him and we went down in a futile deadlock. I didn't want him to holler "uncle," not to me. Letting go, I rolled aside, and for a minute we lay there heaving.

Zoobird was gasping for breath, big hiccups which turned into an awful sort of hysteria. I laughed, too. We lay there and roared with sad hilarity.

After a while we got up and by common consent trooped out and down the stairs, across the street to the café where you could get coffee at any hour. Taking our cups to a table in the corner, we sank into a weary silence.

"Pretty good coffee," I said. It was awful coffee.

He turned his cup around and around. "I'm sorry Bernie. It's the damnable war."

"So what happened last night? You go down to Grange-le-Compt?"

He nodded. "When I got there she had another guy in her bed, a crummy Captain."

I had already figured as much.

"Sorry I made those remarks about you not being good enough for Lindy. I don't even know her."

"Shoot, you were right. She's quality. By the time I get home she'll probably be engaged to some stock broker or lawyer or maybe the Governor of Missouri." I was only half kidding.

"Thing is," he said earnestly, "you *are* good enough — for any woman you want.

If you went to college you could darned well *be* the Governor of Missouri."

Twenty-Three

The new offensive was carried out a little differently. The artillery was to open up at the same time the infantry went over the top. Objectives were too scattered to be taken out by any one Regiment, so targets were assigned on the basis of the intelligence information that had come in from me and others like me. By the 1st of November we had pinpointed the enemy's cantonments, ammunition dumps, balloon hangars, as well as their gun emplacements. Division Intelligence assigned sectors, including a new Division that had come on the line, the 81st from Tennessee, called themselves the Wild Cats. Though the 35th had been withdrawn, our Artillery stayed in support of these raw rookies, who proved themselves to be pretty tough.

They were moving ahead so fast, it was hard to keep up with them. Prisoners were being brought in by the dozen. I heard that many of the Bosch just walked toward our lines with their hands up. And I was assigned to interrogate them.

Once more I was struck by how young they were, most in their teens, skinny, scared kids who were not reluctant to answer my questions, the way the young pilot had been. In fact they babbled about home and family, would gladly tell you where their command posts were. They were very hungry. There had been no fresh provisions along the German line for weeks, I gathered.

One of them who seemed especially articulate even asked me a few questions, about our forces and deployment. Just curious. I didn't give him any answers, but I couldn't help asking him: *"Why are you fighting this war?"*

He looked puzzled at the question. *"We do what we're told."* Then he said, *"Why are you?"*

I searched for the right answer. Patriotism? Not exactly, my country wasn't threatened. Duty, yes, your President says you're needed, you take his word for it. And he was acting on moral grounds. No dictator like the Kaiser should be allowed to take over somebody else's country by force of arms. All I could tell the man was, *"We do what is right."*

"Oh," he gave me a sneer. *"You are a choir boy."*

I let it go, I didn't feel equipped to argue with him over right and wrong. His authority was his Emperor; ours was — I guess — the Bible. "Thou shalt not covet." Somebody once told me most of our laws were based on Moses' commandments. Talk about leadership, I had to hand it to the old boy, parting the Red Sea and so forth. Then I remembered that his offensive, leading the Jews out of Egypt, was done under the direct orders of God. Or so the scriptures say.

Something I needed to think about, only I still tried to keep from thinking too much.

Those days I wished I was out on the line with Zoobird, who was training more forward observers in the art of triangulation. I hardly ever got to see him. This battle was different, not so intense, but it was more tiresome. The bombs fell around us daily, but we rarely bothered to duck. As for me all I wanted was mail call, and when it came there still was no letter from Lindy. That took precedence over my personal anxieties. By now men were going home, wounded, or mustered out, probably her friends, people of her society crowd. I could picture a nice Major with a limp and stories of the Front and his own bravery under fire, killed dozens of men himself, yelling "Onward," to his troops. He'd be about thirty with a neat moustache and stoical gray eyes and a scar along his jaw line . . .

"Lieutenant Jones, you are wanted over at Headquarters. General Berry has called a meeting of his staff." The young Sergeant saluted.

I returned his salute and left the prisoner compound, a little concerned. The General had issued our orders the night before. It was still early morning, barely eight a.m. when a dozen of us crowded into the small room at the Mairie in Sommedieu. Most looked sleepy. Zoobird seemed impatient, he was still in a bear of a mood these days. Around eight-thirty General Berry came in, walking with more of a bounce in his step than I'd seen lately.

"Gentlemen, I have news. An Armistice has been signed between the Allied forces and the Germans. At eleven o'clock today there will be a cease-fire."

It didn't penetrate at once. We all stood there silently, while in the distance the howitzers were still rumbling away.

"We have to keep on fighting until that moment," he went on with a touch of bitterness. "God knows how many hapless men will die in the next two and a half hours. But then the whole thing has been a cruel conflict, waged by cruel men. The Kaiser has abdicated his throne. The Allies have achieved an unconditional surrender. Please pass the word down the line to hold your fire and keep your heads low for a little longer. But know that the war is officially over."

I couldn't get my balance. It was as if we'd all been running for the finish line so hard that when you hit the tape you couldn't stop. Back at Intelligence Headquarters I passed the word and saw to it the runners were assigned to relay it to the various Brigades along the line. But the General had asked me to get back to Headquarters as soon as possible.

It was about ten o'clock when I returned to his office. He had a stack of telegraph sheets, messages for home. "Bernie, what I want you to do is take these to the cable office in Toul and see they get sent. Officers' families, and so forth. Be sure to add your own to the lot. Our people back in the States will be praying that we all came through. Take a staff car and driver," he added. "Be back here by dark."

It was a four-hour drive, so that I happened to be in St. Mihiel at the historic moment the guns stopped firing. Our way was blocked by a small crowd of soldiers, standing at attention as a parade passed by. Down the middle of the street marched three people, probably the only remaining citizens of that ruined village — a woman and two very elderly men in frayed French uniforms. They were singing "The Marseillaise." As they limped down the street between the blasted buildings, from somewhere a church bell tolled the hour, and a great cheer broke forth.

Doughboys fired their weapons in the air, I yelled myself hoarse, yelling away months of tension, sickly fears.

"We beat them! I helped win the war! How do you like that!" I screamed it upward, as if Someone on high had been challenging me. Which was ridiculous, the sky was empty and clean and the air smelled fresh.

By contrast, as we drove on the silence was stupefying. The countryside was quiet as if there was no living thing left on earth. No rumble of guns. The driver kept shaking his head as if he had water in his ears. I wanted to speak, but I couldn't think of anything to say. We just sat wordless until we came into Toul.

There were the real crowds of people all over the streets, cavorting in a scene of mad joy, hooting in demented elation. The town was a central clearing depot for the Army. Well back from the Front, its streets were unpitted, its warehouses undamaged. As we passed the rail yards I saw a sobering sight — stacks of wooden crates all about seven feet long and two feet wide. A silent witness to the toll the war had taken. It bothered me to see them standing there in the elements, not even a tarp over them.

When we got to the cable office I saw at once that it was hopeless. The line of soldiers waiting to send messages was two deep and went entirely around the block. A couple of gendarmes stood by to keep order, but we still got hustled and bustled by crowds from every arm of the service, Marines, sailors, French and English and Americans, celebrating the end to all the misery. By now I didn't feel a lot like whooping it up.

When we went into one of the cafés for a quick bowl of ragout, I finally heard a word from my driver. A red-headed kid named Smedson, he looked to be about fifteen, but must have been older.

With a sigh he said, "That was a sad sight at the station, sir, all those coffins piled up."

Our waitress, a middle-aged woman with bleak eyes, said, "Yes, it is the flu."

I didn't understand. "You mean those aren't casualties?"

She shook her head. "All flu. From the hospital. There is an American hospital here, very much flu."

It jarred things back into some kind of perspective. The world had gone on outside our battleground. An illness this deadly? I'd hardly taken notice of it before, but now it hit me a blow. Who was it had said the disease had reached America?

I took out my notebook and scribbled a message. To Smedson I said, "I've got to get these cables out. You stand by the car," and headed back for that long queue. It took every cent I had, about twenty-five bucks, to bribe one of the men near the head of the line to let me in, and when others glowered I invoked authority. "Official business!"

Lindy, I had written, *stay away from railroad station STOP. Much flu, be careful STOP. I'm fine, be home soon.*

I picked up an American newspaper at a vendor's stand on the street, the New York Herald Tribune. Four days old, its headlines weren't of war or peace. They were all about the flu. Thousands of people were dying —

they called it a pandemic. I had supposed that meant a small epidemic, but it really meant a world-wide catastrophe.

Now, the fact that I hadn't heard from Lindy in weeks raised terrifying new questions. Not the worst verdict, I couldn't face that. But even to picture her ill made me break into a sweat. I had to get home! To hang around France had become excruciating.

We were all feeling the dregs of aftermath that next morning as we reported to General Berry's office for orders. All I could think of was the long journey between me and Missouri. How soon could we start? Would we be mustered out at once, maybe? I'd gladly hit the road walking.

Over in the corner Zoobird was sunk into a chair that was too short for his long legs. Knees sticking up, elbows aslant, he was playing soft chords on the harmonica, his eyes closed, his crest of hair at half-mast. Hobby Carter was over by the window, staring out at nothing, his profile lumpy with an instrument he carried beneath his rain cape. Abe Peters' banjo. A couple of new men, Lieutenants, stood near the door awkwardly as if they weren't sure they belonged here. I hoped they were our replacements.

We all straightened up when the door opened, but it wasn't General Berry. The man who stood there looked familiar — I had to readjust my mind to realize that it was Ookey.

The swagger was the same, yet somehow different. He had an arm in a sling and his gait was crooked with a heavy limp. More than that, he looked oddly compressed as if hours in the cockpit of a plane had concentrated him into a tighter package. Mouth a hard slit in the stubble of jaw and chin, his eyes were wary. All the old toughness was shaped into a hard shell behind which was a man years older than me.

"Well, Hell!" he said with a grin. "You'd think I was a ghost."

"Aren't we all?" I shook his hand and Zoobird put away the harmonica.

"Heard you were stationed down here. Some of the fellows said they ran into a little runty guy and a tall clown with a red nose, had to be you two." He clapped the Bird on the shoulder. "Looks like the old gang made it through all right. I ran into Pug a month ago down in Paris. He's getting fat. Deke, I don't know —"

"I saw him," Zoobird said, "at least through my glasses. He was on an Engineering crew, repairing a bridge the Heinie had blown up, over toward Montfaucon. He was okay as of then, at least. Shells falling all around, but those guys are tough."

"And Dollars is with the supply station at Cheppy," I added.

"Trust him to go where the money is," Ookey said snidely. "They say those Commissary guys are getting rich off selling Army materiél to the natives."

"He was in the line of fire when I saw him," I said curtly.

"Aw Bunk, you're still a dreamer."

"And you're still a smart-mouth." For some reason he was rubbing me the wrong way, maybe it was the Captain's insignia. "Your buddies, that time we ran into them in Sommedieu, they called you 'Scattershot.' "

"Yeah, that would be O'Hara. A little stupid, but he's a fair flyer."

"Said you went down in flames."

"Then he lied. I landed that plane very nicely, thank you, even though I personally took a few bullets." He glanced at his arm. "It'll mend. Plenty of time now, no more joy rides, I guess." He was sorry the war was over, I realized. "Hey, I'm on leave, I've got a car and a month's pay. Why don't we go somewhere? I'd like to drink you guys under the table."

General Berry had come into the room behind him. “At ease, men. I just stopped by with some good news. I’m giving the staff a week’s leave, a few at a time. And you two —” he meant me and Zoobird — “are top of my list. So your coming was in good order, young man.” He turned to Ookey. I introduced them and as they shook hands the General went on. “I suggest you take these men out on the town and paint it red, white and blue. You’ve all earned it.”

Twenty-Four

"Paree, here we come!" Ookey gunned the old Caddy. Weathered and scarred, it was a war veteran too, but the tires looked new, and the engine had a steady efficient hum. Beside him on the front seat I was a little winded. In a hurry, I had packed my overnight gear in a caddy — razor and soap and a washcloth. You don't ever expect those to be provided anywhere. When Zoobird joined us he was in a strange state, oddly excited, wearing his best uniform and shouldering a duffle that could have contained his entire worldly goods.

"Whatcha got there?" I kidded him.

"Change of clothes," he said as he lunged into the back seat. "When I dance I sweat a lot. Girls don't like that."

"Come on, Zoo" I kidded him. "Admit it — you're going AWOL."

"I'm going just as far as the first dance

hall we can find. I heard there's one in Toul."

I said, "It's not far from Grange-le-Compt, either."

"Don't mention that," he warned in a snarl that didn't sound like Zoobird at all.

"We're going to Paris," Ookey said flatly. "And then it's every man for himself."

Just to be difficult I remarked, "I hear the Riviera is nice. Warm, sandy beaches, nude women." Right then the chill of the air made me wish I was a long way from northern France.

"You Missouri pukes are just scared to take on the big bad city," Ookey sneered. "You want dance halls? I'll show you some dance halls. I bet you never saw them do the CanCan."

"You've been there, I take it?"

"Twice. They give us plenty of leave time in the Air Corps. I —" He hit a pothole in the road and swore.

"Hey," I said, "if you're in pain I'll be glad to drive."

"No, let me," Zoobird demanded. "I haven't been behind the wheel of a car in months."

"Fight over it then." Ookey pulled to the side of the road and let Zoo have the front seat, crawling into the back with another wince. “It’s not the elbow that hurts, it’s the stitches in my thigh. I took a whole chain of lead off that Bosch flier before I shot him out of the sky.”

For a minute I envied him that careless arrogance so keenly it twisted my innards. Grimly I said, “With us, it was a different kind of action. An endurance test, to outlast the Hun, wear him down, taking the guns out one at a time as fast as they could bring them up. Like a treadmill with 75 mm shells coming at you.”

“Bore me to death,” Ookey shrugged.

“It’s what won the war,” Zoobird informed him in a heavy tone, almost menacing. “Not the show-off stuff where you take down some pilot and go collect your medal.”

“What’s your count, Ook?” I asked. “How many notches on your gun?”

“So many I lost track. Sky fights, they come at you, you squeeze the handles of the gun, watch a plane explode, turn fast and take on the next one. Medals are a dime a dozen. They give ’em out like candy bars in the Air Force. What matters is being the best at the game. You poor dodos slogging around down in the mud, how do you ever feel like a hero that way? Where’s the glory?”

We had come into the outskirts of Toul, a street of small businesses, where abruptly

Zoobird swerved the Caddy into a spot at the curb. Feverishly he said, "I need some shoes."

"Shoes? Zoo, you got shoes on your feet right now."

"You can't dance in Army boots." He had the door open and was out and gone, dodging through traffic. There was a steady stream of lorries and Army trucks busting along the road with a haste that was infectious. Meanwhile Zoo had gone into a shop that bore the word ***Mercerie.***

"Bunk, what's the matter with him?" Ookey grumbled. "Time is precious. Didn't you dopes learn anything during this war? Time is the only thing worth having. There isn't enough time in all the world."

I felt pretty much the same way, but I was in no mood to agree with him by now. That nickname "Bunk" came from a time way back in our childhood when he had made some overblown claim and I had said, "Aw, that's the bunk." Turned out he was right. He never let me forget it.

Ookey fidgeted. "So is it war nerves? I've seen men jitter around like that after they've been under fire. It's like shell-shock almost."

"Zoobird is the steadiest guy in our outfit," I told him flatly. "He's responsible for more damage to the Bosch than you could inflict in a couple of hundred passes over their guns. He stood out there under fire on Vauquois Hill and located their 75's, passed the information along to our artillery, single-handed. Nobody to spell him or do the arithmetic, he did it all. So don't talk about Zoo losing his nerve. He just had a small problem with a woman over in Grange-le-Compt."

"Not Marietta the Mutt?" Ookey snorted long and loud. "Gawd, I wish I had a nickel for every poor fool got snookered into her bed. She's a legend along the Front. Mama wants her to learn about life. Yeah, and increase the family income by five bucks a night."

"Okay, you know it, I know it. Zoo doesn't know it, so shut up about it." I turned to look over my shoulder at him, as tough a frown as I can put on. But Ookey was peering out the window.

"Where the Hell is he going now?"

Zoobird had come out of the store, a package under his arm, and headed down the street toward another establishment, with a sign above the door: ***Cabaret.*** Probably looking for directions to the dance hall, I thought, but I was beginning to get impatient myself.

"Aw, Bunk, for the love of Pete. Go over

there and find out what he's up to." It had been a good five minutes. "Tell him if it's dancing he wants they've got babes in Paris who'll dance his rump off and then take him upstairs and make him forget Marietta. Wait'll you see those flirty little floozies over on the Left Bank. In fact you look like you could do with a good —"

I was out of the car by then. What I could do with was none of his business. Same old Ookey, I thought, but with a hard edge now, none of the boyhood joy. When I went into the dark little club I made out the Bird hanging onto the bar. He seemed confused.

Behind it, the proprietor was wringing his hands — I never understood the description before — he was actually twisting his fingers in a nervous fit.

"Allez. S'il vous plait." There followed a spate of apology that sounded almost frantic. I could only pick out scraps. He was saying the place wasn't open at this hour, and there was no dancing, and he had to go now and *vive La France.*

"Come on, Zoo," I took his arm. "What's the matter?"

"Just a little dizzy." His eyes weren't quite focusing.

The bartender was backed away from us as far as he could go. Trying to convey some advice, he waved vigorously toward the street. *"Dans l'hopital. La bas."*

"Hospital?"

"Mais oui. Tout de suite." Another rattle of words like an eruption. And finally one that needed no translation. *"La flu."*

It was almost like being on a battlefield of a different nature, the logistical problem of getting Zoobird back across the street against traffic. He tilted and sagged, I had to struggle to get him into the car, settling him on the passenger side. Ookey was already in the driver's seat. Finding the hospital wasn't hard; the tallest building in town, it looked to have been a warehouse, four stories high and square as a breadbox. Barren inside, floors stripped down to bare wood, the place reeked of antiseptic. In the lobby there were a couple of wheelchairs and we got Zoo into one of them. At the desk a volunteer lady in a Red Cross get-up was keeper of the ledger, writing his name in her book, address, next of kin. That question almost made me choke. *He's not THAT sick.* But the nurse who had come with her stethoscope to bend over his long lanky bones was looking grave.

"It's the flu, all right," she said. "In an advanced stage. He needs to be in bed, but we don't have one open in the flu ward.

You'll have to wait." And she hurried off into the elevator over to one side, doors closed, gone.

"Wait? How long?" Ookey yelled in a whisper.

The anteroom was lined with other emergency cases, a man with a wounded leg that was bleeding through his bandages, another who sat and trembled, eyes vacant, hands twitching, couldn't have been much over eighteen, chin hair was just a yellow fuzz. Across the way a soldier sat frowning at his injured foot, from which came the distinctive odor of gangrene. I'd run into plenty of that on the battlefield in the latter days of the Argonne. The medics out there had been great, but the job of hauling off all those wounded was impossible.

The elevator door opened again and our nurse hurried off to get one of the empty gurneys. Snagged an orderly and told him something — he put the gurney on the elevator while she collected Zoobird and wheelchair. "A bed has come vacant," she said, leaving us to follow if we pleased.

A big freight elevator, we all crowded in and it rose slowly to the top floor. Up there another nurse was waiting. She eyed Zoobird and shook her head. "It will just be a minute." And they went off through some swinging doors, wheeling the gurney.

"This is good," Ookey announced. "I mean that we were so close to a hospital. They can get him some help right away. Me, I hope I never see the inside of another one. Those docs — you should have seen 'em stitch me up. No anesthetic, over and done with and I got out of there as quick as I could."

I didn't want to hear any heroics. "How do you feel, Zoo?" I asked, but he didn't answer. Seemed to be humming something under his breath, "In The Good Old Summertime." The anteroom was hot, from a coal stove in the corner. It didn't begin to cut through that awful inner chill I'd had for days now, as if my whole belly was on ice, maybe forever.

"I remember one time . . ." Ookey began, then broke off as the nurses came back, orderly wheeling the gurney, now lumpy with a body draped in a sheet. No need to spell that one out.

"This one can come now." The upstairs nurse took charge of Zoobird.

"Can I stay?" I asked her.

A plain-faced woman with months of weariness in her gray eyes, she gave me a smile that was almost luminous. "That's good, of course you can. It will take me a half-hour or so to get him to bed, and then you can sit with him."

"We're due elsewhere," Ookey began.

I said, "Thank you, ma'am. We'll be back."

Ookey was already at the elevator, punching the button. "Nice lady. We can trust her to do right by old Zoo. Let's go."

As we reached the street outside I said, "We'd better find a room for the night."

"What are you saying? Why do you want to hang around some hotel in a two-bit nowhere town . . . ?"

"You figure to just drive off and leave him here?"

"But they know what they're doing. We'd only be in the way. Bunk, for the love of God, use your head. We'll run down to Paris tonight, have a couple days fun, by the time we get back Zoobird will be better. We'll find him a dance hall."

"I'm going to grab a bite to eat," I told him. There was a café down the street, accordion music, the sound not too different from Zoo's harmonica. I could smell *bouillabaisse.* No appetite, but the soup didn't turn my stomach. Aromatic with herbs, strong of fish, it filled some of the empty gaps inside me, the ones where bad thoughts echoed. *Next of kin, she must have been kidding.*

At another table sat a Corporal who coughed and coughed and coughed.

Ookey hardly touched his food. His face was an odd shade of gray that he had picked up when we were at the hospital. I was puzzled, never figured him to be queasy about — anything. But then Ookey had never been on a battlefield, never seen people cut to pieces, not close-up. His kills were all off in the clouds somewhere. If he closed his eyes he didn't see bloody rows of dead doughboys, arms and legs blown off, heads open and spilling brain-matter. Never found a severed finger stuck to the bottom of his boot. Never seen a man cut in two by a machine-gun burst, or a dead horse with its guts spilling forth.

Back at the car, I reached into the rear seat and hauled out Zoobird's duffle and my own kit. "For now I'm just going to stow these in the hospital," I said, "so nobody swipes them." He could come with me or not. I was a little surprised to find him still with me as we went back up in the ponderous elevator.

"Okay, we'll look in on the boy, make sure he's being taken care of. Then," he said in that old commanding way, "we are going to Paris, you and me. Don't shake your head. What are buddies for? We can be there by midnight."

The fourth floor beyond the curtained doorway was one long ward, a double row of fifteen or so beds. By the cot nearest the door, the nurse was hovering over Zoobird, taking his temperature. They had got him into a hospital bed-shirt. I didn't see his uniform, but beneath the bed his boots stood, looking lost without his long shanks in them. He lay peaceful under the sheets, eyes closed, but his face was very flushed. She had put a damp cloth on his forehead.

"His fever is very high. I gave him a little laudanum to keep him from tossing about. Now all we can do is wait and hope."

"Where are his clothes?" I glanced around.

"We burn them. The flu is highly infectious."

Behind me, Ookey made an odd noise as if he had swallowed a rock. "We'll know more by morning," she added, "if you want to come back then."

"See?" Ookey fidgeted. "I told you, there's not a thing we can do here. Bunk, will you kindly get a move on?"

I was thinking of Lindy as I watched the woman go down the long line of patients, her skirts swaying, her flat shoes making a hushed sound on the wooden floor. No dramatic wounds here, just the miserably sick, tossing and coughing and fighting for breath, groans and feverish mutterings, someone sobbing in fear. She turned aside to comfort him.

"Bunk!" Ookey plucked at my sleeve insistently.

"I am staying right here," I told him curtly.

"What's the matter, you scared to try your luck with those Parisian ladies of the night? I realize you're pretty innocent, but I'll see to it you have a good time."

It dawned on me: that's why he wanted company — to show off, to strut and be the know-it-all, to be Ookey the Great. I said, "After the girls in Anne's Chambers, I'm afraid your little playmates would be a big disappointment." That caught him by surprise. For a minute he looked unsure of himself.

"Well, you might change your mind. Paris isn't in Missouri."

"Yeah, in Kansas City I wouldn't get a case of the clap."

"But I need this leave. I've been in combat for weeks, laying my life on the line —"

"And the rest of us in the Argonne were just a side show?"

Ookey shot me a side-long look. "Bunk, you never used to be sarcastic. It's like I hardly know you any more."

"What's there to know? I'm one of those 'poor dodos' you mentioned, crawling around in the mud, taking territory one kilometer at a time. Like you said, no glory. We — Zoobird and me and the rest — we just got the job done. You'll never understand that, so go ahead, go to Paris. And don't ever call me 'Bunk' again."

At that moment down the ward somebody threw up all over the floor. Orderlies came rushing with mops and buckets. There was a time of confusion. When things got back to normal I glanced around and Ookey was gone.

I looked for a chair and found one near the door. Bringing it to the bedside I sat down beside Zoobird. His eyes were ajar. I told him, "You're in the hospital, Zoo. They're taking care of you. It's going to be okay."

". . . dance hall?"

"We'll find one later when you feel up to it."

He dropped off again, and the next time he opened his eyes the sense had come back into them. "Bernie? What's happening?"

"You've got the flu. But you're getting better now. Go back to sleep."

He frowned. "Did I buy some shoes?"

"Yeah. They're great shoes. I put them in

your duffle, it's right outside. Soon as you're able we'll go look up a dance hall."

"Okay," he sighed. "Only don't wait for me. I feel kind of weak. I'm going to just lie here a while."

As grayness set in beyond the windows the sounds of the ward seemed to grow muted, the murmurs of the patients, the rubber-soled steps of the nurses. *Lindy.* In this place of ugly reality, pain and raw truth and desperation, it came over me like a clean warm miracle. I couldn't fight it off any more. I was in love with the girl. I wished I could have told her that just once.

But of course it would never come to anything. I couldn't expect her to return my feelings, not in the context of marriage, home, kids. Her children would some day grow up in a mansion, be sent to the best colleges, turn out to be judges or generals or run big corporations. Could you imagine her at a cook stove in a hot kitchen in a little bungalow on Oak Street? With a toddler that needed its diaper changed and a dog that was tracking mud on the rug? She's wearing a cheap house dress, because it's all I can afford, as bookkeeper at the Kansas City Bag Company. Her parents are coming over for dinner, that majestic Mrs. Forrest in a fashionable gown. Judge Forrest with his gold watch chain draped across his considerable belly, he's too large a man for our cottage. Lindy still looks beautiful as a picture-book angel, but she sounds tired as she says, "The hash is ready . . ."

Thank you, Sir, for giving me that great image. I'll remember it whenever I get delusions of happiness.

How did He get back inside my head? I guess it was a matter of old habit, to talk to Him upon occasion. I had missed it, for all that I was angry at Him for the war and the blood and the horse. Actually I guess I understood about the horse. Like it says in Zoobird's poem, there's a time to ride and a time to walk. A time to shut up and a time to talk. You could make up verses without half trying.

Glancing at the figure on the cot, each breath coming so long and hard, I was tempted, badly tempted, to demand that the Lord cure his fever immediately and let us get on with our lives. But it might not be the right moment — that's what Zoobird meant, about everything being done on God's schedule.

So okay, take Your time, but do it right. Please.

The twilight outside had deepened into thick darkness. High up in the building you felt as if you were suspended in a void. Dark up there beyond the windows. Maybe if I'm asking favors I should butter Him up a little.

It was nice of you to help us win the war. Zoo says men make war, You try to stop it. Okay. So it's over. But honest, You have to agree that there wouldn't be any point in letting a good man die now, not from a bunch of germs?

I thought of trying to make a battlefield bargain: If You'll just do this one thing I'll go to church forever. But that seemed unworthy of Zoobird, as if he were the prize in a game of pool. Anyway it wouldn't work. The Lord doesn't haggle. Too many fine soldiers went down in the Argonne; obviously He doesn't have time to sort them all out. When it comes down to it, all you can do is beg. I never was great at that.

Over in the opposite row of cots the nurse was bending over a patient who lay motionless. I saw her make the sign of the cross. With a certain caution I went over to her side, I didn't want to butt in, but —

When she glanced up I whispered, "Could you say one of those for my friend over there? I mean I don't know how and you've had a lot of practice, and . . ."

"All too much practice," she murmured, straightening her back as if to get the kinks out. "Right now I need to stay with this one. He's very low and he doesn't have any faith. This afternoon he cursed the Chaplain. The war has set him adrift. He's all alone, and I'm hoping if I pray hard enough he'll go to his Maker in a state of grace."

"Well, my friend believes in the Lord, but he's pretty sick. I think he could use some help."

"He'll be fine." She smiled a little. "If he has faith it will either strengthen him to recover or steady him through to the next life. Don't fret, dear. If you want to comfort him, just say the Lord's prayer. You know 'Our father who art in heaven'? Concentrate on that line: 'Thy will be done.' " She turned back to the unconscious man on the cot.

Adrift, she said. I knew what she meant. For a long time I had felt that disconnection from my innocent younger self, naively believing in a God who could solve my small problems. I had outgrown that, and yet now it was blocking me from making up a proper prayer, as if I didn't really have the right to. Couldn't even remember the words. How did it, go? *Our father who art in heaven, hallowed be thy name,* and then what? I ought to know that.

When I got back to Zoobird's side he was

stirring around on the cot. With sudden violence he flung himself upright. "Marietta! I'm here!"

I made him lie back down. "Don't worry about her, Zoo. She's way off in Grange-le-Compt. We're in Toul, at the hospital."

He blinked at me, but he was seeing something else. "Bernie! Hurry up, those mules are gaining on you. Watch out for the tent ropes." Then sinking back, he closed his eyes.

In a while he let out a sharp order. "Corporal, here's some new coordinates. Go!" His arm waved wildly until I grabbed his hand and held it. I wished I could turn off my mind. I was so completely tired. And that sing-song verse of Mrs. Fleischman's kept churning out new couplets.

A time to think and a time to quit thinking.
A time for rising, a time for sinking. . . .

When I roused again the night had crossed some threshold, as it always did about four in the morning, as if it were darkening down to bitter lees. Not even any yellow patches of light out across the buildings beyond the window. The ward was quiet with a stillness that went deeper than absence of sound, as if it held its breath.

I came alert. Zoobird wasn't breathing. His hand was still clenched on mine, but the redness had faded from his face. It was the color of marble. He was rigid as a carving of a long lost warrior. Belatedly my mind rushed: *Our Father, who art in Heaven . . .* But it was too late for that. I know what death looks like. I know you can't argue with it.

Twenty-Five

Grief comes in different packages. I'd seen men cry, out on the battlefield. Or rush headlong at the guns. Or curse the Lord over the loss of a buddy. With me, it was a huge hole that spilled my feelings out in a gush, leaving me numb and empty. I felt as artificial as the body in the coffin.

I bought him a good one, not one of those jerry-built wooden boxes. He looked peaceful lying there, he just didn't look like Zoobird. In his graduation suit and the new dancing shoes he made a very presentable appearance, which is what I wanted for his mother. As an afterthought I pinned my uncle's medal to his lapel, so she might realize that her son was a hero in every sense of the word. Then I made arrangements to ship him straight out to Joplin. He was not going to be piled up on the station platform, the war owed him better than that.

Through all this I maintained a certain

momentum. It was only after it was all done that I felt the gaping cavern inside me. So much of my life had been removed — not just Zoobird, or the others, Abe Peters, poor old Angus, Fats off in Leavenworth. Deke, I heard, had joined the regular Army and got promoted to Major, stationed in Paris.

Remotely I wondered if Ookey had a good time there. I never saw him again, which was just as well. There was nothing I wanted to say to him. Actually, it felt good not having to envy him any more. But hatred, or the loss of it, can leave a hole, too.

And there were smaller gaps in my torn inner surface. There was the young lieutenant who had taught us how to clean a horse's hooves. In the Argonne one day I'd stumbled across him lying upside-down in a shell hole, his little fuzzy moustache all dirty and a bleeding stump where his left foot had been. By then he was past caring about regulations or anything else. There had been other faces that harked back to Doniphan, I couldn't put names to them.

Some losses are harder to identify. I could barely remember a time of joy. The pleasure of riding down the rope to the tree house, or the expectation of getting rich off panning for gold. The buzz of excitement as you took the floor for the big game. I even missed my fears. On the eve of the Argonne I had felt a soaring terror at the thought of facing the enemy. It was the closest thing to ecstasy. Different from being scared — that was a mean shameful thing which affected the gut. But fear was in the brain, the magnificence of mind over matter. Of course, it was beside the point. When the fighting started you just did what had to be done, and there was no joy in that, God knows.

God knows. Of course You do. I think I understand You better now. You just don't care what it takes to carry out Your plans. Like Zoobird said, we all run on Your timetable. A time to die, we die. You merciless master, so long. I won't bother You again.

One final loss: when I got back to Sommedieu a week later I found that General Berry had been replaced by another General, a younger man who was all business.

"Glad to meet you, Lieutenant. Welcome back. Sorry to learn about the death of —" he consulted a sheet of paper on his desk "— Lieutenant Fleischman. You handled things? Good. Well, we've got our work cut out for us. It's going to take some organization to get this Regiment home."

"Yes, sir."

"I have a memo here that says you and Fleischman were experts on inventory. Can you manage that alone? It won't be quite so extensive this time. We won't be shipping back our kitchen equipment or the stable tack or a lot of other things. Check with my Adjutant, he's got the list."

Those weeks of anticlimax are a blank in my head. The only part I remember was buying a notebook and beginning to put down this account, memories, impressions, discoveries. To make a record of what had happened to me, not just in France, but the years before, the years when I had been so young, when I had first met Lindy. Those daffodils.

Our first mail call in December I got a letter from her. It was short and there was no chewing gum this time. She said she'd been ill with pneumonia, but she was getting better. Maybe it was true, her writing looked so fragile it almost faded into the page. That's what it felt like, we were fading apart. She was happy the war was over. Happy. In times past she would have been punching the words out on paper, elated, thrilled, ecstatic. Instead her letter wilted with overtones of *goodby.*

I didn't answer it. I couldn't find words to be cheerful, or worse still, resigned. I couldn't find "me" inside. You can't write "I love you" if you have no "I." So Lindy joined the procession of ghosts that were heading for the horizon, growing more distant day by day as those long months wore on.

It took us until April to ship out. Checking over the inventory to be loaded into the hold of our vessel I felt a kinship with those heaps of duffles and suitcases full of uniforms that would never be worn again. What's the term? Excess baggage. Made me shiver.

But the cold of France was nothing compared to the icy rigors of the North Atlantic. We were on a liner this time, with shared staterooms for the officers and fancy banquet halls for the men to lounge around and play cards, smoke, brag, tell their tall tales. I couldn't stand it. Frigid or not, I sought out the deck.

And finally found my personal dead end, a niche behind one of the funnels. It was a good place where I wouldn't be disturbed. Nobody in their right minds would have come on deck with that freezing wind sweeping across it. I got some heavy blankets and took them to my cubbyhole. There was a thin warmth from the smoke rising up the stack, but mainly there was isolation.

When I slept I had nightmares. Awake, the sense of motion made me ill. Not seasick. It was the forward movement of my life that made me shudder. When I faced the prospect of my future, all I felt about that was a vague NO.

There finally came a night when I was afraid to sleep, the dreams were so vivid. I left my lair and walked out onto the deck in the cold light of a three-quarters moon. It looked as lopsided as I felt. Standing at the rail I looked down into the bottomless black of the ocean, sliding along the side of the ship. They say it only takes a few minutes to drown. Doesn't even hurt, you just . . . go away. Which is easy if you're already half gone.

Who'd care? My folks, briefly. At some distant time Deke would say, "Not old Bernie? Really? Tough." Zoobird would be out there waiting for me. But when I thought again I realized, I wouldn't be going to the same place he was. Not if I messed up God's timetable, you don't get to heaven by trying to out-think Him. If I went into that water now, I would float off — adrift, as the nurse said. So, what difference?

Lindy might give me a thought. She had written me one more letter, said she was sorry to hear about Zoobird. She'd got the news from my mother. When would she have talked to Mom? I couldn't imagine she'd call the house, so it was probably at one of those social functions. She'd ended the letter, "I pray for you every night. I ask God to bring you home safely."

Lindy, little girl, you don't know it, but the Lord doesn't have time for small requests about people like me.

I still had the letter, maybe I should tear it up and put it down the incinerator. When I went overboard it would get wet, I hated the thought of that. I reached in my pocket and came up with Zoobird's harmonica. For some reason I had insisted on keeping it, so the nurse had dropped it in a dish of antiseptic. Probably ruined the insides, but she wasn't going to let me walk around with a case of the flu in my pocket. Don't know why I wanted the thing, I certainly would never play it. The memories it brought back were so strong it was like an electric wire burning my hand. Do angels dance? Wasn't there something about that in the Bible? Well, if they didn't, the Bird would teach them how. He'd be great wherever he was. Dammit, that should have been me in that coffin.

But it wasn't.

The voice was so real I jumped. No one

else was on deck at that hour. The words had come from inside my head, a powerful deep intonation not like any stray thought I ever had. Hardly believing, I glanced up at the mercilessly cold stars.

"You talking to me?" I had to be mistaken. All the times I had spoken to Him, He had never said a word back. No, this was probably Zoobird. It would be just like him to try to give me advice from the great Out There.

"Zoo?"

But I got no response to that. Whoever had spoken it didn't sound like him. And it certainly wasn't one of my own inner whispers that had been whining around in my head lately. That tone had gone through me like an electric charge. I made my mind a blank, trying to pick up the signal again. I mean, the power in those words . . .

Nothing. I was being stupid. Just a symptom of how much I missed the guy. He always had cared what happened to me — I realized that now. You don't think about it at the time, but he was truly concerned. And he had a wealth of common sense locked away in his curious noggin. I was only now beginning to appreciate that.

He advised you to go to college.

It was back. I held still, waiting on all

edges for a little more, but that was all.

College? The last thing on earth I needed, more classrooms. I wouldn't even know what to study. A degree is a piece of paper you hang on a wall. It's what people like Dolly need to be a teacher. I don't want to be a teacher. Or, I guess you could study world history and politics and wars and so forth. Come in handy if you wanted to run for office, which I don't. Zoobird was only kidding when he said I could be Governor if I wanted to. He might as well have predicted that I'd be President of the United States, as if anybody from Missouri would ever lead the nation.

Of course it would help if I ever got together with Lindy again — I mean to know what it all means, the Allies and the Peace Treaty. For her I would do anything. Even wear a freshman beanie at some school. Is that what I'm supposed to do?

I felt a nudge of excitement. For some reason I wasn't cold inside any more. I was hot as if I'd done some push-ups. I looked down at the harmonica in my hand, and on a sudden impulse I hurled it far out over the dark waters.

"Give that to Zoobird when You see him. Please."

■ ■ ■ ■

After six long days of dodging icebergs and driving through heavy seas we came into quiet waters and saw ahead that unmistakable skyline. It brought a lump to my throat, further proof that I was still human. The last couple of days I'd gone to mess and managed to get down a little of the Army food. I felt ready to supervise the unloading of the baggage and the transfer onto the train west.

Confusion still tangled my mind when I tried to think about the future. All I wanted now was to get back to Missouri and see Dad and my mother and Grossmutter, maybe even a brief encounter with Lindy, just to thank her for all those letters.

As the train wheels clacked away beneath I felt as if I was wasting time. I should be making plans. When we pulled into Cincinnati, the doughboy in the seat beside me collected his gear from the rack and headed for the door, leaving behind him on the seat a newspaper. The New York Times, I'd heard it was almost as good as The Tribune. Out of curiosity I picked it up. The front page was all about the Paris Conference, where Woodrow Wilson had been meeting with the heads of the other Allies. He was proposing something called "The League of Nations," where everybody would sit around a table and discuss the world's problems, try to head off any future wars. It sounded good on paper, but I had an idea it was going to be hard to sell to France and Germany and England. They had hated each other for centuries, right? How do you make them agree on anything?

I turned the page to the Editorial Section and there was a cartoon that said it all: It showed the heads of state of the Allied countries sitting around a poker table playing with money labeled "Reparations." Only Wilson's chips were "The Fourteen Points." The pot was "World Peace," and the caption for the whole picture was "A League of Nations." The message was well expressed, but the artist had made Wilson look like a ninny with his fussy little glasses. I took out my pencil and gave him a better chin, a firmer mouth. I put a harder look in his eye. There was a vacant spot up in the corner. I did a little sketch of Zoobird, lanky and cowlicked, looking out a window with those binoculars, figuring the coordinates on a row of howitzers way off on the horizon.

Shoot, I could have drawn the whole cartoon. It was a great way to get the idea across to people who didn't have time or know enough to read it all in the small print of the newspaper. But to think it up in the first place I'd have to know what the Fourteen Points were and about the reparations and all that. It would take . . .

College.

By now, I knew that tone. "Sir, did You arrange for the guy to put that paper on the seat for me to read?"

He wasn't going to help with that one. It was up to me to believe, and suddenly I did. Once you hear that strong voice in your mind, or maybe it's in your heart, you could never doubt again. I might argue with Him, but I'd never question that He was up there, winding His pocket watch. That He actually had time for me.

In my chest I felt a sort of agitation, as if I were late for a party. With the train moving at a crawl I wanted to get out and push. Tried to sit back and soak up the wonderful sight of the Missouri countryside. It's beautiful in springtime, wild crabapple trees blooming, bittersweet vines trailing off the ledges of rock, studded with dried berries left over from last Fall. The greening hills so healthy and undamaged made me feel a twinge of sorrow for poor old France and its wreckage. Thank God there would never be any bombs here.

At least any time soon. Maybe never, if we play our cards right. But the question left a wrinkle on my mind. The world didn't seem as huge as it once had. We were coming into Kansas City, and yet my mind's eye could see halfway across the world to a little street in Toul, to the barracks in Sommedieu. I could close my eyes and imagine I was back there. France was never going to be that far away.

The train went barreling right on through past the stock yards and on out the other side into Kansas. We were the last contingent of the 129th FA. Most of the other companies had already been mustered out — there had been a grand parade, I heard. I wasn't sorry I missed that, but I wished I could just get off the train and start living my life.

But no, we had to go clear out to Camp Funston to be properly discharged at an Army base. Fort Riley, a hundred miles to the west. I hadn't wanted my folks to feel they must drive over just to meet the train, so I hadn't told them about it. There'd be transportation to take us back to K.C.

It would give me time to rehearse: "Oh, by the way, I've decided to go and enroll at M.U." I could picture their disbelief. At my age? Twenty-two years old approaching forty, I would mingle among the freshmen right out of high-school like a workhorse in a pony farm. Of course it would make Zoobird happy. Who else? Certainly not Lindy.

Why not?

"Are you saying —" No, I thought. He won't spell it out. You're supposed to trust Him. It's enough to know that He cares about me personally. All the rest is gravy.

Lindy will be around — or not. After I have a couple of years of school I might get a job as a political cartoonist on The Star. Well, probably not The Star, but some small paper in Olathe or Springfield. Maybe I might get smart enough to interest her. I'll look her up, if she's not already married and gone. And if she is, then I have to believe it's part of His plan. A new concept for me, but I began to see why it worked with so many people. The idea of faith was like a comfort to my churning questions.

Eventually the train rolled slowly into the yards at Fort Riley. As the big steam engine chuffed its way toward the platform I could see that a crowd had gathered, everybody cheering. Going forward to stand on the top step of the first car, ready to jump off and see to the baggage, I marveled to the train man.

“Where did all those people come from? The Army base?”

He gave me a smile. “Oh, the news was in the Kansas City papers that the rest of the 129th would start arriving at Funston today. I reckon they drove over.”

At that moment I spotted Dad in the crowd. As we glided slowly past he saw me and broke into a huge grin. Beside him was my mother in a big feathery hat, with Grossmutter lurking between them. Dolly stood off to one side, frowning severely, as if she disapproved of this uncouth racket. Scanning the other faces my heart gave a lunge.

She was there among the throng, Lindy, in a little fur bonnet and an elegant coat. She would have looked like a society lady except that she was jumping up and down, waving her arms like a kid at a parade.

The train had stopped. The conductor was setting out the steps. “All right, son, let’s go. Come on, boys,” he chanted, “move on, move on.”

The employees of Thorndike Press hope you have enjoyed this Large Print book. All our Thorndike and Wheeler Large Print titles are designed for easy reading, and all our books are made to last. Other Thorndike Press Large Print books are available at your library, through selected bookstores, or directly from us.

For information about titles, please call:

(800) 223-1244

or visit our Web site at:

http://gale.cengage.com/thorndike

To share your comments, please write:

Publisher
Thorndike Press
295 Kennedy Memorial Drive
Waterville, ME 04901